She laid her head against his chest.

"I haven't danced in years. This is nice."

"Oh, honey, you really are as smooth as Tennessee whiskey," he whispered softly in her ear.

"But sweet as strawberry wine?" She leaned back and smiled at him. "I've been called a lot of things, but sweet is not one of them."

"The sweet is down deep in your soul and takes a special cowboy to find it." Cody was kind of proud of himself for remembering how to flirt.

"Well, if you're thinking you might be that special cowboy, you'd best bring two shovels, because one will get dull before you dig that deep," she laughed.

"I'll remember that," he said and kissed her on the forehead before she could say another word.

High Praise for Carolyn Brown

"Carolyn Brown makes the sun shine brighter and the tea taste sweeter. Southern comfort in a book."
—Sheila Roberts, *USA Today* bestselling author

"Carolyn Brown is one of my go-to authors when I want a feel-good story that will make me smile."
—FreshFiction

"Carolyn Brown writes about everyday things that happen to all of us and she does it with panache, class, empathy and humor."
—Night Owl Reviews

"Carolyn Brown always manages to write feel-good stories."
—Harlequin Junkie

"Fans of romance series filled with small-town charm and a cast of supportive family and friends will appreciate this."
—*Publishers Weekly* on *Cowboy Rebel*

"Lighthearted banter [and] heart-tugging emotion…make this a delightful romance."
—*Library Journal* on *Cowboy Bold*

"There's no one who creates a rancher with a heart of gold like Carolyn Brown."
—*RT Book Reviews*

SECOND CHANCE AT SUNFLOWER RANCH

"Readers will fall for both the endearing couple and the stellar supporting cast. This is a delight."

—*Publishers Weekly*

"A truly enjoyable romance."   —Romance Junkies

"*Second Chance at Sunflower Ranch* is about opening your heart and mind to possibilities that you never expected to face. This could be one of my favorites by Carolyn Brown."   —Fresh Fiction

Also by Carolyn Brown

THE RYAN FAMILY SERIES
Second Chance at Sunflower Ranch

THE LONGHORN CANYON SERIES
Cowboy Bold
Cowboy Honor
Cowboy Brave
Cowboy Rebel
Christmas with a Cowboy
Cowboy Courage
Cowboy Strong
A Perfect Christmas novella in *Little Country Christmas*

THE HAPPY, TEXAS, SERIES
Luckiest Cowboy of All
Long, Tall Cowboy Christmas
The Toughest Cowboy in Texas

THE LUCKY PENNY RANCH SERIES
Wild Cowboy Ways
Hot Cowboy Nights
Merry Cowboy Christmas
Wicked Cowboy Charm

DIGITAL NOVELLAS
Wildflower Ranch
Sunrise Ranch
Small Town Charm

Texas
Homecoming

CAROLYN
BROWN

FOREVER

NEW YORK BOSTON

Copyright 2022 by Carolyn Brown

Cover design by Sarah Congdon. Cover photograph © Chamille White
Cover copyright © 2022 by Hachette Book Group, Inc.

Forever
Hachette Book Group
1290 Avenue of the Americas, New York, NY 10104
read-forever.com
twitter.com/readforeverpub

First Mass Market Edition: January 2022

Forever is an imprint of Grand Central Publishing. The Forever name and logo are trademarks of Hachette Book Group, Inc.

The publisher is not responsible for websites (or their content) that are not owned by the publisher.

The Hachette Speakers Bureau provides a wide range of authors for speaking events. To find out more, go to www.hachettespeakersbureau.com or call (866) 376-6591.

ISBNs: 978-1-5387-3563-3 (mass market); 978-1-5387-3565-7 (ebook)

Printed in the United States of America

CW

10 9 8 7 6 5 4 3 2 1

ATTENTION CORPORATIONS AND ORGANIZATIONS:

Most Hachette Book Group books are available at quantity discounts with bulk purchase for educational, business, or sales promotional use. For information, please call or write:

Special Markets Department, Hachette Book Group
1290 Avenue of the Americas, New York, NY 10104
Telephone: 1-800-222-6747 Fax: 1-800-477-5925

This is for my friend, Laura Drake.
With hugs for all the support!

Dear Reader,

I'm finishing this book just as spring pushes winter into the history books. After this past year with all the problems that covid (I refuse to capitalize that word in hopes that I will offend it so badly that it dies in its sleep) has brought to us, I'm glad to see spring coming around. I'm hoping it will bring new life to the whole world and restore some semblance of normal into our lives.

As always there are so many people to thank for helping me take *Texas Homecoming* from a rough idea to the book you hold in your hands. Some of those have gone on past this lifetime, but they remain in my heart and give me the courage to keep writing. A saying about life says: "You don't meet people by accident. There's always a reason—a lesson or a blessing!" Many of the people I have met have taught me valuable lessons, and many others have brought a blessing into my life.

Today I'd like to thank those who came bearing blessings. To my editor, Leah Hultenschmidt, and all the folks at Forever—you are truly a blessing. To my agent, and the folks at Folio Management—you are truly a blessing. To all my family, friends, and fans—

you are truly a blessing. And of course, as always, to Mr. B—you've always been my biggest blessing.

I hope you enjoy reading Cody and Stevie's story, and that the characters stay with you long after the last page.

Hugs to you all,
Carolyn Brown

Texas
Homecoming

Chapter One

Cody Ryan inched along at less than ten miles an hour on the icy roads. He had driven through sandstorms, out-run tornadoes, and even worked his way over snowcapped mountains, but nothing had ever been like this.

"So much for a big Texas homecoming," he muttered as his truck slid over toward a ditch and then back again to the middle of the road. His windshield wipers were doing double time, but with the blizzard-like conditions, he couldn't have seen the yellow line in the middle of the pavement even if there were one.

So, you're tired of having sand everywhere and living in a tent, are you? The words of his old friend Nate Fisher came back to his mind.

"We don't have much choice right now. We've got to get out of this place, and I'm ready to go home to Texas where it gets cold in the winter." Cody repeated what he had told Nate last summer when he had hurriedly packed his bags and gotten ready to catch the next military truck headed toward a town with an airport.

"But I didn't expect a damn blizzard to settle down right over the top of us just weeks after I got home." His truck tires lost traction again and fishtailed all over the road.

When he finally got control, he hit the speed dial for Sunflower Ranch to let his family know he wouldn't be home as soon as he thought. Addy, his sister-in-law, answered the phone on the third ring.

"Hey, Cody, everything okay?" she asked. "The roads look pretty bad out there."

"Yeah, sorry I'm running late. Please don't hold supper. It'll be a while before I can get back home in this storm," Cody said.

"I'm putting you on speaker. I've got Pearl, Sonny, Mia, and Jesse all here around the table with me."

"Hey, everyone!" Cody answered. "Y'all need to stay inside as much as possible, and off these slick roads. Have you heard a weather report?"

"Uncle Cody, they say this snow isn't going to stop for a couple of days," Mia chimed in.

"Drive safe," his father yelled.

"Will do, and save me some supper," Cody said and ended the call.

Cody's dad had been diagnosed with multiple sclerosis a while back, and a few months ago, he'd had a reaction to the drugs in the clinical trial. That incident had made Cody realize just how much he missed family and being home in Texas, so he'd given up his job with Doctors Without Borders and moved back to Honey Grove.

"But I damn sure didn't miss brutally cold winters," he muttered.

When he came home, Cody had thought about hanging out his shingle for a family practice right there in Honey Grove. After looking around for a place to buy or rent and not finding a thing that he liked, he came up with the idea of doing old-fashioned house calls in the whole community. Elderly folks, like Max Hilton, who needed him that morning but couldn't drive more than twenty miles to see a doctor in his condition, had quickly built up his business. Now, between helping his brother Jesse on Sunflower Ranch and trying to keep up with his patients, Cody stayed busy from daylight to dark most days.

"Poor old Max." Cody kept his eyes on the road, but he said a quick prayer that the ambulance got Max to the hospital without sliding off the slick roads. Max was too stubborn to see a doctor and had said more than once that his time was worth more than sitting in an office waiting for hours for a doctor to see him. But when he found out that Cody would come to his ranch house to see him, he called on him every few weeks. Lately, Cody had been telling him that he needed to see a heart specialist.

"I guess he'll see one now, whether he wants to or not." Cody slowed down another five miles per hour and leaned over the steering wheel to better see the road in front of him.

Addy, Cody's nurse, would be glad that Max would be

getting help. She'd been worried about him after the last two times they had been out to Max's ranch.

Cody hit another slick spot and went sideways in the road for a few seconds before he got straightened out. He started to pull off to the side until his heart stopped pounding, but the smart thing was to keep moving ahead. He made it another quarter of a mile, when a front tire hit a pothole and sent him into another greasy slide. He gripped the steering wheel so tightly that his knuckles ached, and hoped that no one would need his doctor services again until the roads were clear.

"And I thought a sandstorm was the most horrible thing in the world. Thank God you aren't here, Addy. I would never forgive myself if you got hurt and those twins didn't have a mother." He thought of the twin boys his brother and Addy had adopted right after they got married. Sam and Taylor were only about three months old, and Cody loved them almost as much as if they were his own sons.

He leaned forward as far as the seat belt would allow, hoping to get a better view of the road up ahead. "It's only twenty miles to the ranch. Even at this rate I should be there before bedtime. Talking to myself doesn't help, so why am I doing it?"

The words had barely left his mouth when a buck with a huge rack of antlers jumped out right in front of his truck. Instinctively, his foot left the gas pedal and stomped the brake. The deer disappeared in a flash, but Cody's vehicle began to spin like a top, and there was nothing that he could do to stop the motion.

The steering wheel had a mind of its own, and neither

the brake nor the gas pedal had any effect on what was happening. Adrenaline raced through his body, and he covered his face with his arms, expecting his crew cab truck to hit one of the many potholes in the old country road and begin to roll.

Then Cody felt as if he was flying for a split second, and the truck landed with so much force that it jarred his teeth. For several seconds he wasn't sure what had happened, but then he realized all the white stuff around him wasn't snow but airbags. He fought them back away from his face and unfastened the seat belt, only to fall forward nose down.

He slung open the door and rolled out of the truck to land in several inches of snow. When his heart settled enough that he could breathe without panting, he pulled his phone from his hip pocket to call the ranch for help, only to realize that there was no service. He stood up, checked for blood or broken bones, and heaved a huge sigh of relief when he figured out that he was fine.

"Thank you, God!" he said when he recognized an old mailbox. Just last week, he'd met Max at a barn about a quarter of a mile down the lane to check his blood pressure. Cody remembered Max's blood pressure being too high then and had told the octogenarian that he needed some tests done, but the old guy flat-out refused.

"They'll put me on some god-awful diet and tell me to exercise," Max had growled. "I'm going to eat what I want, and I get all the exercise I need right here on this ranch."

Cody visualized an old potbellied stove in the tack room where he'd done what he could for Max. He'd seen a pile of firewood in one of the stalls out in the barn, and there had been a bunch of kittens playing chase in the hay bales. "Maybe there will be phone service when I reach the barn," he muttered as he opened the back door of the truck and grabbed his black doctor bag. "If there is, I can let the folks know where I am."

He pocketed his keys, zipped his coat to his chin, and turned his collar up. Then, bent against the driving north wind blowing snow right in his face, he headed up the lane. He vowed that he would never leave home again without both a ski mask and a stocking hat—even if it was summertime and the thermometer registered over a hundred degrees. At least his cowboy boots gave him protection from the snow.

His nose and ears felt like Popsicles by the time he made it to the barn. He was wearing gloves, but his hands were stiff, and he had trouble sliding the barn door open enough to get inside. Unfortunately, it wasn't any warmer than the outside.

"But at least it's dry and out of the wind," Cody told himself as he removed his cowboy hat and brushed snow from it on the way to the tack room. Bits of snow sifted under the collar of his mustard yellow work coat and down the back of his neck.

The tack room door was already open, and dry wood was stacked neatly in the corner, which, otherwise, was a mess. He threw the stove door open and shoved several sticks of kindling inside, and then stacked three sticks of firewood on top of it. Everything was ready to start a fire, but he didn't have a lighter or matches, so he went in search of something to light it. He found rusty screws stored in peanut butter jars, several cans of beans, tuna fish, and chicken, a container of cornmeal and one of flour, but no matches.

"Why on earth would Max have food here when he couldn't even start a fire to heat it?" Cody muttered.

A cast-iron skillet was sitting on top of an old green rounded-top refrigerator, and because he had left his phone in the fridge one time, he even opened the door to see if there were matches in there. Other than a withered apple and two jars of elderberry jelly, the fridge was empty. In the freezer he found a few packages of meat wrapped in white butcher paper—*steaks* was written on the outside of a couple of them—so he wouldn't starve. He was disappointed when he turned on a burner and found there was no gas.

"Propane tank must be empty, so I guess I'll have to use the woodstove, provided I can ever get a fire going," he said.

He was about to give up ever being warm again, when he glanced around the room and noticed a rusty old match holder on the wall to the left of the stove. The burlap curtain hanging over the window where the vent pipe went outside covered part of it, but still Cody fussed at himself for not seeing it earlier as he made his way toward it. His mama always kept a container of matches a lot like that on the wall beside the stove at the ranch house.

"Country folks put things where they need them," he said and reached for a match, and discovered that there were only six left.

He held one of the matches close to the little chips of wood and struck it against the stove. Nothing happened. He tried again, and the head of the match popped off, but there was no flame. The same thing happened with the second one.

His heart had begun to beat fast, and he had visions of busting a bale of hay and covering himself with a layer of the stuff just to get warm. "Four more tries, and then Jesse may find me frozen when he shows up here." He thought of his brother and the rest of the family, all warm on Sunflower Ranch while the cold was seeping into his bone marrow.

At the thought of his brother, he jerked his phone out of his pocket only to see that the battery was almost dead. He didn't even try to call but sent a text: *I'm fine. Slid off the road not far from Max Hilton's old barn. Will hole up here until storm blows over.* He hit send, and the screen went dark.

He tried the third match. When it flared, he held it carefully next to the kindling until a tiny little blaze started, and then he blew on it to encourage the thing to grow. That tiny blaze meant more to him right then than all the money he had in the bank. When the blaze finally ignited and warmth began to spread out from the stove, he slumped down on the old brown-and-orange-plaid sofa not far away. His eyes slid shut, but he snapped them open and recited the signs of hypothermia out loud, starting with shivering and ending with drowsiness.

Afraid to close his eyes again, he stood and began pacing from one end of the room to the other. On one

TEXAS HOMECOMING

of his trips, he noticed two little beady eyes peeking out
from underneath the sofa and came close to jumping up
on the workbench, but then a little gray kitten inched its
way toward the stove. In a few seconds, a yellow one and
then a black-and-white one did the same. And then a big
calico cat came from the tiny bathroom with a dead mouse
in her teeth. She dropped it beside the kittens, and they
began to growl and fight over their dinner.

"I'm not afraid of mice or spiders, and I've seen rats
as big as possums and spiders that would cover a dinner
plate," he told the cats, "but snakes are a different matter,
and for a second there, I thought for sure you were one
of those."

He went back over the symptoms of hypothermia—
fumbling and confusion. He ripped his gloves off and
held his hands out. No tremors. That was a good sign,
but talking to himself and seeing snakes instead of kittens
wasn't.

The mama cat came right over to him and began to
rub around his legs, her purrs so loud that they covered
up the crackling sounds of the fire. Cody squatted down
and rubbed her fur from the top of her head to the tip of
her tail. "Are you depending on mice to raise these kids of
yours, or has Max got some dry food hiding somewhere in
this room?"

As if she understood him, she went over to a plastic bin
shoved up under the worktable and sniffed it. Cody pulled
the lid off, and sure enough, it was filled to the brim with
dry cat food. He found an empty margarine container and
scooped out enough to fill it, then set it beside the stove.

"That should keep you for a day or two, but you're a good mama to give your kids a taste for mice. That will keep the varmints out of the barn."

His hands and feet finally stopped tingling, so he removed his hat and coat and tossed them on the end of the sofa. The room was warming up nicely, and there was nothing to do but settle in for the duration. He laid his head on the sofa arm and closed his eyes. With all the work going on at the ranch, and his doctoring business, he was usually on the run from daylight until after dark. Jesse would come rescue him by morning, so he might as well take advantage of a free evening.

* * *

Dr. Stephanie O'Dell, Stevie to the folks around Honey Grove, figured when she left her place that morning that the going could get rough. The roads were icy, and noise similar to shotgun blasts filled the air as the tree limbs laden with a thick layer of ice snapped off. But Dale Watson had called with the news that both of his female alpacas had died giving birth that morning. He was able to save one baby, but he had no idea how to care for it.

She had made a call over to the Sunflower Ranch and talked to Sonny before she ever set out on the twenty-mile drive to rescue a tiny little newborn alpaca—a cria. Sonny had alpacas and was more than willing to see if one of his female alpacas—a hembra—would adopt the new baby. She determined that even on slick roads, she should be able to drive to her destination and back in two or three hours, but she hadn't figured on the blizzard-like wind and snow that hit when she was returning home.

The weatherman on the television that morning had said there was a possibility of an accumulation of two to three inches of snow in the area. But after she had picked up the cria and was on the way home, she caught a report on the radio that said the storm had taken a sudden turn. Residents of the area should be prepared for at least a foot of snow on top of the ice that was already on the ground.

Stevie still thought she could make it to Sunflower Ranch, pass the cria off to Sonny, and head back home by suppertime. She sure didn't want to get stuck at the ranch, not with Cody Ryan there. They had dated in high school, and she'd fallen head over heels in love with him, but then he went off to college when she still had her senior year to do. He had his heart set on being a doctor, and according to what he told her that last night they were together, he had to devote all his time to study. He had made the decision to help other people, especially those in foreign countries, and to be involved with a girl would get in the way of his dreams.

"We both knew this day would come," Cody had said. "I like you, Stevie, but…"

He had left the sentence hanging, and she had managed to keep the tears at bay until she got home that evening. When she finally stopped crying, she vowed that she would prove to him that she would have been worth the wait. She would study hard, become a veterinarian, and show him that he made a wrong choice.

She let go of the steering wheel for a brief moment to touch the locket around her neck. Inside was a tiny picture of wildflowers as a reminder to never give every bit of her heart to a man again. She'd taken the picture the last night she and Cody were together, and she didn't have to open the locket to see the photo of the sun setting over a field of yellow, purple, and red flowers. She had taken the picture out the window of the bunkhouse out on Sunflower Ranch. In the foreground was a blue vase filled with wild daisies and small purple flowers. That had been more than twenty years ago, and she had moved on since then, but the picture was still with her urging her to go on with life like the wildflowers that popped up every spring.

Stevie really thought she had moved past that teenage love until Cody Ryan came back to Honey Grove. Just seeing him again made her angry—proving that she still carried a little torch for him.

The cria began to hum, which meant the poor little girl was missing her mama.

"It's okay, sweetheart. In another hour or two, we'll have you in a herd of your own kind, probably in a nice warm barn. You're going to be fine," she told the baby. "Just hang on. I'm going as fast as I can."

Stevie still thought she could get home before the storm hit—right up until the gray skies opened up and began to dump flakes on her so thick that she couldn't see two feet in front of her van. The wipers could hardly keep up, so in between swipes, she felt as if she were driving blind down the country road. She was still a long way from Sunflower Ranch when she felt a pull to the right and realized she was getting a flat tire. At the same time, she remembered that she was already using her spare tire and had left the other one at the garage to be fixed two days before.

"Sweet Jesus in heaven!" She turned in to the next lane she saw. "I hope I'm where I think I am," she muttered as she slowed to a crawl and fought with the steering wheel. "Max Hilton's barn should be right up ahead of us. If I am right, we can stay there until this damn thing passes over us, and we can get some help. Don't you worry, little darlin'. I've got alpaca colostrum in the van to get you started and milk to mix up for you after the first twenty-four hours."

She glanced down at her phone lying on the console. The last time she had come out to this area, she hadn't been able to get a bit of service, but today she could see one bar up there at the top of her screen.

"This is damn sure not what I expected when I made up my mind to move back to Texas," she grumbled.

Up ahead, she saw the shape of the barn and tapped her brakes, but that put her van into a long, greasy slide that ended when she slammed into the big, sheet metal barn doors.

Stevie picked up her phone and tried to call Sonny but got a busy signal. So she sent a text: *Had a flat tire. Am at Max Hilton's old barn. I'm fine. Cria is fine. Send help when this blows over please.*

Sure enough, when she opened the van door and glanced down at the phone to see if she'd gotten a response, she had a NO SERVICE message.

"Hope it went through," she said as she grabbed the handle of the big sliding door and gave it a shove with all the strength she had, but nothing happened. Then a force from the other side slid the door wide open, and there was Cody Ryan standing right in front of her.

"What the hell are you doing here?" she gasped.

Cody folded his arms over his chest. "I might ask you the same question, except that I figure with those two flat tires, you got as far as you could and then tried to plow through the doors and into the barn."

"I just need to get my van inside so my supplies don't freeze, and I've got a baby cria to take care of." Stevie pushed past him. "Don't just stand there letting the snow blow all over you. Help me get the van inside."

"Give me your keys. The tack room is heated up. Take the baby in there, and I'll take care of the vehicle. Tires are ruined anyway so it won't matter if I drive it on the rims," Cody said.

Stevie shook snow from her red hair and slid the van's side panel door open.

"Come on, pretty little girl. Let's get you to a warm place and fix you a bottle. You don't get to join a new herd tonight. You'll just have to make do with me." She crooned as she picked up the cria still snuggled down in an old plush blanket and carried it inside. "I'm sorry your mama didn't make it, but when we get you to Sonny's place, there will be lots of alpacas ready to adopt you."

She took the baby into the tack room and laid her on the floor beside the stove. "You stay right here, and I'll be back in a minute," Stevie whispered as she hurried back out into the barn.

Cody glared at her and pointed to the tires. "Why in the hell were you driving in this kind of weather on tires like these? The two that aren't flat have hardly any tread left on them."

"Don't." She glared at him. "Just don't. It's not easy trying to start a business in a small town. I was trying to get one more month out of the tires before I replaced them."

"You could have been killed, or worse yet, you could have frozen to death if..." He returned the dirty look.

Stevie blinked and then looked around the barn. "Where is your fancy-schmancy truck with all the bells and whistles? Don't tell me..." She got inside the van and began digging around in her supplies. "Let me guess. It's sitting somewhere out there with a flat tire, too, right?"

"Nope, it's at the end of the lane in a ditch," he answered. "A deer jumped out in front of me. I swerved and wound up facedown in a ditch. I managed to send a text to my folks, and then I lost power."

Stevie brought out a bag of powdered colostrum for alpacas and a baby bottle. "Is there water in there?"

"In the bathroom," Cody said, nodding. "Max told me that he built this barn on top of an old well. Since he had water, and since this is so far from his other property, he put a bathroom just off the tack room. Only cold water, though."

"I can warm up some on the stove," she said as she edged past him.

In a few long strides, he was across the barn floor and had opened the door for her. "Guess we're stuck here together until this storm passes and the folks come to help me."

"Maybe they'll be coming to help me. I sent them a message too," she said.

"Oh, really," Cody groaned.

"What are you moaning about?" she asked. "At least I got a message out to tell them where they can find me. That's a good thing, right?"

Cody followed her into the tack room and closed the door. "Can you even begin to imagine the teasing we're going to face tomorrow?"

"Tomorrow, nothing!" Stevie said. "The weather report has been updated. This isn't going to let up for at least two days, and then we'll have to dig out from under anywhere from ten to eighteen inches of snow. They're expecting power to be down for a week. And who gives a damn about teasing? I've got a cria to save who needs others of her breed around her. You want to learn to hum like that baby's mama?"

Cody had been around alpacas since he had gotten home a few months ago, so he knew exactly what she was talking about. They made a humming noise when they were happy, and although it was a little different, they also hummed when they were sad. If they were upset or angry, they made a high-pitched screeching sound that came close to breaking glass.

"I took an oath that I would try to save lives." Cody warmed his hands over the top of the stove. "I guess it doesn't matter if it's an alpaca or a human, so I would be willing to give humming a try if I needed to, but I do believe we've got something better." He stopped and pointed.

The cria had changed position and now had her head up as she sniffed the calico cat, who was rubbing herself all around the cria's neck. The humming had gone from mournful to happy, and all three kittens were playing hide-and-seek under the blanket and romping all over the new baby.

"She's bonding with the cats," Stevie said as she went to the small bathroom and filled the bottle with water. "I've never seen anything like that before, but thank God for it. If she eats...where's something to heat this bottle?"

"We've got a cast-iron skillet, but I haven't found any pans, and is that plastic?" Cody asked as he started looking around for something that might work. "I've got an idea. Let's open up a can of beans, put them in the skillet, and hey, would you look at this?"

He found a camping set in a box under the workbench. "One bowl and three metal plates. And here's a couple of forks and a spoon."

Stevie stooped down beside him and took the bowl from the box. "I can heat water in this, then transfer it to the bottle. I'd rather have a microwave or maybe a stove to sterilize things, but..."

"But we'll take our miracles where we find them, right?" Cody set the box on the workbench. "Like you finding me here."

17

She gave him another dirty look. Finding Cody Ryan was anything but a miracle, she thought. She hated rattlesnakes, but she would rather face off with one four feet long than spend days cooped up in a small room with Cody Ryan.

Chapter Two

Four days was an eternity to be stranded anywhere, but especially with Stevie O'Dell. Cody had known he'd broken her heart when he ended things between them. He hadn't expected her to understand his commitment to following his dream of joining Doctors Without Borders. He wanted to give back to people who hadn't had the good fortune that he'd had after the Ryans had taken him in as their foster son, and he couldn't let a girl or his heart stand in the way.

Cody had thought he might have to spend the night in the tack room, and maybe part of Thursday, but if Stevie was right, they might be stuck here until the weekend. He sunk down on the end of the sofa.

"Haven't seen you around since summer." Cody broke the silence.

"Not since the parade and rodeo," she answered. "No need to come out to the ranch unless I'm called to look after animals. Guess everything out there is healthy?"

"Might not be after this storm," Cody said with a shrug.

"Never know," she said as she used her shirttail for a potholder and gently poured the water back into the bottle. She added powder, shook it up, and offered it to the cria. At first, the little thing turned its head away, but then the cat raised up on its hind feet and licked the nipple a couple of times. When Stevie offered it again, the cria stood, popped its little tail straight up, and took to the bottle.

"God bless that cat," Stevie said. "I'll have to go out to the van and get diapers."

"What's that got to do with a cat?" Cody asked.

"Nothing. I need them for the cria. Unless you want to step in poop?" Stevie raised an eyebrow.

Cody got to his feet and pulled on his coat. "Dad never put diapers on his alpaca babies."

"His crias have mamas to take care of wiping their babies' butts. This little girl doesn't have a mother, and I don't see this cat taking care of her in that area, do you?" Stevie said.

"Where are they in the van?" Cody asked. "I'll go get them for you."

"They were on the right side, behind the passenger seat, but things got shifted when the tire went flat. Green box with a baby on the side," she told him. "And thank you. I'll take care of the feeding if you'll change the diapers."

"Oh, no!" Cody said. "I'll get the diapers for you, but I'm not changing them. This is your baby, not mine."

"Then you don't get a vote on her name," Stevie told him. "No responsibilities. No privileges."

Cody slid a sideways glance at her. "I'll name the cat and all the kittens," he grumbled as he opened the side door of the van and found the box of diapers right where she said they would be. A broad smile broke out across his face when he thought of the Blake Shelton song that said she could name the babies and he'd name the dogs. He hummed the song on the way back to the tack room.

"Leave the door cracked a little bit," Stevie said. "It's getting too hot in here. You don't need to hum. She's happy now that she has cats."

"Yes, ma'am." The cat almost tripped him as it ran out of the room. "After that walk from the road up to the barn, I didn't think I'd ever be too hot again, but I suppose Dolly thinks it's too much heat, too."

"The cria's name is not Dolly," Stevie told him as she offered the bottle to the baby.

"Of course it's not. Dolly is my cat's name, and the kittens are Tammy, Loretta, and the black-and-white one is a boy, so he's Boots." He said the first names that came to mind.

"Evidently you still like country music." She looked up from the cria, who was taking to the bottle. "But I figured the boy would be Willie or Waylon or even maybe Blake. Look! Dixie's tail is standing up. That means she's going to be all right."

"I know a little about alpacas," Cody said, "and yes, I still like country music. No matter where I was in the world, it always reminded me of home."

21

Stevie removed her coat and tossed it over on the sofa. "Dixie needs warmth but not blistering heat. I hope there's more wood because this isn't going to last forever."

"One of the stalls has enough in it to last a few days," Cody answered. "Dixie? Where did you get that name?"

"The Chicks. I've always loved 'Goodbye Earl.'" Stevie gave him a look that said she just might take care of him like the woman took care of a man in the song. "She's downed all her formula, which is great. Now, in four hours, we'll offer her some more."

"Where are you getting that *we* business. That critter is cute, but…"

Stevie lowered her chin. "We are stuck here together, Dr. Cowboy. We don't have electricity, a shower, coffee, or chocolate, except for half a candy bar out in my van. Those are the essential things for survival in my world, and I don't see any of them in this room. Don't test me. I'm not a high school girl with a crush on you anymore."

"Ouch!" Cody laid a hand over his heart.

"Truth is truth," Stevie said.

"If you say so, but we do have electricity—at least, unless and until the power goes out," Cody told her. "I just haven't turned on the light, but the refrigerator works. Evidently the propane tank is empty because the burners on the stove won't light, so we'll be making our food on the woodstove. Max told me that he lived out here for a few weeks last spring when that tornado took the roof off his house, so I found some leftover food and supplies."

"Too bad you can't snap your fingers and make a nice

warm shower, or better yet, a deep Jacuzzi tub appear," she said.

"You haven't lost any of your spunk, have you?" he asked.

"Nope." She pulled a pocketknife from the pocket of her jeans, took a diaper from the box he had set on the floor, and made a hole in the middle of it. Then in a few fluid motions, she put it on Dixie. Still on wobbly legs, the tiny animal began to explore the room right along with the kittens.

"She thinks she's a cat," Cody said.

"Maybe so, but she's alive and responding," Stevie said. "If we've got to stay here for a while, I'm going to put things in order and take stock of what we've got to work with. I had just been to the grocery store when I got the call from Dale about Dixie. There are a couple of bags of food in the van. A loaf of bread and a few other things, but I didn't buy any coffee or chocolate. I didn't know that I was going to be stranded with you, or I would have spent all my money on candy bars. Chocolate calms me when I want to chew up fence posts and spit out toothpicks."

"Looks like it's going to be a tough few days," Cody said. "I'm not easy to live with when I don't have coffee. I drink gallons of it every day. We had a rule in the hospitals. The person who takes the last cup starts a new pot."

"Think we'll survive?" Stevie asked.

"If we don't, maybe Jesse will take care of Dixie and the cats." Cody was glad to hear there were a few more supplies but thought she could have mentioned food before he went out in the cold to get the diapers.

"Two bags?" He stood up again, put his coat on one

more time, and headed out. "Anything else while I'm out there?"

"Thank you, and there's a bag of potatoes and..." She grimaced. "Would you bring that half a candy bar from the console?"

"Sure thing," he answered. "I live to serve."

"If we're going to survive until Jesse gets here, maybe we should cut out the sarcasm." She opened the refrigerator door. "Oh, look! I found some frozen steaks and hamburger. And there's canned goods on this shelf. We might not starve or have to live on baby formula after all."

Cody had worked so hard that he was too tired to eat too many times to count when he was working for the firm that was a lot like Doctors Without Borders. He'd spent almost a decade in third world countries, working from before daylight until long after dark. Beans and potatoes and an occasional steak didn't sound too bad at all to him.

Living with a sassy redhead in a room that was smaller than his bedroom at the bunkhouse on Sunflower Ranch—now that sounded far worse than seeing patients in blistering heat seven days a week, or even sleeping on a narrow cot or shaking spiders out of his boots.

* * *

Stevie stole a long look at Cody as he left the room again. Why couldn't he have gotten fat and bald and started wearing slippers and baggy pants rather than those tight-fitting jeans and those cowboy boots? At thirty-nine, he still looked every bit as sexy as he had when he was a senior in high school.

Burn me once, shame on you, she thought as she set the supply of canned goods down from the shelf and peeled off a paper towel from a roll that she found at the back of the shelf.

Burn me twice, and I'll kick your sexy butt all the way to the Red River. She put a new twist on the saying as she dusted the shelf and the tops of the cans.

"Where do you want these?" Cody asked as he brought in two big brown bags of food and one of potatoes.

"You can just set them on the worktable," she answered.

He pulled what was left of a chocolate bar from his pocket and handed it to her.

"And the most important thing of all," he said with a smile.

She had to remind herself not to smile back. He'd broken her heart, damn it! And as much as she wanted to admit she was over him, she also hadn't been expecting him to move back to Honey Grove when she returned to help after her mom's cancer diagnosis. Cody was supposed to be off playing Dr. Superhero in far-flung parts of the world until the day he died. But Sonny Ryan was having some health issues too, and two of his three sons had come home.

She peeled the paper back and took a bite of what was left of her chocolate, then offered the rest to Cody.

"No, thanks," he said and shook his head, "I would never get in between a woman and her chocolate."

"Smart man," she said. "Truce while we are stranded?"

25

"I didn't know we were at war," he drawled. "I thought we were twenty years down the road from when we broke up."

"Why are you bringing that up?" she asked.

"You said truce, and that means war, right?" he shot back.

"Smart-ass," she snapped. "Can you just agree to be civil while we're here? And FYI, we are years past that time when we broke up. We're adults now, not kids."

"Okay, then, deal," he said. "What can I do to help? I've gotten pretty used to roughing it, and this would be considered practically luxurious compared to some of the places I've worked."

"Oh, yeah?" She stepped around Dixie and a yellow kitten to move cans of paint from a second shelf and squealed when she saw what she thought were two blue cans of coffee right there before her eyes. She grabbed the first one, and to her dismay, it rattled.

"Damn it!" She slammed the can down on the work-table when she found nothing but bent nails inside.

"Thought you had found a gold mine, didn't you?" Cody chuckled.

She shook a finger at him. "This is not a laughing matter."

"Probably find screws in the other can," he laughed, "or worse yet, you'll find coffee, and then you won't find a pot around here or any way to make it."

"And what is this, Dr. Smart-Ass?" She pulled an old blue, granite pot from the shelf. It had no lid and looked like it might have been through a Category Five tornado.

"I thought I was Dr. Cowboy," Cody teased. "Who is

this Dr. Smart-Ass? Can he make coffee in a beat-up pot like that?"

"No, but I can. It might be so strong it will melt the enamel off your teeth, but it *will* be coffee. We will have a moment of silence," she said as she bowed her head for a few seconds and then lifted it.

"What was that for?" Cody asked.

Stevie picked up the second coffee can and shook it. "A moment to pray that this is really coffee before I open it up. It feels about half-full, but it might be sugar or flour or sawdust."

"Or the ashes from a cat or dog that Max had cremated," Cody suggested.

"Yuck!" Stevie shot a dirty look his way. "Don't spoil my moment. I was praying that would be coffee, not screws…" She peeked inside. "And it is!"

"You are probably resurrecting grounds that came to Texas in the days when Santa Anna was roaming around this state. Look at where it was sitting, and all those dried-up paint cans in front of it," he said.

Stevie put the lid back on the can. "Don't be a spoilsport. We have coffee. Do you take yours with cream and sugar? If so, you're out of luck. I haven't found sugar, and the only thing that resembles cream is powdered formula for animals."

"Black," he said. "I take it black. When I was thirteen, I decided to start drinking coffee. I wanted some milk and sugar in mine. Mama shook her head and said that life don't come all sweetened up, and neither did her coffee. I could learn to drink it black or leave it alone."

Stevie set the old pot on the worktable along with the coffee. "Pearl is a smart woman. So, when did you try drinking it again?"

"I bit the bullet, so to speak, and started drinking it right then, that day. My brother Jesse just had to show me up and not even ask for sugar or cream. He's a year younger than I am, so there was no way I was going to let him get ahead of me," Cody said.

Lord, why does the room have to light up when he smiles? Stevie sighed.

"I'm going to put all the paint cans out in the barn. They're dried up anyway and should be thrown away, but for now…" Cody dived into the cleaning project and began to help get things in order.

What light came from the single window in the tack room was fading fast by the time they finished. Then the single bulb in the room blinked once and went out. The refrigerator stopped humming—no lights and no power. Could it get any worse?

"There goes one of your essentials for survival. Chocolate is gone and now so is electricity. No shower either. Do you think you will live until Jesse gets here?" Cody asked.

"Oh, hush! I'm in no mood for teasing. I don't suppose you found a candle or an old lantern out there in the barn, did you?" she asked.

Cody's brows drew down in a frown. "There was one hanging on the side of the ladder leading up to the loft. I'll see if it has oil in it and bring it in if it does."

He returned in a minute with the lantern and set it on the now spotlessly clean workbench. "I'm guessing this thing is about half-full of oil, but we've only got three matches left."

"I've got a pocketknife," she said. "I can always whittle a match and we can use the fire from the stove to set it on fire."

"Regular Girl Scout, aren't you?" Cody said.

"Nope," she answered. "Never was in the Scouts, but I've been in places that didn't have decent cell service too many times to rely on my phone. So…" She held up her arm. "I've got a smart watch, so we'll know what time it is and when to feed Dixie, and what day it is."

Cody pulled back his coat sleeve and showed her his watch. "You're preaching to the choir. Very few of the places I've been these past years had cell service. Folks there could barely afford food, much less fancy phones."

"Speaking of time"—she picked up the coffeepot and headed to the bathroom—"it really is time to feed Dixie again."

"And us," Cody said. "You ever cooked on a woodstove?"

"Nope," she answered. "And not over a campfire either."

"Then you feed the baby, and I'll keep us from starving." Cody got down the cast-iron skillet and two steaks.

"Those are frozen. There's no way you can make those for us," she said.

"No, but they'll be thawed by morning, and we'll have them for breakfast," he said. "I noticed that you bought a pound of bacon, so tonight we're having a skillet meal."

"And what goes in that kind of a supper?" she asked when she returned with a coffeepot full of water.

"Bacon fried crispy and chopped, potatoes fried in the

29

grease, served up with a can of beans heated in the can on top of the stove. You wouldn't happen to have a can opener out there in your van, would you?" he asked.

"I've got a church key to open cans of milk, but we don't need anything to open the beans," she said.

Cody eyed her like she was crazy. "You plannin' on opening them with your teeth, or does that watch on your wrist do magic?"

"No, Dr. Cowboy," she said with a big smile. "The cans on the shelf all have those pull tabs on them."

Chapter Three

Supper over and the skillet and forks cleaned as well as they could be, Cody banked the fire so that it wouldn't go out overnight, and set an alarm on his watch to wake him up in four hours so he could check it. There was no way he would take a chance on starting another one with only three matches. The third might not be the charm the second time around, and then they'd be up the crap creek without a paddle, as his dad said when the situation was bad.

"You want the sofa or…" he started to ask, but Stevie raised a palm.

"The cushions come off, so"—she pulled them off—"we're in luck. One of us gets the floor on cushions. The other one…" She flipped out a bed. "Gets to sleep on this bare mattress."

"I'll take the floor since it's likely you will have to sleep with Dixie," Cody offered.

"I don't think so," Stevie said. "Look over there behind the stove. I may adopt Dolly or rent her if Max will let me."

Cody peeked around the stovepipe, and there was Dixie, curled up on her little blanket. Dolly slept with her head on Dixie's belly, and the kittens were draped over the cria like she was their long-lost sister.

"You really may have to steal Max's cat," Cody said, "or at least, borrow her and the kittens until Dixie gets used to her new family at the ranch. I don't see Max renting her out, though."

Stevie glanced out the edge of the single window located behind the stove. "Do you think this blizzard will last until the weekend? I've never seen weather like this in Texas or in Oklahoma, where I've been for the past few years."

Cody shrugged. "I just know what the weatherman said. Can you see the moon or stars?"

"All I see is white," she said with a long sigh. "I guess we'll be here until it stops snowing and someone can find a way to get to us."

"Yep." He sat down on one of the cushions she had tossed on the floor and leaned back against the end of the bed. "But there is an upside. We've got enough beans and food to last a few days, and there's eight rolls of toilet paper in the cabinet above the toilet."

"Count your blessings," Stevie muttered.

"Speaking of that"—he tossed one of the cushions up onto the bed—"use this for your pillow. You'll have a kink in your neck tomorrow morning if you sleep without one. I've slept on the floor lots of times the past few years. I'll use this second one for my pillow."

"Thanks," she said. "Good night."

"See you in four hours," he told her.

Stevie raised up on an elbow. "Why are you getting up? I can feed Dixie without your help."

"The fire," he answered and held up four fingers.

"I understand." Stevie shivered. "If you don't wake up, you can trust me to kick you until you do. I do not want to freeze or starve or lose a cria, for that matter. That stove is our lifeline right now."

"Yep, it is." Cody closed his eyes and wished for his king-sized bed and nice warm blankets at home.

* * *

A pile of hay in a barn stall would have been more comfortable than the lumpy mattress and cushion Stevie had to use for a pillow. She flipped from one side to the other trying to find a position that was semi-comfortable and had just drifted off to sleep when her alarm went off. She tiptoed around Cody, who was curled up in a ball and trying to use his coat to cover his whole body.

Dixie was sleeping soundly with her newfound feline family, and Stevie hated to wake her, but the little thing needed nutrition every four hours. After the night was done, she could put the alpaca on formula and extend her feedings to five hours, but until tomorrow at noon, she would get colostrum.

"Please let the hembra on Sonny's ranch adopt her," Stevie mumbled.

Cody sat up and rubbed his eyes. "Is everything all right? Dixie still alive?"

"She's fine. I'll put a stick of wood in the stove since I'm up already. Go back to sleep," Stevie said.

"Okay, thanks." Cody pulled the coat back up over his shoulders.

Stevie checked the water she had put on the stove before she went to bed. It was entirely too hot, so she stepped around Cody and filled the bottle half-full of cold and then added what was on the stove. What she wouldn't give for a flashlight couldn't be measured in dollars and cents. There was one in her van, but opening and shutting that squeaky door out into the barn would wake Cody again, so she used the tiny bit of light from the window to get the mixture right.

Dixie was already on her feet and butting her head against Stevie's leg by the time the bottle was made, and she sucked her bottle dry with her little tail straight up in no time. When she finished, she flopped back down with the cats and didn't even wiggle while Stevie changed her diaper.

Cody sat up, felt around in the dark until he had a stick of wood in his hand, and shoved it into the stove. "That should keep us warm until morning."

"I said I would do that," she told him.

"The alarm on my watch woke me," he mumbled and curled up again.

He must have been in some tough places to condition

him to catch sleep in bits and pieces like he was doing. Once Stevie was awake, for any reason, it took a while for her to go back to sleep. She stretched out on her mattress and, like Cody, covered up with her coat. She glanced over at Cody, lying between her and the stove. As the heat from the stick of wood began to fill the room, he pushed the coat off his shoulders.

Cody Ryan had always been a stand-up guy—kind, a little on the shy side, and true to his word. He lived by the cowboy code of ethics that hung on the wall out in the bunkhouse. She had admired that in him even when they were just kids in elementary school. When he broke up with her, she still respected him for his honesty.

She couldn't make out his features, but then, she didn't need to. She had dreamed about him regularly for years even though she had moved on—or thought she had. With his chiseled face, those steely blue eyes framed by those thick brown lashes, and all that blond hair that he usually wore just a little too long, he had taken her breath away when he passed her in the halls of Honey Grove High School.

Finally, her eyes grew heavy and she slept.

The vibration on her wrist awoke her, and there were Dixie's little eyes peeking over the side of the bed at her. "Good morning, little one." She reached out and petted the tiny animal.

"I think your baby wants food," Cody said from the kitchen area. "The water is warm on the stove. I'm going to open the door to let Dolly and the kittens out into the barn. We've got to figure out something for the door. The cat either has to get out of here or else we have to make her a litter box."

Stevie stood, stretched, and rolled the kinks out of her neck. "Thanks for warming the water. We could wire the door open a crack so that the cats can come and go as they please but Dixie can't get out."

"If she was in a natural setting, she would be in a stall with her mama, right?" Cody asked.

"Yes, and the mama would be near her for warmth," Stevie answered as she made a bottle.

"So, she could come back in here when she got cold. I'm sure she would follow the cats wherever they go." Cody refueled the stove. "What I wouldn't give for a good hot shower can't be put into words."

"I can't snap my fingers and make a shower or hot water appear out of nowhere, but I do have an extra toothbrush or two in the van," Stevie said. "I'm glad to share with you if that will help."

"Definitely," he answered. "What else have you got out there?"

"I've got a go bag for when I have to spend the night with a cow that's having trouble birthing a calf. It's got extra clothes, toothbrushes and toothpaste, and deodorant," she answered. "Don't you carry a duffel bag with you?"

"Nope, just my doc bag," Cody said, "but I would love to borrow one of those toothbrushes."

"Nope, you can't borrow one," she said.

"Why not?" Cody asked.

"You can have it to have and to hold for all eternity,

because borrowing it means you'll give it back, and I don't have any need for a toothbrush you have used," Stevie said. "Other than to clean the toilet with, maybe."

"How long are you going to hang on to the past?" Cody asked.

"Me? Hold on to the past or hold a grudge?" She raised her eyebrows. "Never! Why would I be angry with you? You warmed up the place before I got here, gave me the sofa last night, got the water ready for Dixie's bottle, and even did the cooking."

"So, we're not going to talk about the elephant that's been hanging around all these years?" he asked.

"I killed that elephant years ago," Stevie said. "Speaking of animals, other than her legs being longer, Dixie isn't much bigger than your cat. I bet Dolly even weighs more than Dixie."

"You are changing the subject, and the elephant is not dead," Cody argued.

"Yes, it is." Stevie might consider herself strong and smart, but she still got a lump in her throat when she remembered the way she had felt that night when Cody told her that he didn't have room in his life for a relationship. "Someday we might be good enough friends to talk about you breaking my young heart, but *someday* is not *today*. Go ahead and prop the door so she can romp and play in the barn with the cats. We'll see how that goes before we make her stay in the house while they get to go out and play."

Cody put on his coat, crossed the room with the cats right behind him. He waited on the other side of the door to see what the cria would do. When Dixie had sucked down all her bottle, she slowly made her way across the room, sniffed the air out in the barn, and returned to her blanket behind the stove.

"Smart girl," Stevie said with a smile as she put the sofa to rights. "It's cold out there." She refilled the coffeepot with water, added coffee grounds to it, and set it on the stove. The coffee would probably taste like crap, but it had to be better than the road tar they had in the dorm when she was in grad school.

You need to really talk to Cody, not just argue and dance around this attraction. Her mother's voice was in her head.

"We will when the time is right." Stevie missed her mother so much. After the funeral a few months ago, she'd thought she would find closure, but it hadn't happened—not yet.

* * *

"Women!" Cody muttered as he picked up Stevie's duffel bag from the van. "They don't ever forget anything." He went to the sliding door and pushed it open a couple of inches to see just how fast the snow was falling. He could see tree limbs on the other side of the lane, which meant the storm was slowing down slightly. He started to shove the door closed, when he caught a blur of movement in his peripheral vision. The black-and-white kitten made a jump through the open space and landed on top of the snow banked up against the door. Another leap and the little ball of fur disappeared completely into the snowdrift.

Cody had only planned on making a quick trip to the

van and back, so he hadn't put on his gloves. But he couldn't let Boots freeze to death out there in the snow. After all, he and Boots were the only two guys in the barn, and Cody felt like he could use all the support he could get. He dropped Stevie's bag on the barn floor and opened the door just wide enough that he could slip out. Snow came up over his boot tops and filtered right down to his toes. He strained his ears, trying to hear the kitten's cries, but couldn't hear a thing except the tree limbs still breaking all around him. Snow clung to his eyelashes and his hair, and his hands were already freezing. He was about to give up, when he saw a slight indentation about two feet ahead of him, but snow was already filling in the hole.

Instantly, he was down on his knees and shoving his bare hand down into the cold snow, searching for the kitten. After feeling around and finding nothing, he thought he heard a slight meow. The sound was faint, but it was definitely a kitten, and it was coming from behind him. He turned to find Dolly and her other two babies at the doorway, staring at him as if they were begging him to find Boots.

"I'm trying." He raised his voice and then noticed another little indentation six inches ahead of him. He reached out and sunk his hand into the snow again, found fur this time, and brought up Boots all covered in snow and limp as a dishrag.

Cody tucked the kitten into his coat close to his chest, hurried back inside the barn, and pushed the door shut. Dolly and her other two kittens went running to the safety of the tack room, and barely beat Cody.

"Boots got out of the barn and fell in a snowdrift. I tried to get to him faster but..." He laid the kitten on the sofa and jerked his coat off.

Stevie was all over the place. She grabbed Boots and carried him to the back of the stove, where Dixie was sleeping, and then picked up the edge of the blanket and began to rub the kitten's fur.

Cody dropped to his knees beside her. "He wasn't in the snow more than two minutes, tops. Is he alive? I never should have opened the door."

Stevie ignored his question, which made Cody wonder if there was hope for the kitten.

"What can I do?" he asked.

"Keep the barn door closed," Stevie said. "You must have gotten him just as he went under because there's no snow in his nose. That's a good sign. Water in the nose could mean sinus and lung problems later. He's just scared and cold. Look, he's opening his eyes. Time for Dixie to be a good big sister." Stevie tucked the kitten against Dixie's belly, and then Dolly made her way over to him. "It's a good thing you saw him run out of the barn. Now about your hands..."

Cody held out his hands. They were bright red and tingling. Another few minutes and he might have suffered frostbite. "They'll warm up in a little while."

Stevie rolled up on her feet, went to the worktable, and came back with his gloves. She warmed them on top of the stove for just a minute and then stretched them onto his hands. Even though his fingers felt like icicles, her touch shot desire through his body.

"Don't reckon I could get you to pull my boots off?" he asked. "The snow went over the tops, and..."

"Good God! Did you roll in the snow?" Stevie asked.

"Nope, just crawled in it. I couldn't let a kitten freeze to death," he answered. "Are you sure he's going to be okay?"

Stevie nodded toward Boots, who was now up and nursing on his mother. "He's fine, but you've got to come out of those jeans as well as your boots."

"And what am I going to wear?" he asked.

"I've got a pair of sweatpants and extra socks in my go bag. They'll keep you warm while your jeans and socks get dry, but they *are* pink," she answered as she set about removing his boots and socks. "You're a doctor. You know how fast frostbite can set in when you're wet like this. You should have taken all this off while I was working on Boots. Now, you need to get those wet jeans off." She set his cowboy boots beside the stove and started for the door.

"And let you see me half-naked?" Both his eyebrows shot up.

"This is not the time to joke around," she threw over her shoulder as she closed the door behind her.

"Day one, and I have to wear pink sweats," he muttered as he shuffled into the bathroom to take off his wet jeans. "I hope Jesse doesn't get here before my jeans get dry."

"Cody? Where are you?" Stevie raised her voice.

"Bathroom." He cracked the door and held out a hand.

She put a rolled-up pair of sweats in his hand, and he quickly closed the door. He laid everything on the back of the toilet, unrolled the gray sweats and found the toothpaste and brush.

41

"These are not pink," he said as he looked in the mirror. "I'll get back at you for this, Stevie."

Most blond-haired men couldn't grow much of a beard, but Cody was the exception, and a day's worth of his stubble was equivalent to a week for most men. His hair stuck up in all directions, and his eyes had bags under them. He pulled a comb out of the hip pocket of his jeans and tamed his hair with a little water, brushed his teeth, and wished for his electric razor.

"At least Jesse won't find me in pink sweats," he said with a grin.

The sweats were soft and warm, like Stevie had been when he held her in his arms those few months they had dated. He'd missed that feeling when he went to college— maybe even more than he'd missed his family, because he could talk to them anytime he wanted.

Stevie had caught his eye back in junior high school, but it had taken him several years to get up the nerve to ask her out. Looking back, maybe it would have been best if he hadn't ever made that first phone call after they had started school that fall of his senior year. By spring, he had really developed feelings for her, and knew that he had to choose between his dream and Stevie. He couldn't ask her to give up her plans, and Doctors Without Borders didn't need veterinarians.

He brought the sweatshirt to his face and inhaled deeply, and wondered what his life would have been like if he'd made a different choice.

Chapter Four

"In my wildest nightmares, I never would have thought I'd be stuck in a blizzard with Cody Ryan," Stevie said as she picked up her bag and dug around in it, hoping that she had tucked in a candy bar, but all she located was a couple of pieces of peppermint that came in the sack with the last hamburger she got from Sonic.

When Cody came out of the bathroom wearing gray sweats and white socks, he asked, "Are you color-blind?"

"Just messin' with you," she said.

She turned away as if she didn't want him to see her expression, but he thought he heard a catch in her voice.

"I've got another pair of sweats in the bag and they *are* pink if you'd rather have them," she muttered.

"These are fine." Cody hung his jeans, shirt, and a pair of boxer shorts on nails beside the door. "I just hope my jeans are dry by the time Jesse gets here. Thank goodness you're tall so that the bottoms are long enough, but this sweatshirt is a little snug across my shoulders."

She inhaled deeply and let it out slowly. "You'll survive until your clothes get dry. As warm as this room is, I don't reckon it will take long."

"I am grateful for a change of warm, dry clothing, so thank you. What's really on your mind, Stevie? You look like you're about to cry. Did I do something wrong?"

"No, not this time." Stevie kept her back turned to him. She had worked so hard to keep up a brave front in front of him that she was determined not to cry.

"Is it time to talk about that big gray animal?" Cody asked.

"No, that's not what..." Her voice quivered.

"You talk and I'll make breakfast," he said.

She flopped down on the sofa and stared out the window at the sheet of white still falling from the sky. "I'm in a tack room with no shower, no electricity, with a baby alpaca and a litter of kittens, and my mother keeps popping into my head with advice. I don't want to just hear her, Cody. I want to be able to sit at the table with her, to see her smile at me, to hear her talk to her, tell her about my day..."

Cody stopped peeling potatoes and sat down beside her. "This will pass. It will stop snowing, and we'll get rescued, and then you can spend time with your mother."

"My mama died before..." She willed the tears welling up in her eyes not to fall down her cheeks. "Just before Mother's Day."

44

"I'm so sorry, Stevie. I didn't know. Mama might have mentioned it when I called, but then Dad was taken to the hospital when his meds disagreed with him, and with all the excitement of Jesse and Addy getting married, the twins coming into our lives and…" he said, stumbling over his words.

Stevie pushed her curly red hair back behind her ears. "I understand, but I miss her so much."

He scooted over closer to her and draped his arm around her shoulders. "I can't even imagine how it would feel to not have my folks around. When we thought Dad had a stroke a few months ago, it scared me really bad. I was in London, getting ready for another assignment, and all I could think of was why wasn't I home with him and Mama."

"I gave up a partnership in a big vet firm in Tulsa, to move back here." Stevie laid her head on his shoulder, glad for even that much human touch. "When I talked to her on the phone last spring, Mama said she wasn't feeling so well. I started making arrangements to move at that time, but I didn't know until I got here that she had terminal cancer. When I fussed at her, she said that she didn't want to worry me, and she didn't want me to change my life because of her."

"I remember Ruth being a kind, sweet person. She and my mama were on that historical planning committee together, right?" Cody asked.

"She loved to volunteer both on city projects and at the hospital, just wherever she was needed, after she retired from teaching at the elementary school," Stevie said.

"Have you talked to anyone about how you're feeling?" Cody asked.

"What good is talking?" Stevie sighed. "It won't bring her back. If she would have told me when she was first diagnosed, I could have been home six months before and spent more time with her."

"No, it won't bring her back, but talking to someone like a therapist might help you find some measure of closure," Cody said.

"Maybe," Stevie agreed. "Just talking to you has helped. I heard that Sonny had to be taken off that trial medication he was on. Is that why you came home?"

"I felt so helpless sitting there, waiting four hours before I could catch a plane, and that seemed like the longest trip I've ever taken," Cody answered. "My heart was heavy, and I kept asking myself why in the hell I hadn't just gone to ranching. Dad raised all us three, and not a one of us stayed on the ranch."

"But he was and is so proud of all of you," Stevie said.

"I know, but..." Cody sighed. "He was already out of the hospital when I got home, but it could have gone the other way. I understand how you feel, Stevie, and I'm so sorry."

"Thank you." She managed a little bit of a smile.

"Tell me your earliest memory of your mother." He removed his arm and went back to the stove.

"Only if you'll tell me your first memory of Pearl." Stevie missed the warmth of his arm lying softly around her shoulders. "But first I'm going to brush my teeth and put on fresh clothes." She stood up and headed to the bathroom.

"How do you like your steak?"

"Medium rare." She picked up her bag and closed the bathroom door behind her.

Once inside the tiny restroom, Stevie put the lid down on the toilet and then sat down. She leaned forward, covered her eyes with her hands, and let the tears come.

That's enough! her mother scolded. *Wash your face. Get cleaned up and go talk to Cody. You need this, Stevie.*

"What I need is to be out of here and back to work," Stevie argued, but she stood up, ran a basin of cold water, and wet a couple of paper towels. She shivered when she peeled out of her clothing but felt like a new woman when she had clean sweats on her body and her teeth brushed. She even took the time to get all the tangles out of her curly red hair and pull it up into a messy bun.

"Best I can do, Mama," she said to her reflection in the tiny mirror above the sink.

You are beautiful. You are smart. I'm proud of you. Her mother had told her that so many times she couldn't count them on both hands.

"Thanks, Mama," she said, and managed a weak smile.

When she opened the door, the smell of sizzling steaks filled the air, and Cody was singing "Millionaire" and surprisingly enough his deep voice had almost as much grit in it as Chris Stapleton's.

"What brought that song to mind?" she asked. "Is there a woman in your life that makes you a millionaire like the lyrics say?"

"Not yet, but I can always hope there's one out there in the future that will make me feel like I'm rich in a

47

way that doesn't have a thing to do with dollar bills," he answered. "When I was in the Doctors program, I couldn't ask a woman to give up her life and follow me around in countries like I've been in, but now that I'm home, things are different."

Stevie breathed a sigh of relief. "Don't we all hope to find that kind of person. Those steaks about ready?"

"They are, and the potatoes are done too. Wait 'til you taste the coffee," he said.

"Good, bad, or ugly?" she asked as she poured herself a cup.

"You be the judge," he said.

She took a sip and shivered even worse at the taste of it than she had because of cold. "Beyond ugly, even beyond downright nasty."

"It should clean out the bathroom drainpipes," Cody teased as he forked up a steak and put a good-sized portion of potatoes on each plate.

"Probably eat right through them." She opened the window behind the stove and tossed what was in the cup out on the ground, then closed the window. "You can drink it if you want. I'd rather have water."

"Me too, only I poured mine back in the pot," he told her.

"Yuck!" Her nose crinkled. "That's not very sanitary."

"Honey, no self-respecting germ would ever live in that horrible stuff." He sat down on the sofa and began to eat. Dolly came from behind the stove and began to rub around his legs. "I'll save the bone for you, pretty girl, but you can't share with Dixie. Alpacas don't eat meat," he said and then glanced over at Stevie, "unless this redhead wants it. I owe her for saving my hands, so if she wants to gnaw on it awhile, then she should have it."

Stevie picked up her pocketknife from the worktable and sat down on the other end of the sofa. "You're not even funny."

"And I tried so hard." Cody heaved a long sigh but there was no denying that it was all fake.

"Seriously." Stevie rolled her eyes. "You know when I miss Mama the most?"

"At mealtimes." Cody turned serious. "That's when I missed my folks the most."

Stevie cut off a piece of steak and started toward her mouth with it. "We shared two meals a day with each other, even when she was sick. I would carry our plates to her room and sit beside her bed while we ate." She finally put the steak in her mouth.

"I understand," Cody said. "I really do. I thought I was ready to get away from the ranch, but I was so lonely in college that sometimes I thought of quitting and going home. There were people all around me in the cafeteria, but not a one of them to talk to about my day. Mama always said breakfast and supper were our best family times. Even as little boys, we talked about our day at the supper table, and I missed that so much."

"Everyone needs a family," Stevie said. "Look at Dixie. She probably wouldn't survive without the cats. Even though they're two different species, they've bonded to make a family. I hope Max doesn't mind if I take them with us when we leave."

"Max is in the hospital," Cody said. "I was coming from his place when I wrecked my truck. He was having chest pains, so I called the ambulance and sent him to the hospital in Bonham. I'm sure he won't mind if we borrow Dolly and the kittens. In fact, he'd probably be happy to know they were being cared for. Once Dixie is happy in her new world, I'll bring them back."

"I envy you and the closeness you have with your family. Always have." Stevie cut another piece of steak and popped it into her mouth.

"You were close to your folks," Cody said.

"Yes, I was, but I always wanted siblings like you had," Stevie confessed. "Losing Mama would have been a little easier to bear if I'd had brothers or sisters to share the grief, to share the memories."

"I can't imagine not having family. Even when I was thousands of miles away, the highlight of my week was getting to talk to Mama and Daddy and my brothers when I could get phone reception," Cody said. "You were going to tell me your first memory."

"Yes, I was, and I will if you promise not to laugh and to remember that I was just a little girl," she said.

Cody laid a hand on his chest. "Cross my heart, I won't laugh."

"Okay then," she said and nodded. "I must have been about four, and I begged and begged Mama and Daddy for a puppy for my birthday. As you know, we lived in town, not out in the country like you did. I didn't care if it was a mixed breed that came from the pound." She stopped and ate a bite of her potatoes. "I just wanted a pet. I can see Mama standing at the kitchen table, putting icing on my birthday cake, and from the smile on her face, I just knew I was getting what I wanted. But when I opened my presents, all I got was two stuffed animals. One was a mama collie dog and the other was her baby."

"Were you disappointed?" Cody asked.

"Oh, absolutely," Stevie answered.

"Did you throw a fit or cry?"

"Why did you ask that?" Stevie asked.

"Because I asked for a pony when I was about that age, and I threw such a bawling fit that I even had my brothers both crying," Cody answered.

Stevie shook her head. "I was disappointed, but I didn't cry. Even at four, I knew that would hurt my folks' feelings. I took those stuffed animals to my bedroom, made them a kennel from a cardboard box, and fed and watered them every day."

"For real? What did you feed them?" Cody asked.

"Whatever I could sneak away from the supper table. When Mama came to clean my room a week later, she found molded food and ants everywhere," Stevie answered.

"What did Ruth do?" Cody chuckled.

"She explained to me that my dogs didn't eat people food, that they only ate pretend food. Then we took them out in the backyard, she said because they needed some exercise, and she had a tea party with me under the pecan tree," Stevie said. "Not much of a story, but that's my earliest memory, and thank you for not laughing. Now your turn. Was it when you didn't get a pony?"

"Why would I laugh?" Cody asked. "I think that's a sweet

story, and with a mother like that, you had a wonderful role model."

"Yes, I did," Stevie said. "Now about the pony?"

"No, and maybe I should explain the reasoning behind why I didn't get one," Cody answered. "Daddy explained that, to be fair, if he bought one pony, he would have to buy three—one each for Lucas and Jesse on their birthdays too, and we didn't need that many ponies on the ranch. I found out later that he had lost his last horse just before we came to live at the ranch, and it hurt him so bad that he vowed he wouldn't have any more horses on his property. He was saving me from the pain of having to put my pony down later in life."

"So, what *is* your first memory?" Stevie asked.

"That would be when I was three and Lucas was just a baby—barely walking. A lady put us in the car with her and took us to the ranch. The lady said our new mama and daddy were waiting and they would love us. There was another little kid there, and Mama said his name was Jesse. I was scared, but I had to be strong for Lucas, or he would start crying."

"You were adopted? What happened to your real parents? I mean your biological ones. I don't think I ever knew that you weren't...actually Sonny and Pearl's son..." Stevie stammered. "I'm sorry. That didn't come out right."

"It's okay. It's old news and not many people even remember that we aren't biologically Ryans," Cody said. "Lucas and I were taken away from our parents because they were on drugs. They got sent away and we were put into foster care. I don't remember anything about them. I was only two and Lucas was just a few weeks old when all that happened. Later, they died in prison, and we went to live on Sunflower Ranch. After a few months, Sonny and Pearl adopted us, and we had a good life. I couldn't have asked for better parents."

"And then you've got Jesse and Addy and their daughter, Mia, plus the twins they've just adopted. I'm jealous of all those folks in your life, Cody," Stevie admitted. "I guess I've got a lot to be thankful for. I've been wallowing in a pity pool when I should be remembering the good times."

"Grief will do that to you," Cody said.

"I never knew that you Ryan guys weren't all three full-blood brothers," Stevie said.

"I love my brothers, both of them equally, even though Lucas is my only blood brother," Cody said, "but there were lots of times when I would have gladly thrown them out in the yard if I could have been an only child."

"I would have taken them in to be my brothers if you had." Stevie pointed to the window. "Look, it's stopped snowing."

"And now, it's sleeting and spitting freezing rain. The thermometer hanging right beside the barn door says that it's twenty-six degrees. That means ice under the snow and more on top of it."

"And everyone thinks that Texas is a hot, dry place," Stevie said.

"If they want hot and dry, they should spend six months in central Africa, but there was one thing that was definitely better there than here," he said.

Stevie turned to face him. "And that would be?"

"The coffee was a helluva lot better," he answered with a broad smile.

"What we need is a nice pot and a decent can of coffee." She set about eating her breakfast, and when she finished, she laid the bone from her steak on the floor. The kittens came out from behind the stove and pounced on it, growling and slapping at each other.

"They are entertaining but look at Dixie." Stevie nodded toward the cria.

"Poor little thing probably wonders why her siblings are carrying on over a bone." Cody finished off his food and gave the kittens his steak bone also.

"If we had a third one, they could each have one," Stevie said.

Cody shook his head. "Nope, that's not the way it works. Three bones. Three siblings. They'll all want the biggest one or the one with the most meat still on it."

Stevie reached out a hand. "Give me your pocketknife and plate. You cooked breakfast. I'll wash dishes."

He handed her the knife and said, "Thanks, but bring it back open."

"Hey, I was raised in the same area as you, even if we lived in town and not on a ranch. I know it's bad luck to give a knife back to someone closed if he or she gave it to you open."

Cody held up a hand, a half inch between his thumb and forefinger. "I'm just a little superstitious."

"Me too," Stevie said. "I'll give it back to you just like it is, only cleaner."

Maybe, she thought, *being stranded with Cody isn't so bad after all.*

Chapter Five

$\mathcal{S}$hotgun blasts, or was it dynamite, sounded all around Stevie when she awoke the next morning. She blinked against the blinding sun rays coming through the window, wondering for a few minutes why someone was shooting a gun in the middle of town, especially so close to a school. She popped up in bed and rubbed her eyes with her knuckles and looked around at the strange room, and her first thought was that she'd been kidnapped.

Then the whole thing with the winter storm came back to her in a flash. She was in Max's barn with Cody Ryan. Those weren't gunshots but Mother Nature pruning trees, and the schools would definitely be closed due to bad weather. She checked her watch—twenty minutes until Dixie needed to be fed.

"I want a warm shower, but I *need* coffee," she whined under her breath as she wiggled the kinks from her neck.

"Run!" Cody muttered in his sleep and began to flail around. "To the cave," he said as his legs twitched even more. "Go! Don't look back!"

She leaned over to get a better look at him in time to see him reach out and grab Dolly. He cradled the cat tightly against his chest and said, "I'll carry you. Everything will be all right. Hang on, Dineo. It'll be over soon, and we'll patch you up." Then he sat up, and his eyes popped wide open. Tears rolled down his unshaven cheeks when he looked down at the wiggling cat in his arms. "I'm so sorry, son. I'm so sorry."

Stevie slung her legs over the side of the sofa bed and touched him gently on the shoulder. "Wake up, Cody. You're dreaming."

He blinked several times, and his frown deepened the beginnings of crow's-feet around his eyes. Then he freed the cat and wiped his wet cheeks with the back of his hand.

"Are you all right?" Stevie asked.

"Just a nightmare," he said.

"Want to talk about it?" she asked.

"Nope," he answered as he got to his feet and headed to the bathroom.

She hadn't been around anyone with PTSD, but she'd heard it was common among soldiers. Evidently, from the way Cody was behaving, he had a bit of it, and a young friend of his somewhere named Dineo had died. From the nightmares, he wasn't over the death of his friend, and Stevie wondered how old the boy had been.

While he was in the bathroom, she went to the refrigerator and brought out a package of hamburger. Hash wouldn't be a traditional breakfast, but it would keep them from starving. Her mouth watered when she thought about a big stack of pancakes covered with melted butter and maple syrup. That could very well be her first big meal when she and Cody were rescued. She tossed the burger in the skillet and set it on the stove, then made Dixie a bottle of alpaca formula and fed it to her. The cria left a little that time around, so Stevie poured it into the one bowl they had and set it down for the kittens, who fought over it—as usual.

Stevie thought of what Cody had said about siblings having arguments. She didn't care if siblings fought. If she ever got to have a family, she fully intended to have a houseful of kids.

Cody finally came out of the bathroom and sniffed the air. "That doesn't smell like bacon and eggs or sausage gravy."

He wouldn't make a very good poker player, not when he couldn't hide anything on his face. His expression told Stevie that the nightmare had brought on painful memories.

"It's hash for breakfast because we're working with what we have. If you want to run out to the chicken house and gather up some eggs and go out to the smokehouse and bring in a slab of bacon, I'll be glad to make a traditional breakfast." She tried to lighten the heavy mood in the room.

He just shrugged and turned to stare out the window.

"Are you sure you're all right?" she asked.

"I'm fine," he grumbled. "Thanks for making breakfast."

"Think they might rescue us today?" she asked as she filled her plate.

"Nope. All that cracking noise we're hearing is more limbs breaking from trees. They'll be down everywhere, blocking the roads and probably even the lane from the road up to this place," he answered, but he didn't turn around. "No coffee this morning?"

"If you can stand to drink it, you can make it. I can't bear the thought of swallowing any more of that stuff." She took a bite. "This hash needs some onion and Worcestershire sauce."

Cody went to the workbench, picked up a plate, and filled it with the meat-and-potato mixture. He took his first bite and said, "I miss salt and pepper."

"Me too, and you're going to miss potatoes after this meal," Stevie said. "I used the last of them, and there's only one package of meat left in the refrigerator, so we'll be trying to figure out how to use canned tuna and chicken. What's in the fridge is unmarked, so I have no idea what it is. We're down to six cans of beans. What's the first thing you're going to eat when we get rescued?"

"Food is food," he muttered.

"Who pissed in your cereal this morning? I know you were having a nightmare when you woke up. It might help to talk about it rather than ignoring what happened," she said. "If you'll remember, it helped me to talk about my mother, and I'm all ears if you want to tell me what's going on in your head or in your nightmares."

58

"Just leave me alone," he said.

Stevie recognized his expression as the same, rather cold one she had seen when he broke up with her. At the time it was devastating, but now she wondered just exactly what Cody was hiding.

"Talking about it won't help," he grumbled.

"Coming from the man who told me something different about my grief for my mother," Stevie said.

"That's different." He cleaned off his food, washed the dish and fork out in the bathroom sink, and set it back on the worktable.

Leave him alone, Stevie warned herself, but she just couldn't do it.

"What's so different? Is it because I'm a woman and we need to talk, but you're a big, tough cowboy who can keep his feelings inside?" she asked.

Cody shot a mean look toward her. "I'm not having this conversation with you, Stephanie. I'm going out in the barn to work for a while. I'm going to clean out the stalls, and split all the wood that's out there. I need something to do." He grabbed his coat from one of the nails on the wall beside the door.

"If you're going out to work, then by damn, I'm going with you. You don't have to talk to me, but I'm not staying in this tack room all day by myself. I can split wood or muck out stalls right along with you," she declared.

"Suit yourself," he said as he went through the door. Dolly, all three kittens, and Dixie paraded along behind him.

Our first fight, Stevie thought, *and I don't even know*

59

what it's about. But I'm pretty damn sure there won't be makeup sex when it's over. Not that either of us would want that right now after three days with no shower. Thank God it's wintertime, or we would really be smelling ripe by now.

Stevie slipped her coat on and buttoned it up the front. She hadn't realized just how warm the little stove kept the tack room until she stepped out into the cold barn. The aroma of hay and what was just the scent of every barn she'd ever been in was different from the smells of the tack room. She took a deep breath, the cold almost burning her lungs, and went straight to her van, where she rustled up two stocking hats and a couple of pairs of work gloves. Cody had been an old bear all morning, but if he caught a cold or pneumonia, he could be even worse. She found him in the last stall with an ax in his bare hands.

"Put this on!" She laid the cap on the rail and went back to the tack room.

"I've got my cowboy hat. I don't need that," he said.

"If your stupid ears get frostbitten and fall off, how are you going to keep your reading glasses on when you pass forty? You're getting pretty damn close to that age right now," she said, "but have it your way."

He removed his cowboy hat, hung it on the post of a nearby stall, and shoved the stocking hat down over his ears. "Happy now?"

"Frankly, darlin', as Rhett Butler said in *Gone with the Wind*, I don't give a damn, but I imagine your ears appreciate the warmth. And here's something else that your hands might say thank you for." She held out a pair of work gloves. "They're pretty well worn, but they're better than nothing."

"I don't need them, and they probably would be too small anyway?" he said.

"In case you didn't notice, I'm a tall girl. I have big hands and big feet, and if you will remember my sweatpants were long enough for you too. The gloves will fit you, and you are a doctor. Your hands are important, but hey, if your ears are as much as you want to protect from frostbite— not to mention blisters on your hands from swinging that ax—then again, it's your business," she said.

He took the gloves from her and shoved his hands down into them. "Is there anything you don't have in that van?"

"Not much, but this fiasco has taught me to put a box of emergency candy bars and some of those packages of instant coffee in the van before I take it out again," she said.

Cody picked up the ax and started splitting wood again, but he didn't have anything else to say. Stevie went to work shoveling out the three remaining stalls and putting down fresh straw in each one. The barn would be clean for whoever leased or bought Max's ranch.

At noon Cody had finished splitting and stacking all the wood. Stevie was done with the stalls and had even swept up the barn floor. And neither of them had spoken a single word to each other. Dixie had come out to romp around in the few bales of hay stacked against the far wall and play hide-and-seek with the cats.

"Time for your dinner, little girl," Stevie said as she picked up the cria and took her into the tack room that seemed too warm now. She changed Dixie's diaper, fixed and fed her the noon bottle, and still Cody hadn't come in.

"Let him stew out there in the cold," Stevie muttered as she added a can of corn and one of crushed tomatoes to the leftover hash and made a reasonable facsimile of soup. Then she added milk to a few cups of the flour she found in the cabinet and a little of the leftover bacon grease for cooking oil. "I'm having hoecake and soup for dinner. If he wants to starve, that's his business."

"Something smells good," Cody said when he came through the door.

"He speaks," Stevie said. "We're having soup and hoe-cakes. You might know them as campfire biscuits. I had to cook it right on the top of the stove, but I did clean it as best I could."

"You used all the rest of the bacon drippings?" He raised an eyebrow.

"Yes, I did, but if you don't want to eat the hoecake, that's fine by me. I'll put some of that jelly in the refrigerator on what's left over and call it dessert," she told him.

"You're awfully prickly." Cody asked.

"After the way you've been acting all morning, the answer would be 'hell yeah, cowboy, I'm prickly,'" she answered as she flipped the round of bread over so it could brown on the other side.

* * *

Cody deserved that from her. No doubt about it, but it still stung.

"We'll be eating out of our coffee mugs," she said. "Those plates won't work."

"Hot soup and bread to dip in it." He managed a smile. "Doesn't get any better than that."

"Oh, yeah it does," she argued, "but it's the best we can do today, and I'm just grateful to figure out that we could make bread. It won't be as light as Mama's biscuits, but it will soak up the soup pretty good. You ready to tell me what put you in a funk this morning?"

He removed his coat and hung it on a nail beside the door. "That dream took me back to a place where I don't want to go or be."

"I got that much from what you were mumbling about when you were still asleep," Stevie said. "Have you ever talked to anyone about Dineo? Who was he?"

"How did you know that name?" Cody asked.

"You called out his name and then said, 'Hang on, son.' He must've been someone young and also a close friend," Stevie answered.

"I lost a little boy that day, and he was like a son to me. His father had become my best friend." Cody's eyes went all misty, but he blinked back the tears.

"I guess the sound of the tree limbs breaking sounded like gunfire and triggered the nightmare. What can I do to help with lunch?" he asked.

"Don't change the subject," Stevie said. "Tell me about this little boy. Evidently he meant a lot to you."

"He did," Cody said, and nodded, "but I . . ."

Stevie shook her head. "Soup and bread are done. All you have to do is dip up a mug full of soup and break off a chunk of bread. I'm a good listener, so tell me more about the child."

Cody filled one mug and used his knife to cut a piece of bread, handed it to Stevie, and said, "You cooked. I can serve."

"Thank you," she said, and nodded as she took her dinner to the sofa and sat down.

Cody fixed his food and sat down beside her.

"So tell me about that little boy," Stevie said gently.

Cody felt like he owed her an explanation, even if it was a short one. "He adopted me when I was in a little village outside of Botswana. He had a perpetual smile and was always around the hospital tent wanting to help me. He said that when he grew up, he was going to be a doctor."

"How old was he?" Stevie asked.

"About nine or ten. His mama was dead, and his daddy thought he had been born ten summers before. Dineo was always underfoot"—Cody smiled at the memory—"kind of like those kittens over there."

"Did you hate to tell him goodbye?" Stevie asked.

"Two weeks before I left the village of Bere, the guerrillas came in their trucks and..." Cody closed his eyes for a moment, then opened them slowly and went on. "They destroyed our hospital tent and fired their weapons into the air. They were gathering up all the children they could find and taking them away to train them to..."

"That's for real?" Stevie asked. "I thought it was just stuff you see on television."

"It's very real," Cody could still feel the ache he had felt in his heart that day. "Dineo's daddy, Bodi, fought with them when they tried to take his son from him, and one of them shot him. The bullet went through Bodi and into Dineo, so he wasn't any good to them anymore. They only wanted healthy kids. They would have kidnapped me if they realized I was a doctor. I grabbed the boy up and took him to a hiding place. I'd only been there a little less than six months, but Bodi and Dineo had become more than just friends. They were family. Then the noise, the gunfire, the yelling, the sound of the trucks moving away with crying children all stopped. I felt so helpless and heartsick when I realized they were both dead."

He stopped and swallowed several times. "Silence as thick as a dense fog filled the village for a few minutes, and a new haunting sound filled the air as people began to weep over their stolen children. I tried to save Dineo, but he probably died instantly, and the doctors and nurses were taken out of the country the next day to be reassigned. Bodi was the only one who had resisted, but there were two deaths that day. He and Dineo both died, and I didn't even get to attend their funerals."

"I'm so sorry. You were still reeling from that death when you got the news of your father. Man, that had to be tough," Stevie said.

"It was rough, and I didn't want to tell you because you've got enough on your plate, dealing with your own grief."

"Ever think that maybe, by sharing in each other's sorrow, it's helping us deal with the pain?" she asked. "Did you talk to counselors or therapists about Dineo?"

Cody shook his head. "I was sent to London and Dad needed me. I'm a doctor, for God's sake." He stood up and took his empty mug to the bathroom to wash it. "I lost patients before Dineo and probably will again. I shouldn't need therapy every time I lose someone."

"No, but this was a special little boy to you," Stevie said. "Sometimes, like with that little guy and with my mama, we don't bounce back like we want to."

"When did you get so smart?" Cody asked.

"Always been smart," Stevie said. "You just didn't recognize it."

"I deserved that smart-ass remark," Cody said.

"Yes, you did," Stevie said. "Would you have ever believed that the two of us would be stranded together like this?"

"Nope," Cody answered.

"Me either." Her grin got even bigger. "Yet, here we are, and with just a little help, we might even learn to be friends."

"Now wouldn't that be a miracle," Cody said.

Cody hadn't had time for friends in college, and he'd been moved so often that he hadn't bonded with many folks—not like he did with Bodi and Dineo. He wasn't sorry for his decision to put his own personal wants aside to give back to others. Pearl and Sonny had been amazing parents, but there had always been the idea in the back of his mind that he owed a debt to society for all that he'd been given. He had to do something to help others, and from the time he had seen a documentary on television about Doctors Without Borders, he had set his mind to devote his life to that.

Chapter Six

The next morning Stevie took stock of the food they had left. She had a can of tuna fish in one hand, and a can of chicken in the other, trying to figure out what to do with either of them for breakfast.

Mama, you got any recipes that only use what I can rustle up from almost nothing?

A reflection of light bounced off the can of tuna.

"I get the message. Start with that, right?" Then she realized sun rays were coming through the single window. Sun meant she and Cody might get rescued before too many more days. "Cody! Open your eyes!" she yelled across the room.

Cody sat up with a jerk. "What? What's happening?"

Stevie pointed across the room. "The sun is shining. Look!"

He tilted his head to one side and frowned, then got up, put on his boots and coat, and headed out into the barn. "Do you hear that? Am I imagining things?"

"What?" She followed him to the door. "Is that what I think it is?"

"It's equipment of some kind," Cody said, and nodded. "And it's getting louder. I'm hoping it's Jesse in one of the ranch tractors."

"What makes you think it's Jesse?" she asked.

"Because the folks at the ranch are the only ones who know where we are. It could be the county workers trying to clear some of the roads, so we can't get too excited," he said.

Stevie heard what he said, but the words had little effect on her hope. They had been stranded since sometime Wednesday, and this was Saturday. She wanted to go home to her own bed, eat some chocolate, drink real coffee first thing in the morning—enjoy all the luxuries she had taken for granted in the past.

She rushed across the room, righted the sofa, and shoved everything into her go bag together. "We need to get a box ready for the cats, just in case. We can't leave them behind. What do we do with the water to keep the pipes from freezing? Should we leave the fire burning in the stove?"

"Slow down, Stevie." Cody removed his coat and hung it back on a nail. "We'll take care of all that when we figure out if it's really Jesse."

"But we should be ready," she said.

"All right, then." He glanced around the room. "We

haven't cooked yet, so everything is in place. Skillet back where we found it. Dishes on the workbench, which is fine. I'll turn the water to the sink and toilet off at the wall and then drain the pipes. Since the well is under the barn, the pipes should be fine. And if it is Jesse, I can put out the fire with what water is in the coffeepot. Satisfied now?"

"I do feel better," she admitted and went to the window. "Cody, it *is* a tractor. I can see the sunlight bouncing off the windshield. It's coming down the lane, so it's got to be more than just a county vehicle. They wouldn't plow anything but the roads."

"You're sure eager to get out of here," Cody said.

"Aren't you?" she asked.

"I've learned to make the best of whatever situation I'm in," he answered. "Truth is, I've kind of enjoyed being stranded. No technology. Living on what we can find."

"Weren't you bored at times?" Stevie asked.

"Sure, but life isn't all happy times. You got to have some rain before you can fully appreciate the rainbow," he said with a grin.

"Well, I've survived the rain, even if it was frozen, and now I'm ready for the rainbow, which in my mind is shampoo, a long bath, a candy bar, something other than tuna fish for breakfast, and my own bed with real pillows," she told him.

Cody peeked out the window and then crossed the room to the bathroom. "Looks like your rainbow will be here in about five minutes. That's a Sunflower Ranch tractor and that's Jesse in the driver's seat. I'll take care of the water, and we can dump the cat food into a bucket and use that box for the cats."

Stevie sucked in a lungful of air and let it out in a whoosh. When she heard the barn doors open over the top of the noise of the tractor's engine, she was busy making sure Dolly and the kittens were all accounted for.

"Hey, anybody home?" Jesse slung open the tack room door. "Y'all both alive or did one of you kill the other?"

Cody met him in one of those man hugs that ended with both of them patting each other on the back. Jesse was a little taller than Cody, and his jet-black hair glistened in the sunlight coming through the window above the stove. His green eyes sparkled with humor when he said, "Well, I guess that answers my question. You've survived being stranded together for several days and no murder has been committed."

"It's a miracle," Stevie told him. "Thank you, thank you for coming to our rescue." She patted his brother on the back several times.

"Yep, it is," Cody agreed. "But now we're ready to go home."

"I saw Stevie's van. I can tow it and y'all to the ranch, but you"—Jesse took a step back and nodded toward Stevie—"will be staying at the ranch for a while. Trees are down between us and town, and we're just as stranded as you have been. I had to take a couple of dirt roads to get here, and what should have taken an hour took more than two."

"What about my truck?" Cody asked.

"I saw it in the ditch, but, brother, there's a tree lying

across the hood right now. It'll be a few days before we can get to it. I think it's totaled anyway, so it won't matter if it sits right there?" Jesse asked.

"Even if it wasn't," Cody said, "it's more important that we get Stevie's van to the ranch anyway. Her supplies are in it."

"What can I do to help y'all get ready to go?" Jesse asked.

"We've got to…" Stevie started to say and then shook her head. "If you're going to tow my van, I can put the cria and the cats in it. They'll be far happier if they're together."

"Cats?" Jesse asked.

"Long story," Cody chuckled. "I'll tell you on the way home," he said, and then focused on Stevie. "I guess your rainbow isn't so bright, but there *is* coffee and chocolate in the bunkhouse, and you can have my room for privacy. It's got a big bed and a bathroom with a tub."

"Thank you." Stevie was a bit disappointed, but hey, like Cody had said earlier, she would make the best of the situation. She practically drooled at the idea of a cup of coffee waiting on the other end of the trip to the ranch.

They loaded the cats and Dixie into the van. Stevie tossed her go bag into the front seat and made sure all the doors were closed. Then Jesse and Cody hooked the vehicle up to the back of the tractor and Jesse pulled it out of the barn.

"You ready?" Cody asked Stevie.

"For a cup of coffee, I'd walk from here to the ranch," she said as she climbed up into the cab of the tractor.

"I wasn't talking about getting out of here." Cody

71

followed right behind her. "I meant, are you ready to share the seat with me? This tractor only has two seats." He picked her up and set her in his lap. "Unless you want me to sit in your lap, this is where you'll be for the next two hours."

"You did say there was chocolate at the end of the road, right?" Stevie wasn't quite ready for the sizzle the contact with his thighs made her feel, but she was determined not to let him know that he affected her so much.

"Yep, and about five miles down the road, we will probably have cell service. Mama and Addy are putting supplies in the bunkhouse for you—girl stuff," Jesse said. "She said that if you think of anything special, to call her." He drove the tractor slowly down the lane. "She and Addy were making cookies and talking about what to fix for lunch when I left. I reckon there'll be a hot meal waiting for y'all."

"That is so sweet of them." Stevie's voice cracked.

"Now, tell me about this cat thing. Why are we taking a mama cat and kittens to Sunflower Ranch?" Jesse said.

Cody explained how Dixie had adopted the cats, and ended the short story with "I'll take them back when the cria adapts to her new family on the ranch."

Jessie stopped at the end of the lane and pointed to his right. "See what I'm talking about?"

Stevie and Cody both turned their heads at the same time. The entire cab and hood of Cody's truck was covered with snow, and all that they could see of the back end was the tailgate. A huge tree was lying over the top and spread out all the way to the other side of the road.

"I guess I'll be looking for a new truck when this thaws out," Cody said. "What's the weatherman saying?"

Jesse shifted the tractor into gear and pulled out onto the road. "We've got sunny days until the first of next week, but the temperature isn't going to be above freezing. Dad thinks it will be the end of next week before the roads are clear into town. And we got news about Max. He had a heart attack, and he's still in the hospital, but he's not going back to his ranch when he gets out of the hospital. He's going to live with his son in Oklahoma."

Stevie heard what they were saying about Max, but it was like words coming through a staticky phone line. The last time she'd felt such a rush of emotions had been when she and Cody were dating back in high school. So much for being completely over him and moving on with her life the past twenty years.

* * *

Cody felt like a little boy at Christmas when Jesse made a turn down the lane onto the Sunflower Ranch. Even with snowdrifts as high as the porch, the house was a welcome sight, but then Jesse drove right past it, toward the barn.

"What are you doing?" Cody asked. "You could let us out at the house."

When Jesse was close to the barn, he drove the tractor off the plowed path and turned it around so he could back into the barn. "Somebody—that would be you, brother—has to get out and open the barn doors and help me get Stevie's van unhitched."

73

"And then we can have coffee?" Stevie groaned.

Jesse kept an eye on the rearview as he slowly backed up to the barn doors. "You haven't had coffee for four days, for real?"

"We had coffee one morning," Cody answered.

"That wasn't coffee," Stevie protested. "That was something between road tar and mud from the bottom of the Red River."

When he braked, Cody slid Stevie off his lap, got out of the tractor, and opened the barn doors. Once both tractor and van were inside, he closed the door and went around the tractor to help Stevie, but she was already headed for the van. He had liked having her so close to him on the trip home. She had been a beautiful girl, but she'd grown into an even more lovely woman—so warm and kind and funny that he was already wishing that they were back in the tack room with just Dixie and the cats to keep them company.

Jesse was right behind her. "There's a mama alpaca in one of the stalls. She gave birth a couple of days ago. Hopefully, she'll adopt your cria and raise it with hers."

"If the hembra won't take on another baby, then we can put Dixie in a separate stall, and I'll come feed her every four hours," Stevie said. "Hopefully, the cats will bed down with her once they check out the place."

Stevie opened the side door of the van before it was even unhitched. Dolly jumped out and meowed several times. Kittens came from different corners and followed her over to where the hay was stacked up. She flopped down on her side and started to purr, and soon all her babies were kneading her belly and nursing.

"I guess she figures a barn is a barn, no matter where it is," Stevie said as she picked Dixie up and carried her toward the stalls.

The mama hembra began to hum when she saw Dixie, and her baby ran over to stick her little nose out from between the rails. Dixie wiggled as if she wanted to be free from Stevie's arms, so Stevie opened the stall gate, set her down, and removed her diaper. The hembra sniffed the new baby all over, and her daughter headbutted the newcomer. Stevie moved slowly into the stall with all three alpacas and put Dixie's nose against the hembra's milk bag. Dixie's tail shot up and she started nursing.

"Thank you, Miz Hembra," Stevie sighed.

"Would you look at that?" Cody came up beside her. "Looks like you won't have to come to the barn every four hours in the cold to feed the baby. I was going to suggest that we take her and the cats to the bunkhouse if Maggie didn't adopt her."

"That's sweet, but she's so much better off here, and the cats have probably never known anything but a barn. They'd feel all cooped up in a bunkhouse," Stevie said.

"I'm not surprised." Jesse joined them. "Alpacas are herd animals, and they're loving toward their own. The only trouble you're going to have now is if you try to take that baby back from Maggie. She *will* fight you for it."

"I'm just glad she's found a good mama. I think the cats saved her life, but she needs her own kind," Stevie said.

Jesse's phone rang, and he slipped it out of his hip pocket. "Hello, darlin'. Yes, we're in the barn and yes, Maggie has taken to the cria, so all is good."

He listened for a few minutes and then said, "That's a great idea. I'll tell them."

"Tell them what?" Cody asked.

"Mama says that she's put food in the oven at the bunkhouse, and that she's pretty sure Stevie would like food and a bath before she comes up to the ranch house." Jesse put his phone back into his pocket. "Mia has plowed a path from the ranch house to the bunkhouse and out to here. You can either use the work truck or walk, but be careful. It's still pretty slick."

"And?" Cody asked. "I can see by that grin you can't wipe off your face you're hiding something."

"Y'all just go get cleaned up, have some food, take a nap, watch television or whatever you want to do. Supper is at five so be there for that," Jesse chuckled.

"I'm heading straight to the bunkhouse," Stevie said. "I'm going to eat and then take a long, hot bath. Tell Pearl and Addy I love them both for everything."

As soon as she was gone, Jesse chuckled again.

"What's so funny?" Cody asked.

"You and Stevie O'Dell stranded together," Jesse laughed, "and now you're going to have to live with her for another week. That's funny, I don't care who you are."

"I may be moving up to the house and sleeping on the sofa," Cody said, "but even that would beat the hard floor of that tack room."

"Good God, brother!" Jesse gasped. "You could have both slept on the sofa."

"Yep, and it even made out into a bed—with a bare mattress that was lumpy—but..." Cody shrugged. "We were like a couple of banty roosters, ready to spar most of the time. I wasn't about to suggest that we share the sofa bed, and she didn't offer."

Jesse shook his head. "Missed your chance, brother. Has it been so long that you need one of those how-to books to learn how to flirt?"

Cody clamped a hand on Jesse's shoulder. "If you've got your book still hiding up in the house, I might borrow it. Seems like you sure needed it when you came home and found Addy living here. Ever think that maybe I preserved my life by not suggesting we share that bare mattress?"

"You going to give Stevie your room and king-sized bed?" Jesse asked.

"Yep, but after the past three nights, one of those bottom bunk beds sounds like heaven right now." Cody got his doctor bag and Stevie's go bag from the van and followed Jesse outside. "Thanks for the rescue. See you at suppertime."

"You'd do the same for me. If me and Addy ever get stranded, don't come get me for at least a week." Jesse closed the barn door and took off in half a jog toward the ranch house.

The sunshine was a sight for sore eyes—one of Sonny's favorite sayings—but it did little to warm the bitter cold wind blowing in Cody's face. Tex, the ranch dog, met him halfway to the bunkhouse and followed him the rest of the way. When Cody opened the bunkhouse door, Tex ran in ahead of him, jumped up on the sofa, and curled up with his paw over his nose.

"Who's that?" Stevie asked from the kitchen table.

"Tex, meet Stevie." Cody dropped her go bag and his doctor bag on the coffee table. "Stevie, meet Tex. He's part ranch dog, part spoiled pet. He's a big baby, so you've got nothing to fear. Tex, Stevie is all redheaded fire, so be afraid. Be very, very afraid."

"That's not funny," Stevie told him. "I've set the table and there's a breakfast omelet in the oven, along with biscuits and a pan of gravy heating on top of the stove."

Cody went straight to the kitchen sink and washed his hands in warm water. "I will never take hot water for granted again."

"Me either. Or jelly, or salt or..." She nodded toward the coffeepot that had just gurgled and finished dripping.

Cody filled two mugs, handed one to her, and held his up. "A toast to surviving the business of being stranded."

She touched her mug with his. "To hoping we make it through the next week."

"We've already made it through the worst of it." He took a sip and held it in his mouth for a few seconds.

"Heavenly," Stevie whispered.

"Amen," Cody agreed. "The gravy is bubbling, and I'm about hungry enough to drink it like a warm milk-shake."

"Me too," Stevie agreed as she set the pan on a trivet in the middle of the table, and then brought out the biscuits and the omelet. "This right here is better than what we could get at a five-star restaurant."

"And this old bunkhouse is better than a five-star hotel." Cody sat down at the table and bowed his head. "I can't eat this food without giving thanks. We could have frozen to death or been killed out there. Let's have a moment of silence."

Stevie bowed her head. "I agree."

Cody said a short prayer of gratitude and then raised his head. He didn't know if Stevie was giving thanks or if she was asking God to help her make it through the next week, but it was a full minute before she opened her eyes. She picked up a biscuit, split it open, covered it with sausage gravy, and moaned when she put the first bite in her mouth.

"Hey, I thought my steak and potatoes were pretty good," he said as he followed her example and then dipped out a big helping of the omelet.

"They kept us from starving, but this is amazing," Stevie said. "It's just like Mama used to make."

"See, another good memory," Cody said. "Wonder what she would think of this situation."

"She would say that things happen for a reason." Stevie spooned omelet onto her plate. "I don't have any idea what the reason for this might be, but that's what she would say," she answered. "Yes, having breakfast with Mama is a good memory, and I do need to dwell on more of those, not the pain of her being gone."

"And me, too, when it comes to Dineo," Cody said. "The good should outweigh the bad, right, love?"

Stevie eyed him without blinking.

"What'd I say?" he said with a twinkle in his eyes.

"You almost sounded British when you said that word, *love*," Stevie answered.

"Sometimes a little of what I listened to over there

comes out. My only consistent friend for the past five years was Nate Fisher. He was born and raised in a village outside of London," Cody explained. "We're both doctors, and after our first six months, we asked if we could be stationed close by each other. They did what they could, so we spent a lot of time together. I picked up on his Queen's English, and he learned a little of my Texas drawl."

"I like the Texas drawl better," Stevie said, and went back to her breakfast.

"Well, then, love, I'll do my best to talk like a true Texan," Cody said with an almost flawless British accent.

Stevie poked her fork at him. "Don't call me *love*."

He went back to his normal drawl. "Yes, ma'am, darlin'."

"Or that either," she told him.

"Little cranky today, are you?" Cody asked. "I thought you'd be ecstatic we're in a place with hot food and water."

"Sorry about the attitude," Stevie said. "I do appreciate everything your mama has done so much for me. There's a note in the bedroom from Mia. I met her a couple of times when I was called out here to the ranch. I wasn't sure if she wanted to learn more by watching me treat the alpacas or if she was making sure I knew what I was doing."

"Mia is a good kid," Cody said. "I just wish Addy would have told us that Jesse fathered her before she was nineteen years old. I've had a niece all these years and didn't even know it."

"But she and Addy have lived here on the ranch for years." Stevie frowned. "How did you not know? She's even tall like Jesse and has his dark hair. I'm glad she's tall and close to my size because she sent flannel pajamas and other clothing for me to borrow while I'm here."

I bet you're even cute in flannel pajamas. Cody wondered where that thought came from. He hadn't blushed since he was a sophomore in high school, but he almost did right then. "Mama and Dad did figure it out, but they didn't say anything. Addy did good raising her as a single mother," Cody said.

"I got to admit, I was shocked when it came out that Jesse was Mia's father. Addy sure kept that secret well for almost twenty years," Stevie said, "but then I would have done the same thing if I'd been in her shoes. Has Mia settled down after that rebellious streak she had last summer?"

"Yep, good as gold," Cody said. "She realizes she dodged a bullet by leaving that worthless Ricky kid in Las Vegas and coming home where she belonged. She's a wonderful big sister to the twins Addy and Jesse adopted, and she's taking online courses at home to finish up her education, plus she's a fine hand on the ranch."

"I agree on Ricky being worthless. I heard that he's got a baby in Honey Grove and one in Bonham, and he's only about twenty. Sometimes, the DNA will surface. His daddy was a bad boy, and his mother was wild," Stevie said.

Oh, yeah! Cody thought about his biological parents, who'd been addicted to painkillers to the extent they could no longer take care of him. Cody was aware of all the pitfalls he may have inherited, but was also thankful he'd grown up in such a loving and nurturing environment, never tempted by bad habits.

"I'm glad Mia got away from Ricky. Whatever happened to open her eyes was worth it. Sometimes it takes a shake-up to realize what you've got right in front of your nose. I'm talking about all this." Stevie waved a hand around to take in the whole bunkhouse. "I didn't even have to ask, and your family came to our rescue like true friends. Addy sent shampoo, conditioner, and sweet-smelling bath salts, and Pearl changed the bedsheets," Stevie said. "I shouldn't be cranky, but I am."

"We are all your friends." Cody laid a hand on her shoulder. "Finish eating, go take a bath, and sleep off the crankiness. Everything will be just fine, and we'll get you back in your own home as soon as we can."

"As cold as it is right now, that might be spring," Stevie grumbled, "but thank you for trying to make me feel better."

"Anytime, Miz Stevie"—he grinned—"and since you set the table and got everything ready, I'll take care of the cleanup."

* * *

"That's so sweet." Stevie was surprised that she had gotten all misty eyed. She tried to convince herself that it was relief at being rescued, but down deep she knew that she would miss the time she'd spent with Cody in the tack room. "I don't deserve it, but it's nice to have friends."

"Why wouldn't you deserve friends?" Cody asked.

Seeing what she took as a look of confusion on Cody's face, Stevie said, "I have been downright mean to you ever since you came home, and here your family is being nice to me."

"Everybody needs a helping hand sometime," Cody said. "Now finish up your breakfast and go run a hot bath."

She cut her eyes around at him. "I don't take well to bossing."

"No bossing intended. I'm being selfish, actually. I want to take a shower and to sink down into one of those bunk beds over there, and you are holding me back by either arguing or being too grateful for little favors," he said. "I'm not sure which it is."

"You've always been blunt." Stevie finished the last bite on her plate and picked up her empty mug. "I shouldn't expect you to change now, should I?"

"I'm too old a dog to start changing, but, darlin'"—he dragged the endearment out—"you are the pot calling the kettle black, when it comes to bluntness."

Stevie refilled her mug and topped Cody's off, then put the pot back on the warmer. "You don't change a zebra's stripes."

She carried her mug to the bedroom, stopped inside the door, and turned around. "Do you need to come in here and get clean clothing or anything from the bathroom?"

"Yep, I do." He pushed his chair back, popped the last bite of a biscuit filled with strawberry jelly into his mouth, and crossed the room in a few long strides. It only took him a few minutes to gather up whatever he needed. "Have a good nap," he said as he eased the door shut behind him.

Stevie took stock of the bedroom and adjoining

bathroom. Back in the day when the bunkhouse was full, this would have been the foreman's quarters, but both had been remodeled in recent years. She figured the closet had been built in since the original foreman stayed in this room, and most likely, the first foreman didn't have a king-sized bed with a memory-foam mattress. The bathroom offered a nice claw-foot tub with a shower, a vanity with a mirrored medicine cabinet above it, and a toilet. Nothing fancy, but that tub looked like it had been dropped out of heaven to Stevie.

She adjusted the water in the bathtub and poured in some of Addy's bath salts, then dropped her clothing in a pile on the floor. Before the tub was half-full, she sunk down into the water and closed her eyes at the wonderful sensation of warmth surrounding her body. She leaned her head against the end of the tub and had almost dozed off when she came awake with a jerk and quickly turned off the faucet.

"I would have felt terrible if I had run this tub over," she muttered as she dunked her head under the water and then worked shampoo into her wet hair, rinsed, and used a coconut-scented conditioner. After that she just leaned against the sloped back of the tub and didn't waste a single bit of the warmth.

Once the water went lukewarm, she stood up and wrapped a wonderfully thick and fluffy towel around her head, and another one around her body. Towel-drying her curly, shoulder-length hair, she noticed a hair dryer on the vanity, and a broad smile broke out across her face.

"So, cowboys do dry their hair," she said to her reflection

in the mirror. "Why does that surprise me. They are proud of their hair, and as women, we wouldn't want to go out with a guy with nasty hair."

You take time to make yourself presentable too, her mother's voice in her head reminded her.

"Whose side are you on?" she asked as she used the dryer.

Her mother didn't have anything else to say, so Stevie fumbled around in the suitcase at the end of the bed and brought out a pair of underpants and pajamas. The flannel brought back memories of long nightgowns in the same fabric that her mother always bought special for her at Christmas. Little girls, according to her, should wear a granny gown when they opened their presents from under the tree.

"Little girls?" Stevie smiled at the memory. "I was thirty years old when you bought me my last flannel gown. I still have it, Mama, even though I only wore it the one time for a picture beside the tree."

Stevie crawled in between sheets that smelled like she imagined heaven would—all fresh and sweet like her mother's did right out of the dryer. Cody said that good memories would help her find closure. Maybe he was right. She snuggled down into the pillow and closed her eyes.

In seconds, she was asleep and dreaming of that day all those years ago when Cody Ryan told her that he had to follow his dreams and help other people. Only instead of turning away with tears in her eyes, in the dream she wrapped her arms around his neck and planted a hot, steamy kiss on his lips.

85

Chapter Seven

*I*n a work of literature, the villain defines the heroine.

Stevie had learned that in her English Comp class—which she hated. That idea came back to her as she unbuttoned the shirt of her flannel pajamas and then took off the bottoms. She tossed both pieces on the end of the bed and got dressed in borrowed jeans and a sweatshirt with a picture of Luke Bryan on the front. Evidently, Mia liked country music too.

If Stevie were writing a book with herself as the heroine, then who was the villain, and who was the hero? she wondered. She sat down on the edge of the bed and pulled on a pair of clean socks, another thing she would never take for granted again.

Is Cody Ryan the villain in my story? she asked herself and nodded while she stomped her feet down into her cowboy boots. "Maybe not *is*, but *was*," she whispered.

Can a villain also be a hero? she asked herself as she braided her hair and let it hang over one shoulder.

She would have to consider that more later because it was time to go to the ranch house for supper, but the idea had stuck firmly in her mind. She would be like a hound dog pup with a soup bone—bury it but keep going back to dig it up and think about it for weeks—until she had a satisfactory answer.

Cody was slouched on the sofa, his boots propped up on the coffee table when she went out into the bunk-house living area. He turned off the television and laid the remote to the side. "Are you hungry?" he asked. "You sure look a lot less cranky since you've had some rest."

"You read people pretty good, Dr. Cowboy," she said with half a smile, still trying to figure out if he could possibly change from bad to good.

"Thank you." Cody stood. "I'll take that as a compliment."

At just two inches shy of six feet, Stevie had always felt like a giant among the other kids she had gone to school with, especially the girls. But Cody was taller by a good six inches, and she felt especially feminine when he picked up her coat and helped her put it on.

"Jesse brought the ranch work truck down for us to use. I thought we'd take a side trip to the barn and check on the livestock," he asked.

"Since when have cats become livestock?" Stevie teased.

Cody straightened her collar, and as his fingers brushed against her neck, she felt a tingle shoot straight down to her toes.

"This is a ranch. Cows are animals. Alpacas are animals. Cats are animals. Cows are livestock. Even that bad-tempered donkey we keep around is an—"

Stevie raised a palm. "I get your point, and yes, I would love to go check on Dixie and the cats."

Tex hopped down off the sofa and followed her outside while Cody put his own coat on. The sun had done very little, if anything, to melt the snow. If it didn't warm up soon, Stevie was afraid she might really be living at the ranch until spring. When she opened the truck door, the dog jumped in ahead of her and settled in the middle of the bench seat.

"Looks like you're pretty familiar with this truck, Tex," she said.

When she'd closed the passenger door, he put his head in her lap and looked up at her with begging eyes. "You are so spoiled," she said, and patted his head.

"Yep, he is." Cody slid behind the wheel. "And he loves this truck better than my new one or any of the tractors. He missed Henry a lot when he retired. Do you remember our old foreman, Henry?"

"Of course, I do. He was one of the wisest ranchers I've ever met. I've only been out here on vet business a couple of times since he left, but I've missed him too. He always had a joke or a story to tell me. I imagine Tex was lost without him," Stevie said.

"So, you had already met Tex?" Cody asked.

"Not formally," Stevie answered. "We had just seen each other in passing. I think he likes me."

"Of course he does," Cody said. "You're petting him. I'm wondering how he's going to tolerate the cats."

"You're going to be nice to them, aren't you?" Stevie sounded like she was talking to a baby, but she didn't care if Cody liked it or not. "Yes, you are. You're not going to chase them or try to kill them, are you? Has he"—her tone changed—"ever been mean to cats?"

"Nope, but then the barn cats are wild, so they run from anyone who gets close to them, especially Tex." Cody drove slowly from the bunkhouse to the barn and parked beside an end door. "Thought it might be better if we go through the tack room rather than opening up the big door."

When Cody stopped the engine and got out of the truck, Tex followed him. The dog took time to turn a patch of snow yellow and then waited for someone to let him in the barn. He dashed inside ahead of Cody and Stevie, ran through the tack room, and headed toward the stalls.

Stevie and Cody made their way to the left side of the barn and stopped at the stall where Dixie and her new little sister were curled up next to each other in a bed of straw. Sunflower Ranch seemed to be a place for adoptions. First the three sons, then Addy and Mia, even though no one knew at the time that Mia was truly Sonny and Pearl's granddaughter. Then the twin boys Jesse and Addy had adopted, and now, they were giving Dixie a home.

And you too, Stevie's mother's voice whispered softly in her ear.

Stevie ignored the voice and said, "I'm so glad that the mama took her."

"Seems like adoption is a way of life on this ranch," Cody said with a smile.

"I was just thinking the same thing," Stevie admitted.

"Look over there behind Dixie." Cody pointed at the sleeping crias.

Stevie moved over a couple of feet and saw a pile of fur cuddled up to Dixie's back. "Well, now that surprises me. I would have thought the hembra—Maggie, right?— would have thrown a fit over cats next to her babies."

"As many times as they've all crawled all over Dixie, they probably smell like an alpaca," Cody suggested.

"You're probably right." Stevie nodded in agreement.

"Did that hurt?" Cody asked.

"What?" Stevie was a little cold, but she wasn't hurting anywhere.

"Admitting that I might be right?" Cody raised an eyebrow.

"It doesn't mean that you've always been right," Stevie told him.

"No, but I am today. Dr. Smarty-Pants just said so," Cody said with a big grin.

"Speaking of being right," Stevie said, "I'm glad that I was right when I told Dale that the alpacas here would adopt Dixie. He didn't think they would."

"I'm glad they did too," Cody said. "I've kind of gotten attached to the little girl, but I'd rather she be raised by her own kind than in the bunkhouse with us."

"Me too," Stevie said, but the way Cody's eyes were

boring right into hers, she wondered if he wanted to say more. "What are you thinking about?" she asked.

"That I'm already missing being stuck in that old barn," Cody said. "I believe that's the first time since I went to college that I didn't have some kind of control over the next thing, whether step or decision, in my life."

"Me too, again," she whispered. "Think we'll look back on those days in a few years and consider them good memories?"

"I will," Cody admitted. "Guess we'd better get on to the house, or supper will be cold."

"After what we've been through, I'd eat it right out of the fridge," she said with a grin. She started back toward the other end of the barn with Cody right behind her. Just like last time, as soon as she opened the door, Tex hopped into the truck and flopped down in the middle of the seat. Stevie slid in beside him, and somewhere out of the clear, blue sky a country song by Cross Canadian Ragweed came to her mind. The song had come out right after Stevie got her bachelor's degree—hardly seemed possible that was thirteen years ago.

"What are you thinking about so hard?" Cody pushed Tex over a little bit to make room for himself.

"A song just popped into my head," she said. "Ever listen to Cross Canadian Ragweed?"

"Yep, loved them. Hated to see them break up," Cody answered. "Which song?"

"'Seventeen,'" Stevie said. "It talks about always being seventeen in your hometown. No matter what you do with your life, or how long you've been away, folks still think of you like you were that same kid who left at seventeen. Coming back to Honey Grove, do you ever feel like people look at you like you're *that kid* again?"

Cody started the engine and turned to face her. "I'm running those lyrics through my head. The song came out about the time I was doing my clinicals. I'll always be one of the Ryan boys in Honey Grove. You'll always be that little red-haired O'Dell kid who lived a block down from the school. We can't change that or what people think of us. Does it bother you that folks still look at you like you're that age?"

"Sometimes," she admitted.

"Then chalk it up to being their problem." Cody shifted into gear and drove toward the house. "You've done a lot with your life, Stevie, and you're giving back to the community by coming home and putting in a vet business."

"Thanks," Stevie muttered.

"Anything else before we trade the peace and quiet for chaos?" Cody parked the truck close to the back porch.

"Not a thing." Stevie slung open the passenger door and stepped out of the truck with Tex right behind her. "And after the past few days, I'm ready for chaos."

Cody stepped out of the truck, crossed the short distance to the porch, and stood to one side of the door. "Ladies first," he said.

"Who are we kidding?" Stevie said with a smile. "We both know the second I open that door, Tex will beat me inside the house, so in reality it's dogs first."

"Such is life," Cody nodded.

The aroma of marinara and fresh bread wafted out to meet her the moment she and Tex stepped into the kitchen. Then Stevie got a whiff of something chocolate, and her mouth began to water. Coffee and candy had gotten her through too many long nights to count—from cramming for tests in college, to hours and hours of waiting for a calf to be born, to the times when she couldn't sleep after her mother's death—and she had sorely missed it while she and Cody were stranded.

"Hey!" Mia looked up from the counter where she had been spreading butter on the tops of hot yeast rolls. "Y'all made it just in time. We're about to put everything on the bar and serve it up buffet tonight."

Mia's dark hair was pulled up into a ponytail, and she wore faded red sweatpants, an orange sweatshirt, and mismatched socks. Stevie wondered if the girl's peers in school had called *her* a giant too. Nowadays, they called it bullying and were a lot quicker to take care of the issue than they had been twenty years ago. Stevie found herself hoping that Mia had never had to put up with those rude comments.

"Thanks for loaning me—" Stevie started to say.

"No problem. Good thing we're both tall and the same size. As you can see, we all got dressed up for supper tonight," Mia joked.

"You look beautiful to me." Stevie remembered coming home crying because some little girl had made fun of her height or of her curly red hair, and her mother telling her that the important thing was to be beautiful on the inside.

The kids who were mean to you are ugly on the inside. You are pretty and smart, and they're jealous, Ruth had said. *Let's have some chocolate cookies and milk. That will help you feel better.*

Mia crossed the big country-style kitchen and gave Cody a hug. "We missed you, Uncle Cody. Dad said your truck is totaled. That's scary."

Cody gave her an extra hug. "Truck is, but I'm just fine. Is that lasagna I'm smelling?"

"Nope," Mia answered. "Mama made rigatoni and Nana made the chocolate cake." Then she turned around and wrapped Stevie up in her arms for a hug and whispered for her ears only. "Did everything fit okay?"

Stevie nodded.

"Let me know if you need anything else." Mia took a step back.

"What can I do to help with supper?" Stevie hadn't been hugged since her mother's funeral, and warm feeling brought tears to her eyes.

Addy came from the dining room and gave Stevie a second hug. "We've got supper covered. Not that you had much choice in the matter, but we're glad to have you spending some time with us here on the ranch."

Addy's dark brown hair hung down her back in a single long braid, and like Mia, she was dressed in sweats—only her top and bottom matched—and thick, fuzzy socks, one blue and one red.

Pearl and Sonny came into the kitchen. "We were glad to get that note from you before you lost cell service. We would have been worried about you and a baby cria stranded out in the middle of the blizzard with no help or warm place to hole up until it blew over. We've called around and made sure everyone on this side of Honey Grove has what they need. Jesse went out yesterday in the tractor and delivered some supplies to two of our neighbors."

Sonny's sickness had taken its toll on Pearl. Her face seemed a little more drawn to Stevie than it was the last time she had been at Sunflower Ranch to check the cattle before the fall sale. Her hair had more salt than pepper in it these days, and somehow, she seemed even shorter.

"That's so sweet of y'all, and thank you for everything you're doing for me," Stevie said.

"Got to take care of our favorite vet." Sonny leaned heavily on his cane, but he had a smile on his face. "Did our boy here behave while y'all were stranded?"

"You should ask if *she* was good instead of me," Cody teased. "She was a cranky butt the whole time, and I *even* gave her the bed."

"Tattletale," Stevie said.

"See, Mama." Jesse carried in two infant seats and set them at the end of the table. "I told you that he tattled all the time when we were little boys."

"Pot and kettle, both black." Cody went over to the twins and dropped down on his knees. "They've both grown a foot since I left on Wednesday."

"That's what babies do. You'd be worried if they weren't right on schedule at two and a half months old," Mia said.

"How do you tell them apart?" Stevie was drawn to them like a bee to a honeypot. She'd always loved babies

95

and made quite a bit of money with her babysitting jobs from the time she was fourteen. "Look at those blue eyes and all that dark hair. They'll have to have a haircut before they're a year old."

"Sam has a dimple on the left side." Mia bent down and touched the baby on the chin, and he gave her a big toothless smile. "Taylor's got two. I'll show you." She made a face at the other baby and he showed off his double dimples. "Other than that, they're identical."

"And I'm their favorite person," Cody declared.

Mia air-slapped him on the arm. "You might be their favorite uncle now. When Uncle Lucas comes home, he might argue with you over that. But I'm their favorite person because I'm their sister, and that takes precedence over uncles."

"An ongoing argument in this house," Sonny chuckled. "If you want to know the truth, Stevie, I'm the favorite over all of them. I made them smile for the first time, and yesterday Sam giggled when I was making faces at him."

"I bet you are." Stevie could almost feel the love the family had for one another wrapping around her like a thick, fuzzy blanket on a cold night.

"All right, everyone, I'm putting the pot on the counter, and tonight I'll ask Jesse to say grace," Addy said. "After that, you can line up and help yourselves."

Jesse slipped his arm around his wife's waist and bowed his head. "Our Father…"

Stevie didn't hear the rest of the prayer, because she was thinking about what her mother said about being beautiful on the inside. Right then she couldn't claim a bit of that beauty, because she was bullfrog green with jealousy.

She had heard the gossip about Mia taking off with Ricky last summer, and also the rumors about Addy when she had finally come clean and revealed Jesse was Mia's father. True enough, the family had had their hurdles to jump over in the past, but that night they were perfect, and she wanted to be a part of something just like this—someday.

What do you mean by someday? Her mother was back while Stevie's head was bowed for grace. *Your biological clock is ticking so loud I can hear it all the way to the pearly gates, girl. If you want a family, you'd best quit wasting time.*

"Amen," Jesse said.

"Guests first." Cody took a step back from the counter and motioned for Stevie to go first.

"Oh, no!" She shook her head. "The only thing I love better than hot rolls is Italian food. If I go first, there won't be anything left for the rest of you."

"Well, I'm not bashful." Mia picked up a plate and covered one side with pasta and the other with salad, then added two hot rolls to the top.

"That's the Ryan genes coming out in you, girl. When it comes to food, not a one of us is shy," Cody agreed. "Mama, are you really going to let her get by with taking two hot rolls? You would have fussed at us guys for that."

"I'm her favorite," Mia teased as she carried her plate to the table. "And I plan to have two pieces of Nana's chocolate sheet cake when I'm done. Feeding cattle in all this snow uses up a lot of energy."

"And plowing pathways from one place to another, I would imagine," Stevie said, and got in line behind Pearl.

Mia stopped, looked over her shoulder, and flashed a bright smile. "Us girls have to stick together, don't we?"

"Yes, ma'am." Stevie was glad to be included in the family, even if it was only for a little while.

"How hungry are you, darlin'?" Pearl asked Sonny.

"Not quite starving, but I'm like Stevie when it comes to Italian food, so give me plenty so you don't have to go back for seconds for me, sweetheart," Sonny answered.

Stevie wanted a relationship like Pearl and Sonny had, one that could endure decades of ups and downs, and she would still love her partner enough to call him *darlin'* at the end of the day. She blinked away more tears and took the serving spoon from Pearl when she'd finished making Sonny's plate.

"This looks so good," Stevie said.

"We've been making pot meals," Mia said from the table, "as in simple things, not pot as in weed, since we've been snowed it. They are my favorite in the wintertime."

"After scrounging for food for four days, this is a pretty fancy supper," Cody said, "but Stevie did whip up a reasonable vegetable soup one evening and some hoecake to eat with it."

"Thank goodness Max left some food." Pearl took Sonny's plate to the table, then returned to fix her own. "I worried about you kids having to hunt rabbits for food in that blizzard."

"I'm not sure I could eat a rabbit. They're so soft and

cuddly and have those big eyes, so I'm glad there was some food in the tack room." Stevie carried her plate to the table and stopped and looked around, not knowing where her place was. Before her mother passed away, she always sat on one side of the table for four and Ruth's place was right across from her.

"Sit anywhere, darlin'," Sonny said. "We don't have assigned seats, except for Jesse and Cody. They can't sit beside each other because they still don't know how to behave."

"It's Jesse's fault." Cody brought his food to the table, set it down, and pulled out a chair for Stevie. "You can sit beside me. You're prettier than my brother anyway."

"That wasn't very nice." Jesse took a seat at the head of the table. "I even drove to the barn and rescued you."

"Whoa!" Addy threw up a hand. "Tell me more about these cats."

"It's like this…" Stevie continued to tell the story of the cria and how the cats took her under their wing, so to speak. "We were afraid Dixie might die if your hembra didn't adopt her, so we brought them with us."

"Cats, as in more than one?" Mia asked.

"A mama cat named Dolly and her kittens Boots, Tammy, and Loretta," Cody answered. "They're out in the barn. Well, they're actually in the stall with Maggie, the new cria, and Dixie. I can take them back when the roads are clear if you don't want them out there, Dad."

"Poppa…" Mia whined. "If no one buys that ranch for a long time, they might starve."

Sonny's old eyes sparkled. "What do you think, Pearl,

darlin'. Can our budget afford to feed a mama cat and her babies?"

Pearl pretended to have to think about the finances for a while, and then finally she nodded. "Well, if she's a good mouser, she might be worth keeping around, but no cats or kittens in the house, Mia. I hate the smell of a litter box."

"Thank you, thank you!" Mia squealed. "I'm going out there to get acquainted with Miz Dixie and the cats soon as we get done with supper. I love their names, Uncle Cody, but why didn't you name the boy Waylon or Willie or even Blake or Twitty?"

"Because he's black and white and has four white feet. He looked like a Boots to me," Cody answered.

"And, Mia, Boots Randolph was a fantastic country music saxophone player, so he's kind of named after a star anyway," Sonny said. "Look him up on that fancy phone of yours and listen to him play 'Yakety Sax.'"

"I will," Mia said, "but before I do that, I want to go see the new animals. I've tried for years to tame those wild barn cats. Now I'll have kittens I can hold and love on."

"And a brand-new baby cria," Addy reminded her.

"Life is good in spite of the snow," Mia sighed.

Yes, it is. Stevie agreed with a slight nod. In this household, she wasn't a seventeen-year-old kid anymore. She was an adult who, like Cody reminded her, was an intelligent woman and a help to the community.

"I'll go with you," Stevie offered. "I'd like to check on Dixie one more time before bedtime, just to be sure she's settling in all right. But not before chocolate cake."

"Oh, Dr. Stevie, nothing comes between me and Nana's chocolate cake, not even new pets," Mia said with a giggle.

The twins began to fuss and gnaw on their fists at the same time, and Addy pushed back her plate. "That's my cue for bedtime. They've had their baths, so it's bottle and rocking time. Save me a piece of cake!"

"I'll do daddy duty." Jesse got up from the table and picked up one of the carriers. "Mia helped with baths, and she needs to go check on the new animals."

"Thanks, Dad," Mia said. "You're the best. I promised to help with the bedtime duties tonight, but I really want to see the new cria and the kittens."

Jesse shook his finger at her. "But if there's not any cake left when I get done, you're in big trouble."

"Must've been nice growing up in this house," Stevie whispered to Cody.

"Yep, it was, at least, part of the time, but we weren't the Waltons. We had our fair share of problems," he told her. "You had mealtimes with your family, didn't you?"

"Not like this. Think about it. Mama, Daddy, and one child. We talked about our day, but when supper was over, Mama and I cleaned up. Daddy took care of whatever jobs needed attention around the place, and then we all went our separate ways. I did a lot of reading in my room," she answered.

"I didn't mean to be eavesdropping on your conversation with Cody, but you missed not having brothers or sisters, didn't you?" Pearl asked.

Stevie nodded. "I really did, and it's even worse now

since Mama is gone. There's no one to share the memories with, or to fuss about tattling when we were kids."

"I'll be your little sister," Mia offered. "We've already got stuff in common. I like alpacas and cats, and so do you. And I can argue with the best of them. Just ask Mama."

Addy and Jesse had each picked up a baby carrier and were headed out of the room, but Addy turned back and nodded. "She's a professional at that for sure. But she's too young to be your sister. I'll take that job and she can be your niece."

"Aww"—Cody nudged Stevie with his shoulder— "they're fighting over you."

"Too young!" Mia said. "There's nineteen years between me and the twins. I bet there's not that many years between me and Stevie."

"See what I mean," Addy said with a smile. "She's good at arguing."

"There's probably about nineteen years between us too, but I've never had a niece." Stevie remembered when she had first heard that Addy had a baby and that she wouldn't tell anyone who the father of the little girl was. She had envied her for having that much backbone and for doing what she wanted, no matter what anyone else thought of her.

Mia raised her chin. "Then I'll be your niece, Aunt Stevie. Does that mean you'll spoil me since I'm the only one you have?"

"As long as you don't expect me to give you my last bit of chocolate. I'm very stingy with that."

Pearl giggled. "Honey, you could be blood kin to Mia if you like chocolate that much."

"She does," Cody said. "If it hadn't been for two bites of a candy bar she had in her van, she wouldn't have survived being stranded in the barn as long as we were."

Stevie shot a dirty look at Cody. "I'm not all that bad, but I will admit to being a chocoholic."

"Which would you rather have," Mia asked as she carried her empty plate to the sink and cut herself a nice-sized wedge of the cake, "a cold beer on a scalding hot day, or a candy bar?"

"Candy," Stevie answered without hesitation.

"Yep, we are kin, Aunt Stevie," Mia told her and then asked, "want me to cut a piece for you?"

"Love one," Stevie answered.

"And me?" Cody asked.

"Are you asking me for a piece of cake?" Mia asked. "Or are you asking Stevie if she loves you?"

Cody's face turned scarlet. "Cake please."

"If I'm going to be the waitress, I'll put a tip jar on the counter," Mia teased.

"I hope you aren't planning on buying a new truck with all those tips that you'll get for serving dessert," Cody said.

"Pennies mount up to nickels, and nickels to dimes." Mia shot a look toward Sonny. "Poppa told me that, and Poppa does not lie."

"That's my girl," Sonny said with a broad grin.

Stevie remembered her mother saying those very words to her just before she slipped into a coma. She couldn't recall what they were talking about just before that, but her mother's last words had stuck with her.

The stars looked like diamonds on a bed of black velvet, and the quarter moon shone down on the white snow, giving the world an ethereal look that night as Stevie and Mia walked from the house to the barn. Stevie could tell that Mia was so excited about going to see the new animals that she didn't even notice the beauty all around her, but then Stevie had been the same way when she was Mia's age.

When they reached the barn, Mia flipped on the lights and hurried back to the stall where Maggie and the babies were. She was already inside and sitting on the floor when Stevie propped a boot on the lower rail and peeked over the top.

Mia gathered both crias in her arms like twin babies and began to rock back and forth. "If Maggie hadn't taken her, I would have volunteered to take care of her. I wish I'd never gotten crazy and sold my flock of sheep."

"Why did you?" Stevie asked.

"I thought I was in love," Mia answered.

"We all do stupid stuff when we fall in love," Stevie said.

"I bet you didn't." Mia looked up at her with eyes as blue as her daddy's. "I can't see you letting any guy lead you down the wrong path."

Before Stevie could figure out what to say, Dolly slipped under the bottom rail and stretched out beside Mia. All three kittens tumbled over and under the rails to join the party going on up next to this new person in their lives.

Mia laid the crias over close to their mama and picked up the cat. "You are beautiful, Miz Dolly," she crooned. "I can't believe that Maggie isn't screeching at you, but I'm glad she isn't. And just look at these babies of yours." She picked each one up and kissed its little nose. "This is almost as good as candy."

Stevie was still thinking about what Mia said, and had to agree that no man had led her down the wrong path. She had taken that fork in the road all by herself. She realized in that moment that she had judged all the men she had dated in the past twenty years by Cody. That hadn't been fair to any of them or to herself, and it was time to get past it and move on.

That's my girl, her mother whispered softly in her ear.

With all the emotions of the evening lying on her heart, Stevie needed a little time alone to think about laying the grudge aside and really moving on with a clean slate. Cody would probably spend most of the evening with his family, so she could have the bunkhouse, and even better, that big bathtub all to herself.

"I'm going to go on to the bunkhouse," Stevie said. "You going to be out here awhile?"

"Oh, yeah!" Mia answered without looking up from her lap full of cats. "I'm glad that things have worked out so you can be here with us until things thaw, Stevie."

"Thank you," Stevie said.

"Hey, a new face in the family is fun, and besides, I've been needing a friend to talk to about some stuff. Not tonight though. Mind if I come see you sometime tomorrow?" Mia asked.

"Not one bit," Stevie answered. "It's not like I can go anywhere."

With a wave over her shoulder, she turned and walked away. Heading toward the bunkhouse with only a little bit of moonlight to guide her way, she touched the locket around her neck and wished for the wildflowers of spring instead of all the snow and ice.

Chapter Eight

"Well, son, you had enough layin' around with nothing to do?" Sonny asked when Stevie had left.

"I kept busy, Dad," Cody assured him. "I didn't want Max to feel like we were eating all his food and using up his wood, so I chopped a whole stall full of wood, and Stevie and I cleaned the tack room for him."

Jesse pushed back his chair and brought the coffeepot to the table. "And now Max won't ever know what y'all did, because he's going from the hospital to his son's place."

Cody held up his cup for a refill. "That's a decision he probably should have made five years ago, and it's all right if he doesn't know about the work we did. Doing it made me feel good."

"I'll make a deal with you." Jesse refilled all three cups. "I'll use the tractor to get you to any patients you might need to visit if you'll help me do chores the next few days."

"I told you before that I'm willing to help any way you need me," Cody said.

"I know that, and you have helped a lot, but I'm going to depend on you even more for a little while," Jesse said in a low voice.

"Mia is worth her weight in gold"—Sonny lowered his voice too—"but all this cold has created extra chores—shoveling, chopping through ice on the water troughs—and I can tell it's wearing her thin. I don't want her to hear me, but I'm going to tell her that I need her in the house a couple of days to catch up on the computer work."

"I understand. What time do you want to get started tomorrow morning?" Cody asked.

"Soon as breakfast is done," Jesse answered. "It's been taking me and Mia until almost noon to get everything taken care of, but I reckon the two of us can be finished a little earlier than that. The water pipes from the well froze up today, so tomorrow we're going to have to carry water from the barn out to the pasture."

"Thank goodness we got a little forewarning and moved all the herd to the forty acres behind the barn, or y'all would have been running all over the ranch trying to feed and water," Sonny said. "I hate that I can't help you guys."

"You help us by supervising," Cody said. "We were raised on this ranch, but we were gone for a long time. We still need some help from a wise old head like yours."

"It's old, all right," Sonny chuckled, "but I'm not so

sure about the wisdom in it. I'll tell you one thing, there's more smarts up here"—he tapped his forehead—"than that rotten weatherman has. Telling us we might not get more than an inch of snow, and then changing his mind just about the time the blizzard hit. Your mother was the one who said we'd better get prepared for a big storm. She's the smart one in the family."

"The storm made a sweep to the south that no one expected. Maybe Mama ought to take that weatherman's place on the morning news," Cody said.

"She'd do a better job, but rest assured, there's a reason for everything." Sonny's tone was dead serious. "We might not know what it is right now, but in ten years, we'll look back and see things clearly."

"What do you see clearly, Dad?" Jesse asked.

"That adopting you three boys was the best thing that happened to me and your mother. It's time me and Pearl went to our house, if I can drag her away from Addy. When we first moved to Henry's house after he retired, it felt strange, but now it feels like we've always lived there." Sonny picked up his cane and headed toward the living room.

"Need some help?" Cody asked.

He had thought his folks might move to the house on the property across the road—the ranch they had bought from Addy's parents when they sold out and went out to the Panhandle—when Jesse and Addy got married, but they'd opted to take over Henry's place that was still right on Sunflower Ranch.

"Not tonight but thanks." Sonny leaned heavily on his

109

cane as he shuffled out of the kitchen. "When I do, I'll ask for it."

"Just remember, we're all here for you, and don't be too stubborn to ask," Cody said with a smile.

"I wouldn't be where I am today without being stubborn." Sonny disappeared around the corner and into the hallway.

Jesse waited until he was out of sight to ask, "In your opinion, what happens next with him?"

"Who knows?" Cody answered. "MS varies with the patient, and like he said, stubborn has taken him a long way, but I would think that he'll need a walker before long." Thinking about not being home to help his dad put a lump in Cody's throat. He believed that nothing should ever be more important than family, and yet he had let his job stand between him and those most important to him. "One day at a time. That's all any of us get anyway."

Jesse stood up and clamped a hand on Cody's shoulder. "You might do well to remember that."

"What's that supposed to mean?" Cody asked.

"Just think about it," Jesse said. "If you were a woman, your biological clock would be tickin' pretty loud. If you had a child in a year, you would be retirement age before that kid got through college."

"Old doctors are like old farmers," Cody chuckled. "They never retire."

"Who's retiring?" Pearl asked as she and Sonny had passed through the room and stopped in the utility room that was right off the kitchen.

"No one," Jesse said. "According to my brother here, old doctors and old farmers don't know what retirement is."

"I knew I'd raised some smart kids." Sonny shifted his cane to his left hand so Pearl could help him with the sleeve of his coat. "See y'all tomorrow."

Pearl slipped on her coat and then pulled a stocking hat down to her ears. "With all this snow, we've been coming up here sometime in the middle of the afternoon and having supper together, Cody."

"You and Stevie are welcome to join us every evening. Addy and Mia appreciate seeing some faces other than mine since we're all stuck in the house," Jesse said.

Cody stood and headed toward the utility room, where he'd hung his own coat. "I know I'd love that, and I'm pretty sure Stevie would look forward to having someone to talk to other than me. I'll see you in the morning, brother. And, Mama, if y'all need anything, we can be there in five minutes or less." Cody turned back to Jesse. "Mind if I take a couple of slices of that cake with me?"

"Not one bit. Addy said she was making pies for tomorrow's dessert," Pearl answered and came back into the kitchen. She cut two wedges of the cake and put them on a paper plate, then covered it with plastic wrap. "Since she's not been able to get out and go places with you and the doctoring business, she's been keeping busy in the kitchen. We'll all have to go on a diet when this snow is melted. And, son, you know you can drop in at our house anytime you don't want to make food for yourself."

"And bring Stevie with you. I like that girl," Sonny said.

"Thanks." Cody picked up the cake. "I might do that."

111

"Y'all ever going to get past the fact that you broke her heart?" Jesse asked when Pearl and Sonny left.

"Ever think that I had my reasons?" Cody asked.

"Never doubted it for a minute," Jesse said. "I'd love to hear them sometime, but right now, I've got a beautiful wife waiting for me in the living room. She told me that we're watching a movie tonight. Want to join us?"

"No, but thanks anyway. Besides, you've got one kid at the barn playing with the new cats—you are welcome for that—and the twins are asleep. Might be nice for you and Addy to have a few minutes to yourselves." Cody winked as he opened the door. "I'm going to leave the work truck and walk back to the bunkhouse. Tell Mia thanks for plowing a path for us, will you? I forgot to."

"Hey, that's not all she did," Jessie said. "She worked over that forty acres the cattle have been moved to so they wouldn't have to stand in a foot of snow. Sure makes the feeding and watering easier because we don't have to wade it up to our knees."

"That girl is a born rancher," Cody said and waved as he closed the door behind him. He paused on the porch steps and thought about what Jesse said. He and Stevie definitely needed to bury the past and move on with their lives, but Stevie O'Dell could teach even Sonny Ryan a few lessons in stubbornness. If he tried to explain the whole story to her, she would set her heels for sure, and besides, he wasn't sure he wanted to be completely honest about his excuse for rejecting her. That would mean he would have to voice the reasons out loud, and that would make them even more real.

Out there in the distance, light glowed through the barn window and around the big sliding door like a beacon, but he didn't want to butt in on Mia and Stevie's time together. Mia had hit a really rough patch the last year and hadn't fully dug out from under her mistakes. Her friend Justine had helped, but she was about Mia's age. Stevie was older and wiser, and then on other hand, Stevie had lost her mother and felt guilty. Sharing their feelings, like women did, would be good for them both.

Tex came out from his doghouse located beside the porch, tail wagging and head down. He butted Cody's leg with his nose, as if pushing him to start walking.

"Well, old boy, all we're doing out here is getting colder by the minute." Cody headed toward the bunkhouse. Frozen grass made a crunching noise under his feet, and a couple of times his feet came close to slipping out from under him.

"I hate ice and snow almost as much as I did sand," he muttered to the dog.

Tex bounded ahead and rushed into the bunkhouse the second the door was opened. Cody opened the door, Tex rushed inside and curled up in the middle of the sofa.

"Hey." Stevie stepped out from the kitchen area. "Is that for me?"

Cody handed the plate to her before he even removed his coat. "One piece is. The other one is for my bedtime snack."

"Thank you, but why wait until bedtime." Stevie peeled back the plastic wrap, ran her finger through the icing, and then licked it. "We need to talk."

113

"About?" Cody could tell by her expression that she didn't want to discuss the snow, the ranch, or the chocolate cake. Even though he would have liked to have more time to think about the issue, if Stevie was ready to talk, then he'd plow through the discussion as best he could.

* * *

Stevie removed the rest of the wrap and tossed it in the trash. She carried the cake to the sofa and sat down on one end. She should have driven out to the ranch and had this conversation with Cody when he first came home, she had decided since she left Mia in the barn. But she'd been downright hateful and belligerent every time she saw him. Her mother always told her that every choice had consequences. That was the absolute gospel truth, she thought as she waited for him to come over to the living area. Today it was time to pay the fiddler, and Stevie was ready to get it over with and off her heart and mind.

"You can bring the forks and two beers. I'm glad I don't have to choose between beer and chocolate tonight. I need both," she said with a long sigh.

"So, it's a serious talk?" Cody took two forks from the drawer and a couple of long-neck bottles of beer from the fridge and joined her on the sofa.

"This is more like a 'come to Jesus' talk for me, starting with I'm sorry for treating you the way I have since you came home, and especially since you've been so nice to me. I thought I was completely over you since we broke up in high school, and I thought I had moved on, but evidently I hadn't." Stevie was glad that Tex was between them.

"Well, then let's hear it, *love*." He set the bottles on the coffee table.

"I told you not to call me that, and this is serious, Cody, and this is not the time to tease me," she said.

"Okay, then spit it out and let's get it over with." He said.

She took a deep breath and let it out slowly. "It's tough to talk about the way I feel, and even harder to admit that I'm to blame for most of it." She took a fork from him and cut off a chunk of cake with the edge of it. "I was in love with you when we were dating..." She sighed. "I know we were both just kids, but I would have followed you to the ends of the earth."

"I know," Cody whispered, "but I couldn't ask you to do that, Stevie. We both had dreams to follow, and we would have both regretted not..." He hesitated. "At least I know I would have if I hadn't..." Another pause. "Damn it, Stevie. This is hard. I just couldn't let myself have a serious relationship with anyone. It wasn't just you, but I did have feelings for you. That's why I broke up with you that spring. If I was going to be a doctor, it would take all my time and energy. You deserved more than a small piece of me. You deserved someone who would give you one hundred percent, not two percent."

"I understand that now, but it's taken me a long time to sort it all out. It's in my nature to finish a project before I start another one, so I thought I couldn't fall in love with anyone else as long as you were around. This all sounds crazy, but bear with me," she said as she took another sip of beer.

"I'm all ears," he said, "and I do not mean that to be joking."

Stevie took in a deep breath and let it out very slowly. Thank God for chocolate. That always helped get her through tough times. "I couldn't believe you asked me to the homecoming dance that fall. I was a gangly red-haired girl with braces and freckles who wasn't popular. I was smart, but not someone that a handsome Ryan boy would give a second look," she said.

"Did you ever think that what you felt was just infatuation and not love?" Cody twisted the top off his beer and took a long drink. "I had a big crush on Brenda Jones when I was a freshman in high school, but she only had eyes for..."

"Darrin Black." Stevie finished the sentence for him. "I remember them coming to church and holding hands when I was in elementary school. But you aren't wired like I am. You got over your crush. Did you put her on a pedestal and measure every woman by her for the next two decades?"

"No, I did not." Cody frowned. "Are you telling me that you did that with me?"

"I told you, I have to finish a project before I start another one," she answered. "So, yes, I did. I told myself that I had moved on and didn't even realize that I was measuring every guy by your yardstick. I've dated guys. First dates, second, and even a few third. I've had three fairly serious relationships. I can see now that the reason none of them worked out was because I was trying to put them up on a pedestal beside the one I had built for you."

"Good Lord, Stevie!" Cody took a long draw from his beer. "Why would you do that?"

"I made you into this perfect person in my mind. I was devastated the night we broke up, but I told myself that you were doing it for the greater good." Stevie shrugged. "Remember earlier this evening when we were talking about always being seventeen in our hometown?"

Cody nodded. "What's that got to do with this?"

"Everything," Stevie answered. "Being seventeen in Honey Grove isn't important. What is important is that when I'm around *you*, that I'm still seventeen again. I don't know if I was your first, but you were mine."

"I knew, and yes, you were," Cody whispered.

"They say you never get over your first love, your first experience in sex, your first anything. I guess I didn't," she told him.

"Now that I recognize the problem, I *will* get over it. It's been pretty damn immature of me not to own up to it and admit it before now. I hope that going forward we can be friends," Stevie said.

"Whew!" Cody said. "That's a lot of honesty for one night, but I'd like it very much if we could be friends."

"I feel better for having said it," Stevie told him. "It's not fair to either of us for me to blame you for my failed relationships, and like you said, what I felt was pure infatuation, not love. You were wise enough to see that. I wasn't, but I do now."

"We were both too young to make a lifetime commitment or to change our plans to suit the other one," Cody said. "I knew that you wanted more, and it scared me, because to give you that, like I said, it would have taken more than I had to offer at the time. The feelings I had for you back then scared me."

In all the scenarios that had ever played out in her head, this one had never entered Stevie's mind. She'd always thought the Ryan boys were super sure of themselves. In her eyes Cody had always been ten feet tall and bulletproof.

"I can't imagine you being scared, but I understand," she said.

"You've figured out things for yourself, and it took a lot of courage to talk to me about this," Cody said, "and, honey, you are not seventeen in my eyes anymore."

"Thank you for that." Stevie felt as if a weight had been lifted off her heart.

"I'm glad we had this talk," Cody said.

"Me too. We've kind of taken care of the elephant, haven't we?" Stevie smiled.

"We have," Cody agreed.

"Speaking of elephants, Mia and I had a little visit out in the barn. She feels so bad that she sold off her flock of sheep and ran away with Honey Grove's most notorious bad boy, and used up every bit of her money. Talking to her is what gave me the courage to tell you how I felt."

"From what Jesse told me, they were heartsick for Mia," Cody said. "And she's paying dearly for her mistakes now."

"How's that?" Stevie asked.

"She lost her position overseeing some of the hired hands. Addy made her take her courses online this semester because last semester she flunked them all, and she had to interview with Jesse for a job as a ranch hand," Cody answered.

"Tough love." Stevie finished off her piece of cake and stole a bite of Cody's. "Mama applied some of that several times when I was growing up, and even after I came home."

"Dad will never get better." Cody's tone went all hoarse, like he was trying to talk past a lump in his throat. "I couldn't bear to have one of my kids do that to him in his last days."

"So you are thinking about settling down now? I figured after you saw that Sonny was all right, you might go back to Doctors Without Borders again."

Cody took another drink of his beer. "I do miss that life, but my place is here, and to answer your question, I have thought about a family, but that's as far as it's gone. Right now, I'm just trying to take care of Dad, this ranch, and my practice."

"And again, you've got too much on your plate for a serious relationship, right?"

"That's pretty much the way of it," Cody answered.

"From the time we spent in the tack room, I'd say that you're a normal old cowboy looking for peace, love, and contentment," Stevie said.

"I'll take *normal* anytime, but I'll argue that *old* point," he teased.

119

"You're staring forty in the eye," she reminded him. "Like I said, I finish a project before I start another one. Consider yourself all done. I'm moving on. You can do the same or not—that's your choice."

"What do you want out of life . . . *love?*" he teased.

"I don't have to decide tonight, but I don't intend to waste any more time on measuring all guys by your yardstick. I'm not seventeen, in this town, or in my own eyes when I'm around you. I'm an independent woman who is building a vet practice." She picked up her beer and finished it.

"You are definitely independent," Cody agreed. "You remind me a lot of Addy."

She stole another forkful of his cake. "I'll take that as a compliment." The piece of cake slipped off the fork and was on the way to land on the sofa when Tex gobbled it down in one bite.

"I meant it as a compliment. Addy is amazing." Cody loaded his fork with the last bite of cake and offered it to her. "Thanks for the talk. Think we might be friends?"

"Right back at you for being honest with me, and I'd like for us to be friends." Stevie steadied his hand with hers so that the cake made it to her mouth. "And thank you for sharing your last bit of cake with me. Anyone who gives me chocolate is well on their way to being my friend. I'm going to bed now. What time should we be up and around? I can help with ranch work if you need me. Guess we won't be going to church since we can't get there past the roads that are blocked with broken-down trees."

"Jesse and I can take care of that, but breakfast is early.

We only have supper together in the ranch house. That way Jesse and Addy can have time to be a family," Cody explained as he carried the plate and empty beer bottles to the kitchen.

"Then I'll be up at the crack of dawn, and we can cook breakfast together," she said. "But really, I would be glad to help with whatever. I could check the cattle and make sure they're all right in this kind of weather."

"Make sure your phone is charged." Cody covered a yawn with his hand. "That way, if we need you, we'll call."

"You got it," Stevie said. "I'm surprised that I haven't got texts or calls from folks in town who need help with their animals."

"Mama has probably let her friends all know you are stranded out here on the ranch and couldn't get to them even if you wanted to," Cody said.

"Hadn't thought of that." Stevie headed toward her bedroom. So now she and Cody were friends, but there was a little piece of her heart that still wanted more, whether she would ever admit it out loud or not.

Chapter Nine

$\mathcal{T}$he past several days had all run together, and Stevie had to check her phone to see what day it was when the alarm awoke her that morning. "How did it get to be Sunday?" she muttered as she padded to the bunkhouse kitchen in her pajamas and socks.

"I don't know, but I don't think we'll be going to church this morning." Cody handed her a cup of coffee. "Seems like a month ago that we were stuck at Max's barn."

"And yet we were only rescued yesterday." Stevie opened the refrigerator door and took out bacon, eggs, and cheese. "Got any oatmeal? You're going to need a big breakfast to keep you warm out there in the weather."

"In the pantry," Cody answered. "I can't make biscuits fit to eat so I usually just have toast. There's a couple of loaves of Mama's homemade bread in the freezer."

"I'll make the biscuits this morning. We can thaw out a loaf of bread for sandwiches or maybe potato soup for lunch." She went into the pantry and came out with what she needed.

Cody turned on the oven and brought pans out from the cabinet. "I could get used to this."

"Oh, yeah?" Stevie raised an eyebrow. "Would that be having a woman in flannel pajamas and her hair all messy making biscuits?"

"That would be having a friend to talk to while we make breakfast, and then sharing conversation while we eat," he answered, "and you are definitely not that little girl in braces anymore. Even with your bedroom hair, you are a beautiful woman."

Stevie couldn't remember the last time she had been paid a compliment like that, and she'd never had anyone tell her she was beautiful when she looked like she did right then. But the expression on Cody's face told her that he wasn't joking—and he hadn't added the word *love*.

"Thank you," she said, and wondered how both of their lives would have changed if Cody had even told her something like that when she had seen him at the rodeo a few weeks ago.

To everything there is a season. Your time will come. Be patient. Her mother had told her that many times, especially when her relationships went south.

For the days to be in such a jumble, the time that it took to make breakfast and eat it went fast. Stevie was just drying the last fork and putting it away when she heard the noise of the truck. Cody grabbed his hat, settled it on his head, and then put his coat on.

"See you at noon or before," he said on his way out the door with Tex right behind him.

She raised her voice and yelled, "Call if you need a vet."

She had no sooner said the words than her phone rang. She raced to the bedroom, grabbed it, and answered without even looking at the caller ID. "Hello, this is Dr. Stevie O'Dell."

"Oh, Stevie," Gracie Langston whined, "Fifi is sick. I need help."

"What's the matter with her?" Stevie had gotten a call like this about every two weeks since she had come home to Honey Grove. The first few times she had rushed across the street to her mother's best friend's house and checked on the ten-year-old poodle. Then she realized that it was Gracie who wanted company, and she was using the miniature poodle as an excuse to get Stevie to visit her. Then, of course, while she was there, Gracie would either pump her for gossip about what she might have heard when she was on vet business, or else Gracie wanted to spread rumors to her. Most of the time, she just steered the conversation away from the folks she did business with, and then let the rumors go in one ear and right out the other.

"I'm so, so sorry, Miz Gracie," Stevie said, "but as you probably know, I'm stuck at Sunflower Ranch. Trees are down between here and town, and it will probably be next week before I can come home. What's wrong with Fifi? Tell me how she's acting."

"I heard you and Cody Ryan were stranded together," Gracie said. "Is there something going on between you?"

"No, ma'am," Stevie answered. "Now about Fifi?"

"Your folks was good people, and they raised you up to be a good girl. Don't you be lettin' that Cody Ryan ruin your reputation," Gracie scolded.

"I'll be very careful." Stevie bit back a smile. "Is Fifi running a fever? Is her nose dry and cold? Are her eyes all watery?"

"No, none of those things," Gracie sighed. "I think she's depressed. Can you call the pharmacy and have them bring me some antidepressants for her?"

"I'm sorry," Stevie answered, "but no. Does she stare at the door and whine?"

"Yes, but she's been using her little potty pads since she can't go outside. Before all this storm hit, she would bark at the door when she was ready for me to take her for a walk around the block," Gracie answered. "Since Fifi is your patient, can I tell you something under that patient-doctor confidentiality rule?"

"I don't think vets work that way, since animals don't talk to us," Stevie said.

"Well, I think she has a crush on that corgi that Eva has next door, but I'm not having her out there flirting with that short-legged little mutt," Gracie said. "I don't like Eva and her pompous ways, and I sure don't like that dog of hers. When she takes it for a walk, it hikes its leg on my flowers, and she doesn't even apologize."

"Has someone shoveled your sidewalk?" Stevie asked.

"Yes, and from my house to the end of the block, but

what's that got to do with my Fifi?" Gracie's tone said she was getting tired of the conversation.

"She's bored," Stevie said. "Poodles are temperamental and like a schedule. She's used to you walking her every day. Put on your boots—the ones with fur around the top—and take her for a stroll down to the corner and back. That should make her happy again."

"But it's cold out there," Gracie objected.

"Bundle up real good and call me later if she doesn't feel better. I've got to hang up now and take this next call." Stevie hit the right buttons and said, "Hello, Mia. Is everything all right?"

"Yes, but I was wondering if you were awake and were up for some company for a little while," Mia answered.

"Always," Stevie answered. "I'll put on a pot of coffee."

"I'll bring a package of cookies," Mia said, "and be there in ten minutes."

Stevie hurried to the bedroom, changed into sweats, and brushed her hair out. She'd just finished when she heard a knock, and then Mia's voice yelling, "I'm coming in. Is everyone decent?"

"Just me here, and yes, I'm decent," Stevie answered. "Come on in out of the cold and have a seat. Coffee is done."

"I brought chocolate chip cookies. They're not home-made, but they aren't bad." Mia laid the package on the coffee table and removed her coat, hat, gloves, and boots.

Stevie poured two mugs full of coffee. "Sugar, cream, or both? And, honey, there's no such thing as bad chocolate, unless it's burned fudge, and then it goes beyond bad and becomes a sin."

"Just black, and you are so right about chocolate." Mia sunk down on the end of the sofa and sat cross-legged. "I couldn't sleep so I got up real early and got the computer work caught up for Poppa and made breakfast for the family."

Stevie carried the coffee to the living area and set the mugs on the coffee table. "We just finished a big meal, so I'm going to wait a little while on a cookie," she said. "I had trouble sleeping last night too. I'd like to blame it on the fact that I had such a long nap yesterday, but I would be lying to myself."

"Uncle Cody?" Mia raised a dark eyebrow.

"Yes, and no," Stevie answered, not sure if she wanted to take Mia into her confidence. "Who kept you awake?"

"I'll show you mine if you promise to show me yours." Mia picked up her coffee and held it in her hands. "I like the way it warms my hands and smells as much as I like the flavor."

"Me too," Stevie said. "You go first. Who have you been worrying about and why?"

"I made a big, huge, colossal mistake a year ago. I was the lucky one of at least three different women. I didn't have Ricky's baby, but that doesn't mean I wasn't just as taken in by him as the other two girls," Mia said.

"Is he back in town and wanting to see you again?" Stevie asked.

"No," Mia said, and shook her head, "and if he was, I might be tempted to thump on him a little bit. But...it's hard to explain..." she stammered. "I probably shouldn't talk to you about this. Promise you won't tell Mama and Daddy. I just need a sounding board, and you're here, and—"

"And it's easier to talk to a stranger than to your folks about whatever this is, right?" Stevie asked.

"Yes, only I don't feel like you're really a stranger. You kind of fit in with the family, and I bet you had some of the same problems I did when you were my age. Were you a bit of a misfit, what with being almost six feet tall, and I bet you liked animals more than people most of the time, right?" Mia set her coffee on the table and opened the package of cookies. "I need chocolate."

"I didn't make friends well in high school or in college," Stevie admitted. "I wish I would have had one of those BFF girls in my life to talk to, but I didn't, so I hit the books hard, and tried to forget a certain young man who broke up with me and broke my heart."

"Was it with Uncle Cody?" Mia asked.

"Yes, it was, but you were telling me your story." Stevie urged her on with a smile.

"I'm over Ricky," Mia said, "but I don't trust myself. He paid attention to me and told me I was beautiful, and even talked me into a tattoo. I learned later that three of us in this county alone have the same tat, like he was marking his harem. There's no telling how many more there will be before he's done."

"That's his problem, not yours," Stevie said. "Let me see the tat."

Mia shifted her position and pulled up her shirt to

show a rose on the small of her back. "Justine has one just like it, and a girl over in Bonham. They both have babies with him."

"As long as you think about Ricky and consider that tattoo as his mark, he has power over you. You can't change him, but you can change the way you view that beautiful rose. Start to think of it as a warning to never let a guy sweet-talk you into doing something you know in your heart is wrong again," Stevie advised her.

"I like that," she said. "Now, for the reason I can't sleep. I met this really sweet guy at the feed store. He's working there part-time and taking online courses just like me to get an agribusiness degree."

"Do his folks own a ranch around here?" Stevie asked.

"No, but his grandpa does. He came down here from Colorado to help out when his grandma died last summer," Mia said. "Do you know Beau Martin?"

"Kin to Vernon Martin, who owns Bois D'Arc Ranch?" Stevie asked.

Mia nodded. "That's Beau's grandpa."

A picture of Vernon flashed in Stevie's head. He was about six feet four inches tall and had a big smile and kind eyes. Here lately, when she was called out to his ranch, he'd talked about his grandson being such a good boy to come stay with him, and how much he missed his wife. "The Martins are good, solid ranching people in this area. Why are you worried?"

"Everyone in town knows that I messed up real bad," Mia answered. "I don't want Beau to..." she stammered, "to think I'm a slut, or his granddad to..." She frowned. "Be ashamed of the girl Beau is dating. There, I said it."

"Don't do that to yourself," Stevie said. "Don't let one mistake with Ricky define who you are."

"But what if Beau thinks I'm just a pushover like I was with Ricky? What if I am?"

"Ask him," Stevie said.

"Just be blunt like that?" Mia asked.

"I was every bit that straightforward and honest with Cody last night, so yes, ma'am, just be up front and honest and ask him about it."

"I've only ever been with Ricky, and you know how that turned out." Mia almost blushed. "I fell over backward for him and let him control my life for months."

"Then don't do that again." Stevie wondered if she would have fallen over backward for Cody when she was Mia's age. Would she have given up her dreams of being a vet to support him through medical school? "Be yourself. Be totally honest and agree to a date or two with him when we get rid of all this snow. If you like him, then invite him to Sunday dinner. You can figure out what kind of guy he is by how he reacts to your family."

Mia dipped a cookie in her coffee. "Ricky wouldn't ever even come in and let me introduce him to my folks, and Beau and I've already talked on the phone and went on a couple of drives together. Matter of fact, we've been talking every night, and he texts me several times a day, I do like him, and I want to see what Mama thinks of him, but what if he refuses to…" Mia sighed. "What if he's just trying to butter me up for sex?"

"Don't do what I've done and let a good guy slip out of your life because you are judging him by someone else's actions," Stevie said.

"What if I invited him to dinner, and he says he doesn't want to meet my folks?" Mia asked.

"Then tell him to get lost," Stevie said. "He can come to Sunday dinner, or he can go find another young woman to flirt with."

Mia nodded. "I knew you'd be the one to talk to. Now, I guess I should tell Mama and the rest of the folks."

"That would be a good idea, for sure." Stevie picked up her first cookie.

"Time for you to need chocolate too?" Mia asked.

"Oh, yeah," Stevie answered, "and it wasn't your uncle Cody who kept me awake last night, but I did dream about him. It wasn't the first time either, and it all started more than twenty years ago."

Mia sat up a little straighter, and her eyes widened. "I knew there was something between y'all. I just knew it. He looks at you like…" She started on another cookie.

"Like what?" Stevie asked.

"Like Daddy did and still does at Mama," Mia asked. "Now I want to hear the rest of the story."

Stevie told her a little bit of the story, ending with *it was all probably just an infatuation*. "I bet that's what you had with Ricky, right?"

"Probably," Mia said, "but it felt real at the time."

"So did what I felt," Stevie said, "but it wasn't real love. You are smarter than I am. You're not letting your experience define who you are, but be careful that you don't let it ruin any potential relationships you might be destined for."

Mia was quiet for several minutes, as if she was letting what Stevie had said soak into her heart and soul. "What did he say when you talked to him last night?"

"We decided that we should be just friends, and I'm not angry with him anymore. After all, we've got a lot in common, and we have to be together for a few days until the roads are clear. It would be better to be friends than to be enemies right now, don't you think?"

Stevie's phone rang before Mia could answer. She picked it up and said, "Hello, Gracie. Is Fifi happier now?"

"Poor little darlin' is tuckered out from her walk, and so am I," Gracie answered. "We're both cuddled up under a blanket in my recliner and watching game shows on television. Getting out is just what she needed. Now, let's talk about this thing with you being out there with Cody Ryan. You know that folks are already talking, don't you?"

"I can't help that or the fact that trees are down," Stevie answered. "I'm just glad that I'm not stuck on the side of a backcountry road with two flat tires in that blizzard anymore."

"Bless your heart," Gracie said. "I guess it could have been worse. Commercial is over. Back to my show. Thank you for taking care of my Fifi."

"You are so welcome." Stevie ended the call.

"I wasn't eavesdropping, but Gracie has one of those voices that carries halfway to the barn when she talks. So, there's gossip?" Mia grinned.

"Isn't there always?" Stevie asked. "That's part of living in a small town."

"But neither of us want to live in the big city again, do we?" Mia asked.

"You got that right. A toast to small towns." Stevie held up a cookie.

Mia tapped hers against Stevie's. "And to a new friend that isn't a stranger anymore."

"Amen," Stevie agreed.

Chapter Ten

"Come on, Mama, you can do this," Stevie crooned to the heifer that was trying to deliver her first calf. "I know it's a bad time, and you didn't want to bring a baby into the world when it might freeze, but you're in the barn now. I don't want to have to pull your calf. It will be healthier for both of you if you do this on your own."

She felt Cody's presence long before she glanced over her shoulder and saw him peeking over the top rail of the stall. Infatuation or not, he still made her pulse race just like it did when she was fifteen years old. But Stevie couldn't be distracted by her emotions when she was on the job, not even by Cody Ryan.

"You always talk to the animals?" he asked.

"Do you talk to your patients?" she shot back at him.

"Of course, but they answer me," Cody answered.

"So do mine." She rubbed the heifer's heaving sides when she contracted again. "She's saying that she likes for me to be here, that she trusts me to make the right decisions, and...all right, Mama, I see hooves. You are doing good. One more big push and we'll have a baby on the ground."

"I'd forgotten that calving season started in January," Cody said.

"This is one of those unusual winters that come along every hundred years. It's not normally so cold at this time." Stevie was all over the place the second the calf was born, but once the mama was on her feet and washing the new baby, she stepped out of the stall. "What was I saying?"

"That you're a hundred years old," Cody teased.

"I look pretty damn good to be that old, don't I?" No way was Cody getting ahead of her, not when she had a healthy calf on the ground, and a heifer that was doing what she was supposed to do without any coaxing.

"Oh, honey..." Cody laid a hand over his heart.

Was he flirting? She was prepared for bantering, even arguing, but not flirting.

"What I was saying is..." She tried willing her pulse to slow down, but it didn't work, so she took a deep breath, let it out slowly, and went on, "That the rest of this week is going to be a real trial for you and Jesse. With a herd the size of what you're running, you could see half a dozen calves dropped every day. January is always cold, and babies can survive in normal cold, but this is far from our usual winter weather. They'll have trouble in ice, snow, and below-freezing temperatures. I'd suggest that you put up some temporary panels and turn this whole barn into stalls. Tomorrow or the next day this lady and her baby could probably be turned out into the corral, but you could need extra places for newborns for a couple of days."

"You're the doc," Cody said. "Jesse and I'll get busy bringing the panels and gates in from one of the other barns. Maybe you should start riding with us tomorrow morning."

"I told you, I'm more than willing to help," Stevie said. "We've got a while before supper. Mind if I take one of the four-wheelers and drive through the pasture while y'all put up some temporary stalls?"

"Keys are hanging inside the door of the tack room. Call me if you run into trouble," Cody said.

Stevie grabbed her coat from the stall gate and patted the pocket. "I won't be out that long. I just want to take a look at the pregnant cows. I'll be back in time for supper."

Cody nodded and was talking to Jesse on the phone when Stevie fired up one of the four-wheelers parked over against the wall. She drove it around her pitiful-looking van, which was leaning to the side because of its flat tires, and stopped at the barn door. Before she could shut off the engine, Cody had jogged over and slid the door open for her.

"Thanks," she yelled over the noise of the vehicle.

Freedom! she thought as she shifted into gear and headed around the barn. The cold wind bit into her face. When she reached the gate leading into the pasture where the herd milled about, she stopped the four-wheeler and opened the heavy gate. "This is why you always bring backup," she muttered. "That way someone else can take care of gates."

The cold wind practically took her breath away as she drove around the edge of the pasture. Any cows about to deliver would find a secluded spot, maybe close to a mesquite thicket. She didn't see any, but she did see a pack of coyotes tearing across the next pasture over, and there were tracks right up to the fence line.

"Where's a donkey when you need one?" Stevie asked. "Or Tex, for that matter?"

As if in answer to her question, a braying sound filled the air. Stevie whipped her head around to see a little spotted donkey making his way from the middle of the herd toward the fence.

"I think this four-wheeler scared them off for you," she said as she drove on a little farther. "But you keep up the good work."

Donkeys protected cattle from coyotes pretty much the same way alpacas protected sheep from predators. That thought caused Stevie to wonder why the Ryan family had kept the alpacas after Mia had gotten that wild hair and sold her sheep. She was wondering about that when she made the corner and started along the fence that marked the very back of the forty-acre pasture.

"I'll have to ask Cody about that when I get back to the bunkhouse," she said, and then silently gave herself a scolding for talking to herself.

Her focus shifted in a hurry when both front tires of her four-wheeler dropped off into a massive hole that was hidden by the snow. Everything happened as if in slow motion. One second, she was studying a cow that was moving away from the herd toward a big scrub oak tree with broken-down limbs. The next Stevie was flying head over heels through the air toward a grove of scrub oak trees just a few feet from the hole. She threw out her hands trying to grab onto something to break the fall, but all she got was arms full of cold air. One of the lower ice-covered branches of the tree broke her fall, but in doing so ripped at her face and arm. She landed on her back, and the gray sky seemed to fall right down on top of her, sucking all the air from her lungs. Then everything went black.

* * *

There was no path to the barn where the panels for temporary stalls were stored, and that barn was almost two miles away. The trip that should have taken five minutes even over rough pasture took half an hour. They had to drive through a foot of snow that was lying on top of a couple of inches of ice.

"I will be *so* glad to see bare ground again," Jesse said when they finally reached the barn.

"You are preaching to the choir," Cody told him. "I may never even listen to that song about dreaming of a white Christmas again."

"I hear you, brother." Jesse backed the truck up close to the barn. "Let's get this stuff loaded. Mia can help us put up the pens tomorrow after we do chores. Stevie has come up with a good idea here. Who would have ever thought we'd have to do this in our part of Texas?"

"That's the truth." Cody got out of the truck, sunk down to the top of his boots in snow, and growled.

Cody slipped his phone from his hip pocket. "I'm going to check on Stevie and get her opinion on the cows."

"Kind of nice having a vet on the property." Jesse picked up a panel and carried it to the truck.

"Huh, her phone is going straight to voice mail," Cody answered.

"Probably lost service if she's at the back side of the forty," Jesse said. Y'all ever get around to having that talk? Seems like she's not as prickly as she was when I rescued you."

"We decided that we might be friends," Cody said and then frowned. "We've never had service problems anywhere in the pasture. I called Mia yesterday to ask her to look up a cow's number for us and had no trouble getting through, remember?"

"Maybe Stevie's having second thoughts about the idea of friendship and she's flown the coop," Jesse chuckled. "Hey, Mia told us at the breakfast table this morning that she's going to invite Beau Martin to Sunday dinner when we dig out from under all this mess. Seems she's been talking and texting him for a few weeks, and they even went on a couple of drives through the country together."

Cody had heard that name, but he couldn't put a face with it. Was it someone he had treated in the last six months? No, but Martin rang a bell. A visual of a little lady with gray in her hair came to his mind, and then he remembered Vernon Martin's wife.

"Libby Martin of the Bois D'Arc Ranch?" he questioned.

"That would be his grandmother. Vernon is his grandpa. He works at the feed store part-time and helps Vernon run the ranch since Libby passed away. Seems like a good kid," Jesse answered.

"I met him just before Libby died," Cody said as he helped load up the panels. "His grandparents seem like good people."

"And that boy likes ranching?" Cody asked.

"I guess he does, or he wouldn't be down here helping Vernon and working two days a week at the feed store, plus taking online agribusiness courses," Jesse answered.

"I bet Vernon is happy that he's finally got a family member interested in ranching," Cody said.

"I would be if I was in his boots." Jesse said as they put one last panel on the truck. "I'm so glad that Mia loves this lifestyle and hope the twins grow up to love it as much as she does. That's a load. I reckon we should get on back and get them unloaded. We'll have just enough time before supper to come back for the gates. We could even leave them on the truck if it's going to cause us to be late."

Cody tried to call Stevie again, but it went to voice mail. He left a message and shoved the phone back in his pocket. "I wonder if she's got a cow down and is pulling a calf. Maybe I should drive out there and see if she needs help."

"Maybe you should let well enough alone," Jesse suggested. "She's been cooped up with you for days. She might need some time to herself. Addy gets like that every so often, like now, and believe me, when she does, I take a step back and give her some space. I'll be glad when you two can get back to seeing patients again. She enjoys that."

"Me too," Cody said.

When they had reached the barn and unloaded the panels, Cody tried again to reach Stevie, but got nothing. "She might want time alone, but I'm driving out that way to see about her. If she wants time alone, she's just honest and blunt enough to tell me. Stevie speaks her mind—loud and clear. I'll go get the gates tomorrow morning while you and Mia build the stalls."

Jesse gave a quick nod and tossed the pickup keys across to him. "I'm headed to the house then. Call me if you need another set of hands."

Cody had a gut feeling that something was wrong—and Cody's gut had never lied to him. He drove the old truck down the grooves the four-wheeler had cut in the snow. Deep boot prints told him that Stevie had gotten off the vehicle to open the gate into the pasture. She had driven through, then more prints said that she had gone back to close it again. Cody did the same thing, and then he was driving on slick grass instead of in deep snow. Mia had done a good job of plowing the pasture so that none of the cattle had to wade in it halfway to their bellies.

He drove slowly, keeping an eye on the tire prints ahead of him. When he turned the corner at the back edge of the field, he noticed the donkey with his head up and ears back, braying at a couple of coyotes out there beyond the fence line. There was a whole pack of them, most likely lying in wait for a cow to drop a calf, and then they would swoop in for the kill.

"Good boy," Cody said, "keep them away from the herd, and especially any baby calves."

He'd barely gotten the words out of his mouth when he noticed the four-wheeler nose down in a hole. He hit the gas pedal a little too hard and fishtailed all over the pasture for a few seconds before he got control. When he came to a stop, the pickup's bumper was just inches from the rear end of the four-wheeler. He grabbed his phone from his pocket, slung open the truck door, and called Stevie. Surely she was on her way back to the ranch house or was already there.

Cody could hear the phone ringing in the distance, and he started to run that way. He slipped and fell flat on his butt, and that's when he saw Stevie, lying next to an old scrub oak tree. He crawled over to her and laid a finger on her neck. Her lips were blue, and she had a nasty gash on her forehead, but she had a pulse. As a doctor, he knew he should put a neck brace on her and use a board to move her, but he had neither one and he had to get her to the house. He took time to check her pupils and they were only slightly enlarged. He ran his fingers down the bones in her neck and back. He couldn't feel anything broken, which were all good signs.

"Hang on, love," he said, hoping that would make her open her eyes, but it didn't.

He gently laid her on the bench seat and cradled her

head in his lap all the way back to the bunkhouse, where his supplies and doctor bag were. "Wake up, Stevie. Please, wake up," he begged as he moved her head to the seat so he could get out and open the gate.

When he finally reached the bunkhouse, he called Addy, told her in a few words what had happened, and then carried Stevie inside. He laid her on the sofa, checked her to be sure no bones were broken and that the only blood was coming from the gash on her forehead. Then Addy was there, running her fingers over Stevie's scalp checking for knots or soft spots.

"Here it is," Cody said when he had wiped all the blood away. "See this indentation. This could possibly be a concussion. We need to get her to a hospital for tests," he said as he applied butterfly bandages to hold the wound together.

"Not possible. We'll have to do the best we can right here," Addy said. "Her lips are getting color back in them, and she's breathing normal, so I don't think she has punctured either of her lungs. We'll have to wait for her to wake up to make sure she can walk and there's no damage to her back."

"I should have gone out there the minute she didn't pick up when I called," Cody said.

Addy laid a hand on his shoulder. "You can't blame yourself for this. Let's get these wet clothes off her and wrap her up in warm blankets. I'm glad she had gloves on her hands. As cold as it's been, they probably protected her from frostbite." She talked as she removed Stevie's boots, socks, jeans, coat, and everything else, down to her bra and underpants.

Cody brought a stack of blankets from the end of one of the bunk beds and began to cover Stevie with them, when her eyes finally fluttered open. "Where am I?" she muttered.

"You had a wreck," Addy said.

"No, I didn't"—she shivered—"I made it to the barn on flat tires, and Cody was there with a fire already going."

"You are at the bunkhouse on Sunflower Ranch," Addy explained. "You were checking the cattle when the four-wheeler must have thrown you."

Her eyes darted around the room. "I'm so cold."

Cody shook out two more blankets and piled them on top of her. "I'm Dr. Cody Ryan. I'm going to check your eyes." He leaned in close to her face. "You hit your head on something when you wrecked the four-wheeler."

Stevie closed her eyes, and then opened them wide. "I'm so sorry. I'll pay for the damages. How did I get here? The last thing I remember was landing on my back with the wind knocked out of me and then I kind of woke up and saw a donkey."

"I hope it's just a concussion," Addy whispered, "and not a brain bleed. Did you notice if she had hit a rock?"

"I remember flying through the air, and hitting the low limb of a tree," Stevie said. "Then the fall must've knocked the wind out of me. I couldn't breathe and everything went black." Stevie sat up and pulled the top blanket up to her chin when she realized that she was only wearing her underwear. "How did I get from the pasture to here?"

"Now, she's coming around," Addy smiled.

"I think I hit a pothole," she said with a frown. "There were coyotes, and I thought they were coming to eat me."

"Your memory is coming back," Addy said. "Do you feel dizzy or nauseated? Your pupils are slightly dilated, so I believe you have a concussion. Hopefully, only a mild one, but all the signs point to one."

"I'm not nauseated. I do feel a little dizzy," Stevie admitted. She reached up and laid a hand on her forehead. "My head hurts. Are these stitches I'm feeling?"

"No, that's just strips holding the wound together. It's not deep, but head wounds bleed a lot. The donkey out there in the pasture kept the coyotes away from you," Cody explained. "Can you see me? Is anything fuzzy?"

"I'm fine," Stevie said. "My brain got a little scrambled. The wind got knocked out of me, and I was so cold. I'm warming up, so I'm good."

"I'm going to call the folks and let them know she's going to be all right." Addy slipped her phone out of her pocket. "Then I'm going back to the house. If you need me in the night, just holler."

"Thanks, Addy," Cody said. "I've got it under control now."

Stevie frowned and then flinched. "Wake me every hour. Tell you if I'm nauseated. This isn't my first concussion. I know the drill."

"You gave us a scare, *love*," Cody said.

"I told you not to call me that," Stevie scolded.

"I think we'll be fine," Cody said with a wink at Addy, "but I wouldn't turn down some of that chili Jesse told me you were making."

"Or some of that chocolate pie Mia told me about this morning." Stevie stretched back out on the sofa. "It feels so good to be warm. Do you think chocolate pie will cure a concussion?"

"Of course it will," Addy chuckled as she left.

"Why didn't you call some of us?" Cody tucked the blankets back around Stevie's shoulders.

"I don't know," she answered. "It was all surreal, and then it was cold and dark."

"When did you have a concussion before?" Cody asked as he stood up. "Talk to me while I make you something hot to drink. Do you want tea, coffee, or..."

"Hot chocolate please." Stevie shivered so hard that the blankets shifted. "I've had two concussions. One when I was in college during spring break. The one and only time I tried to use a skateboard, and tequila was involved. The second was about five years ago when a nasty-tempered cow kicked me. I never passed out on either of those times, but I did have a headache for a couple of days. If the four-wheeler is wrecked, how did I get from there to here?" She sat up and then stood to her feet and wrapped a blanket around her like a sarong.

"You need to stay on the sofa," Cody told her.

"I need to go to the bathroom," she said, "and then I'm going to put on flannel pajamas and some socks."

"Are you dizzy?" Cody rushed across the room to support her with an arm around her shoulders.

"Just a little, but I'll be fine." She leaned against him.

"You have to be truthful with me, Stevie," Cody told her.

"The room took a couple of spins when I first stood

up, but it's all better now." She shrugged off his arm and stepped inside the bathroom. "I can do this without you."

Cody closed the door. "All right then, but I'll be sitting on the edge of the bed so I can hear you if you call me."

* * *

That she didn't wet herself when she landed on her back was a mystery to Stevie. The last time she'd gone to the bathroom had been hours before the accident, and her bladder felt like she'd drank three pitchers of beer all by herself. She dropped the blanket on the floor and took care of business, then she checked her reflection in the mirror above the sink as she washed her hands.

Her hair was a mess. There was still a little smear of blood on her cheek. Three strips held the head wound together. There could be a scar to go with the freckles. She soaked a washcloth in warm water and wiped away the blood and a smudge of dirt on her jawline, and then noticed the bruises. One on her upper right arm, and one on her left hip.

"I'm lucky I'm alive," she muttered.

"What did you say?" Cody called out.

"I said that you can go now. I'm going to get dressed," she yelled through the closed door.

"I've seen you in your underwear, Stevie. I'm staying right here," he said, "your pajamas are still on the end of the bed, where you left them. I'll help you get into them."

147

She threw the door open and glared at him. "I'm perfectly able to dress myself."

"I'm your doctor right now, and I'll make that decision." He met her glare without blinking. "I'm not leaving until you are wearing those pajamas, and your hot chocolate is getting cold. Your choice, *love*."

"Oh, all right," she said, "but only because I'm ready for a cup of something warm."

"Sit down right here." He patted the bed.

She took a couple of long steps and sat down. "Guess maybe I do have a concussion," she muttered.

Cody helped her into the flannel shirt and then buttoned it for her. Every time his fingertips touched her bare skin, she was reminded again of the feelings she'd had when she was younger.

Maybe it wasn't just an infatuation, the aggravating voice in her head said. *Ever think that those feelings could have been real?*

Cody kneeled in front of her and slipped each foot into the pajama pants and then said, "Stand up slowly."

The edges of his palms brushed against her legs as he pulled the pants up to her waist. *This is not a teenage crush,* she thought.

"Now lean on me, and we'll go back to the sofa," Cody said. "When you're settled, I'll put your socks on your feet."

"Thank you." Stevie stood up and the room did a couple of spins before it finally settled. "How can I be so lucid and yet dizzy?"

"Concussions seem to have a mind of their own," Cody

said as he slipped his arm around her waist and helped her back to the sofa. Her body had warmed up, but his hand still felt hot enough to leave a print on her back. No, sir, the way her heart threw in that extra beat and her pulse raced told Stevie that what she was feeling had nothing to do with the concussion.

Chapter Eleven

Sometimes you don't know what you've got until you lose it. That was just one example of Pearl's words of wisdom that came to Cody's mind as he helped settle Stevie on the sofa.

"I'm sorry to be such a bother," Stevie said. "I hate having to depend on anyone for anything."

"You're not a bother." Cody shook his head. "I should have come looking for you the first time you didn't answer your phone. I understand about not liking to be dependent, but sometimes you've got to let your friends help you."

"What are you talking about?" Stevie frowned. "I'm glad you came to find me. It would have been a long walk back when I came to, and who knows, as cold as I was, I could have frozen to death."

"It's just that you..." he started. "Do I smother you?" he asked.

"No. What brought all this on anyway?" she asked.

Cody raked a hand through his hair. He wasn't about to throw his brother under the bus, or the tractor as they said on the ranch, so he chose his words carefully. "I've learned that when a woman gets cranky, it's time to let her have a little space. You seemed to need to get away from everyone when you went out on the four-wheeler, so I waited to check on you. That's all."

"I. Am. Not. Cranky," she said through clenched teeth.

Cody bit back a chuckle. "Your words say one thing. Your tone and body language says something else altogether. What was your first thought when you drove out toward the pasture?"

She set her mouth in a firm line and turned her face away from him. "Freedom," she finally answered.

"Been there. Done that," Cody said. "In the villages where I worked, I seldom got a free minute to myself. It was too dangerous to walk more than a little way from the hospital, and even then, there were always people around wanting to talk to me."

"I don't mean to be unappreciative." Stevie's tone changed.

"I know," Cody assured her.

"Hey," Mia yelled. "Y'all ready for some chili and a spoiled dog named Tex? If so, someone needs to open the door for me."

Cody rushed across the floor to let her in and took the box from her arms. He took it to the kitchen, set it on the table, and returned to the living area. Tex beat Mia inside and ran right to the sofa, where he curled up beside Stevie and laid his head on her lap. Mia took off her coat and hung it on the back of a kitchen chair, then sat down in the rocking chair. "Mama says you could have a slight concussion. How are you feeling?"

"If I've got one, it's not a bad one. I've had a couple before, so I know how they work. Thanks for supper," Stevie said.

"How'd you get that cut on your forehead? Do you remember?" Mia asked.

"I thought I was a flying squirrel and could land on a branch of a tree. I went through it and the ice on the limb cut me, then I landed on my back, and it was lights-out." Stevie rubbed Tex's head the whole time she talked. "Where have you been, old boy? You could have helped the donkey keep those coyotes away from me."

"What coyotes?" Mia's eyes widened out. "Did you have to fight them off?"

"No, the donkey you talked Dad into buying did his job," Cody answered for Stevie. "But when I got out there, the donkey was braying, and they were out there by that grove of scrub oak trees."

"I knew that donkey would pay for his keep," Mia said. "I don't know where that lazy dog has been, but it wasn't at the ranch house. He was on the porch when I got here."

"He was with me and Jesse." Cody dipped chili into two bowls. "Crackers or cornbread?"

"Crackers," Stevie answered.

"Do you have a headache?" Mia focused on Stevie.

"See double? I had a concussion a year ago when…" She stopped talking and put a hand over her mouth.

"When what?" Cody asked. "You never told me that you'd had an accident."

She removed her hand, but two scarlet spots dotted her cheeks. "It wasn't an accident."

"Did someone hurt you?" Cody handed Stevie a bowl of chili and a package of crackers on a lap tray, and then brought food to the coffee table. He sat down on the floor and took the first bite.

"It wasn't any big deal." The blush deepened even more. "I shouldn't have said anything."

"Was it Ricky?" Stevie asked.

Mia nodded. "He pushed me one night when I told him we had to keep back part of the money I made that week for groceries. He wanted to use my whole paycheck to place a bet on a game. I fell and hit my head on the edge of his gaming system."

"Did you tell Addy and Jesse about this?" Cody laid his spoon to the side and his hands knotted into fists. Anger rose up from depths that he didn't even know he had. Losing Dineo and Bodi had made him both angry and sad, but the thought of Ricky hurting Mia went above and beyond that.

"No, I didn't," she said and shook her head. "How could I? Mama and Daddy both thought that I was still living in the dorm and going to class, not working for minimum wage in a café. But I did go to the health clinic and they diagnosed me with a concussion. I had a headache for a few days, but I didn't miss any work.

In those days, I didn't even blame Ricky. I figured I deserved it because I didn't let him make that bet." Mia clamped her mouth shut tightly and then said through clenched teeth, "He didn't ever let me forget it either. Even though his team didn't win, and he would have lost the money anyway, he said I was bad luck because we had to use his betting money for doctor bills and medicine for me. I was pretty stupid, wasn't I?" She glanced up at Stevie. "And I didn't mean to bring all this up."

"You didn't," Stevie said. "We kind of pried it out of you."

"But I do feel better for talking about it," Mia admitted.

"He was a real loser," Cody growled. "Why did you put up with that kind of abuse?"

"Ricky is what happens to us girls who feel too ugly for boys to notice," Mia declared, "but it won't happen again. I don't want to talk about it anymore. Now, eat up because I brought chocolate pie too."

"I have to know one thing," Stevie said, "Why would you ever feel ugly? You look like a runway model."

"Ricky used to say that, but hearing it and believing it is two different things," Mia said.

Cody was glad that Stevie could talk to Mia, because at that moment all he wanted to do was find that kid and give *him* a concussion. No wonder she hadn't dated anyone since she'd come home.

"I understand." Stevie nodded and went back to eating.

"Knowing I'm not the only one who has felt that way helps more than you'll ever know," Mia said. "Mama says to tell you that Cody is supposed to bring you to the house tomorrow morning."

"I would love to spend the day with y'all, but I don't really need babysitting," Stevie said.

"Then consider it as you keeping us sane rather than us watching over you. We're all getting stir-crazy. I actually wished someone would need Uncle Cody and Mama to go do some doctor stuff so she could get out for a little while," Mia said.

"In that case, thank you," Stevie said, "and thank you for this supper too. After four days of scrounging for what we could make in Max's barn, I won't take food for granted again."

"You are so welcome." Mia's face lit up in a smile.

History can't be changed, Cody thought. *But if it could and Stevie and I had gotten together when we were young, would we have a daughter just younger than Mia?*

Mia left after a few more minutes, and Tex followed her. When Cody was sure that she was gone for good, he looked across the coffee table at Stevie. "You said you understood. Did someone like Ricky hurt you?"

"Not physically, but I grew up thinking that because I'm tall and have freckles and red hair, that I was ugly. My first boyfriend in college told me I was beautiful, and I was putty in his hands for about six months," she answered.

"And after six months?" Cody asked.

"I found out that he was cheating on me with a petite blond cheerleader, or maybe he was cheating on her with me. That's the more likely story. He took her on real dates, not just rides in his car for ice cream and a booty call in the back seat," Stevie said.

"I'm sorry. Seems like you and Mia didn't have much

luck with past boyfriends." Cody felt horrible for both of them even if he couldn't do anything about the past.

"Thanks for that. It took me a while to figure out that all guys aren't trustworthy. Enough about all that. Didn't Mia say she brought chocolate pie?" Stevie started to get up.

"Oh, no!" Cody said. "You sit still. I'll get the pie."

* * *

Stevie awoke the next morning, and for a split second, she wondered where she was. Nothing looked familiar, and then in a flash, the fog cleared, and she remembered everything.

"Good morning!" Cody brought her a cup of coffee. "How are you feeling today. Headache? Memory problems?"

"I feel great," she answered. "Why did you let me sleep so long? The sun is already up. Shouldn't you and Jesse be taking care of chores, or do you have doctor appointments today?"

"Jesse is picking me up in about ten minutes," Cody answered. "After being wakened every hour all night, I thought you could use two full hours of sleep. If you have a concussion, it's a minor one. Mia says to call her when you get dressed, but not to bother with breakfast. They've got waffles up at the ranch house."

"Did you already eat something?" Stevie threw off the blanket, sat up and glanced across the living room at the bunk beds. "Your bed hasn't been slept in."

"I sacked out on the floor beside the sofa in case you needed me in a hurry," he said. "It was better than the floor in the tack room. I had several blankets under me, a real pillow, and the room is warm."

"Thank you for doing that for me." Stevie remembered being downright grouchy a few times when he woke her from a deep sleep to ask her a stupid question like what her mother's name was, or what the name of the ranch was where she was staying.

"No problem," Cody said, "you would do the same for me."

Would you? the voice in her head asked. *After all these years of being angry with him, would you take care of him if the roles were reversed?*

"Have a good day." Cody put on his coat and settled his cowboy hat on his head. "Weatherman says this is supposed to start melting today, so maybe by the weekend we can get into town."

She cut her eyes over at him. "You ready to get rid of me and have your bunkhouse to yourself again?"

"Been kind of nice having someone around, so that would be no," Cody answered as he shoved his hands into his gloves. "And there's Jesse. See you at noon."

"Be safe," she said. "There's potholes out there."

"I will," he threw over his shoulder as he left.

Stevie stood up slowly, but there was no dizziness. In her opinion, she didn't have a concussion at all, but all those symptoms she had experienced were from having the wind knocked out of her, and from lying so long in the extreme cold. She went to the bedroom and changed into jeans and a sweatshirt, then sat down on the edge of the bed to put on her boots. She had sat right there in that same spot when Cody dressed her in the flannel pajamas. She closed her eyes and got the same sensation of his hands on her bare skin as she'd had the evening before. The time had come for her to figure things out where he was concerned, but she didn't even know where to begin.

Her phone pinged and she picked it up from the nightstand to find a message from Mia: *Call me when you're ready. I'm waiting to have breakfast with you.*

Stevie's thumbs quickly typed out, *I'm ready now.*

She shoved a stocking hat down over her red hair and put on her coat. She stepped outside and heard the rattle of a four-wheeler coming down the path. A visual of the gray sky dropping down to cover her with darkness made her chest tighten. She wasn't ready to get back on one of those vehicles, but the sound was getting louder and louder, and then Mia was right there at the end of the porch steps.

"Crawl on behind me," Mia said.

Stevie wanted to shake her head and say that she would walk, but Mia needed to see a strong, fearless woman, not a whimpering weakling that was afraid to get back on the horse—so to speak. She walked down the porch steps, slung a leg over the seat, and willed her heart to stop beating so hard.

The trip up to the house only took a few minutes, but Stevie gripped the edge of the seat so hard that her knuckles began to ache. A coyote howled out in the distance, and she remembered that scary feeling when she barely came to and thought the coyotes were going to eat her.

"We're here." Mia's voice came through her fear. "Are you okay, Stevie?"

"I'm fine"—she managed a weak smile—"just thinking about the other four-wheeler and hoping that it can be repaired."

Mia had killed the engine and was already off the vehicle. "My dad can fix anything. Trust me. Let's get inside where it's warm and have some breakfast."

Stevie let go of her grip and got off the vehicle. "After that supper you brought us and a second piece of pie before I went to sleep, I shouldn't be hungry for a week, but I'm starving."

"It always seems like we need more food when it's so cold." She held the back door open for Stevie to go inside ahead of her. "The weatherman said that the temperatures will start rising today and tomorrow. That means by the weekend, the roads might be clear, and we can go back to normal."

Stevie wondered just what her new normal would be when she got to go home. Would she slip right back into her veterinarian job, and into the depression she'd been fighting since her mother's death? No answers came floating down from the ceiling, so she tucked her hat and gloves into the pocket of her coat and hung it on a hook right inside the door of the utility room.

"Good morning," Addy said from the kitchen. "How are you feeling?"

Stevie crossed the small utility/mudroom and stopped in the kitchen. "I'm really fine, not sure I even have a concussion. I think maybe what I was feeling was the result of getting the wind knocked out of me and being so cold."

"Better treat it as a concussion and be safe rather than sorry," Addy told her. "Pour yourself a mug of coffee and have a seat at the table. Mia made waffles and sausage this morning, and she's got strawberries and whipped cream if you'd rather have that instead of syrup."

"I feel like I'm saying this all the time but thank you. Can I help with anything?" Stevie asked as she filled a mug with coffee.

"Yep, you can." Mia poured batter into the waffle iron. "I'm studying agribusiness so I can understand more about running that end of the ranch. Here lately I've been thinking that I would like to be a vet tech, so I enrolled in a couple of animal husbandry courses this next semester. Can I pick your brain a little while you're here?"

"Sure, but why do you want to do that in addition to the business part?" Stevie took a sip of her coffee, made strong like she liked.

"That way, I can be of more help on the ranch. I could do some of the things that you do," Mia answered.

"The courses will help, but hands-on will teach you a lot," Stevie said. "I can't pay you much, but if you want to assist me a couple of days a week, I'd be glad to have you."

"Are you serious?" Mia squealed and dashed across the room to give Stevie a hug. "I would love that." Then she hesitated and looked over at Addy. "Mama, can you and Dad spare me two days a week?"

"Of course we can when it's all about learning more," Addy said, "and we should be paying you, Stevie, just like we pay for college hours."

Stevie shook her head. "Not after what all y'all have

done for me. Besides, it would be nice to have a sidekick a couple of days a week."

"What days?" Mia asked.

"You talk to Jesse, and y'all decide that. I'm on call right now seven days a week," Stevie answered. "So, the days and times could vary, but if you're busy with something here, we can always get together on another day. We'll just keep it flexible."

"I'm not glad that you've got two flat tires, but I'm glad you got stuck with Uncle Cody." Mia dished up waffles onto a plate and set them in front of Stevie.

Stevie slathered butter on her waffles and then covered them with maple syrup. "It's crazy how all this has happened, but I'm glad it did."

"Us too," Addy said. "Why did you decide to go to vet school?"

"I loved animals more than people, or I would have been a doctor like Cody, or maybe a nurse like you," Stevie answered between bites. "Do you like being a concierge nurse with Cody?"

"Love it," Addy said. "I've got a support system with Pearl and Sonny and Mia to help with the twins, so I don't have to feel guilty about leaving them. But then, I can do what I love at the same time. It's the perfect job for me."

"It's not so different from what you do." Mia brought her breakfast to the table. "You go to the animals. Folks don't bring them to your house. Mama and Uncle Cody go to the houses of the older folks and those who don't want to go to a clinic. It's about the same thing only the patients have two legs instead of four."

Stevie nodded in agreement. "That's pretty much it in a nutshell."

"I know your mama was sick, but why did you stay after you lost her?" Addy finished making a pan of yeast bread and set it to the side to rise. She poured herself a cup of coffee and sat down across from Stevie. "If that's too personal, you don't have to answer it."

"I might ask you the same thing. Considering the circumstances of Mia's birth, why would you ever come to work here on Sunflower Ranch?" Stevie asked.

"Fair enough," Addy answered. "This was home, and something kept drawing me back here. Maybe it was Fate, or just a longing in my heart, but whatever, I'm glad I listened to it. When the Ryans offered me a job helping take care of Sonny after he was diagnosed, well..." She took a sip of her coffee. "I learned years later that they figured out that Mia was their granddaughter and considered it an extra bonus to get to spend time with her and have me as Sonny's private nurse."

"When did you tell Jesse?" Stevie asked.

"He kind of figured it out on his own," Addy answered. "Now, your turn? Did you come back to get closure with Cody?"

"Not really, but that is an added bonus to my Texas homecoming." Stevie finished off the last bite of her waffles. "I've tried to steer clear of him the past six months, but I guess Fate, as you called it, had different plans."

"Sometimes it works that way," Mia said, adding her two cents. "I couldn't wait to get out of this place, but before many days passed, I felt like the prodigal son. I didn't care what I had to do, I just wanted to come home. I guess age doesn't matter when the heart longs for home, does it?"

"You are so right about that." But if that was the case, why did Stevie feel more at home in Addy's kitchen than she had anyplace she'd been in a very long time—including her own house?

Must be the town of Honey Grove, or maybe the state of Texas calling us home, not a particular house, she thought.

Chapter Twelve

Cody had been in and out of the bunkhouse since he was a toddler. There were times when it was completely full, and when Henry had the foreman's bedroom. In those days, the place seemed huge to him. As years went by more and more of the hired hands lived in town and commuted to the ranch. Nowadays with the newer equipment, they could make do with hiring spring, summer, and weekend help, and there were always teenage boys willing to work. And somehow, as Cody grew up, the bunkhouse got smaller. There were now two sets of bunk beds on the far wall, the foreman's bedroom and bathroom with a tub and shower, and a large living room, kitchen, dining area all combined.

"Did things seem bigger to you when you were a kid?" Cody asked as he brought a beer and a bottle of sweet tea out of the kitchen, twisted the top off the tea, and handed it to Stevie.

"Thank you, and of course they did. I remember when our backyard was enormous and the walk to school, which was barely a block, seemed like a mile," Stevie answered.

Cody settled on the other end of the sofa from her, laid his phone on the coffee table, and hit an icon. "Here's to country music at the end of a long day." He held out his bottle of beer toward hers.

Stevie touched her bottle with his. "Music and cold beer. It don't get no better than this."

"If you get tired of it, we can watch something on television, or just talk," he said.

"I don't get tired of music." Stevie swayed to Chris Stapleton singing "Broken Halos."

"Do you think of Dineo when this song plays?" she asked.

"Yes, I do," Cody answered. "But I got to admit that I didn't do what the lyrics say about not asking Jesus why, because I did many times."

"I've seen my share of broken halos too, and I didn't let it go without asking God why he had to take them from me since they were all I had. First my dad and then my mama, and I still want answers *now*, and I don't want to wait to get them until the by-and-by, like the words say."

"Evidently, we aren't supposed to know the reasons why." Cody took a long drink of his beer. "Are you still feeling all right, Stevie? It's been twenty-four hours since your fall, and a brain bleed can hide and present a little later. I would sure feel better if we could have gotten an MRI."

"I feel just fine," Stevie assured him. "Not even a headache. Did y'all get the four-wheeler checked out? Did it need an MRI?" Her eyes twinkled when she joked.

"Nope"—Cody flashed a smile—"when I set it up on all four wheels and turned the engine over, it started right up. I drove it back to the barn. Nothing wrong with it but a slight dent on the front, which matches the one on the other side where Jesse dented it last fall."

"I'll be glad to have that repaired," Stevie offered.

"It's a farm machine, and they get dinged up. Don't worry about that," Cody told her. "Did you enjoy the day at the ranch?"

"Yes, I did." Her expression said as much as her words. "I'm excited about Mia working with me a couple of days a week, but in a couple of years, she'll know enough that y'all won't even need me out here on Sunflower."

"I kind of doubt that," Cody said, "but it's good to see her so excited about something. She's bouncing off the walls about the idea, but Addy was right in saying that we'd pay you what we would have to for college classes. She'll get one-on-one, hands-on training this way, whereas she'd only get book learning with online courses."

"We came to an agreement this evening while we were cleaning up the kitchen after supper. She works for me free, and I don't charge anything. It's a win-win situation," Stevie said. "Getting back to the day, Addy's twins are so cute. They'll be crawling soon, and that playpen won't hold them then."

"They grow up fast, don't they?"

"Yep, they sure do. Jesse and Addy seem to be enjoying

every minute of each phase, though," Stevie said. "Speaking of that, Mia and I went out and checked on Dixie this afternoon. Her new mama has adapted to her new herd so well that a stranger would never know that she was once an orphan."

"Kind of like the twins, right?" Cody didn't give her time to answer. "Or like me and Jesse and Lucas?"

"Just look at how good y'all all turned out." Stevie locked gazes with him.

He felt as if he was drowning in her mossy green eyes. Every little yellow fleck glittered and beckoned to him to dive right into her soul.

"Yep, all for the best all the way around," he said.

Cody laced her fingers in his and stood, pulling her up with him. "May I have this dance, Stephanie O'Dell?"

She got to her feet. "No, but Stevie loves to dance. Stephanie is a little bit shy."

"I don't believe that any of your personalities have a shy bone," Cody chuckled as he draped an arm around her waist. He sang the lyrics to "Tennessee Whiskey" right along with Chris Stapleton.

Her arms snaked up around his neck, and she laid her head against his chest. "I haven't danced in years. This is nice, but I'm not believing a word of what you're singing."

"Oh, honey, you really are as smooth as Tennessee whiskey," he whispered softly in her ear.

"But sweet as strawberry wine"—she leaned back and smiled at him—"that's definitely not me. I've been called a lot of things, but sweet is not one of them."

"The sweet is down deep in your soul and takes a special cowboy to find it." Cody was kind of proud of himself for remembering how to flirt.

"Well, if you're thinking you might be that special cowboy, you had best bring two shovels, because one will get dull before you dig that deep," she giggled.

"I'll remember that," he said.

When the song ended and "Millionaire" started playing, Cody kept two-stepping around the floor with her.

"You only asked for one dance," she told him.

"This second one is a vertical MRI. It's for medical purposes only, to see if you get dizzy when you move around the floor," he teased.

"You, Dr. Cowboy, are full of…" she started.

He kissed her on the forehead before she could say another word.

"Is that medical too?" she asked.

"Yes, ma'am. It's to test your endorphins. If you have a brain bleed, a kiss from a sexy cowboy might cause dizziness." He reached up and removed her hands from around his neck and swung her out, then brought her back to his chest with a thump. "Your heart is beating fast, and your eyes have even more gold flecks in them than usual, which tells me that you are enjoying this."

"I'd have to be stone-cold dead to not think you are sexy. I've already told you that I had a crush on you for five years," she said. "I wouldn't have wasted my time and energy on a cowboy who wasn't good-looking."

"Thank you, love." He gave her another kiss on the forehead.

"Just stating facts...*love*," she shot back and then asked, "Do you really think that love is more precious than gold?"

"Yes, I do," Cody whispered in her ear. "A man can have empty pockets and still feel like a millionaire if he's got love to spare like Chris is singing about. I see it in Jesse and Addy and have always seen it in my folks. If and when I ever find that kind of love, I'll be a millionaire, even if I don't have two dimes to rub together in my pocket."

When that song ended, Cody brought Stevie's hand to his lips and kissed her knuckles. "Thank you, Stevie, for the dances. Maybe someday, we'll go over to the Rusty Spur and dance some leather off our cowboy boots."

"Why would we go to a crowded bar when we've got music, a dance floor, and beer right here?" She sat back down on the sofa and picked up her beer.

Tex woke up, stretched, and hopped down off the sofa. He made his way to the kitchen, where he lapped up water from a bowl and ate a few bites of his dry food, then he flopped down under the table.

"Because I might want people to think we were out on a date," Cody answered.

* * *

Had Stevie really heard Cody right? She wondered if maybe she ought to ask him to repeat what he'd said, then realized from the quizzical look on his face that he had indeed just said something about a date. She jerked her head around, almost choked trying to get the

169

swallow of beer down, and gasped. "You're asking me on a date?"

"Yes, I am, but from that reaction, I guess that I'm going to suffer from rejection." Cody picked up his beer and took a long drink.

"You aren't God, so you don't know what I'm thinking," she told him.

"Then you're saying yes?" Cody asked. "But going out dancing was just a suggestion. If you'd rather go out to dinner and maybe to a movie, that's fine with me. The snow is melting, and we've gotten word that the road from here to town will be clear by day after tomorrow. I want to spend more time with you."

"After you broke up with me, I never thought you'd ever ask me out. But I would like to spend more time with you too, so once I'm back home, give me a call. You've got my number," Stevie said.

Twenty years ago, if Cody Ryan had called her for a second chance, Stevie would have danced a jig around the floor. Her heart would have thumped right out of her chest, and sucking on lemons wouldn't have been able to wipe the grin off her face. Ten years ago, when she came home and saw him at church that Christmas, if he had asked her out, even just for ice cream, she would have probably told him to drop dead and go to hell.

Time and life change the way we look at things. Those were some of her mother's last words before she died.

You are so right, Mama, Stevie agreed now.

"I will call you, but how about Sunday?" Cody asked. "I'll pick you up for church, and afterwards, we can go over to Paris for dinner, and then maybe take a long slow drive back home."

"I'd like that," Stevie answered as she recognized the piano lead-in for "Broken Roads" by Rascal Flatts. "Hey, this song could be Jesse and Addy's theme song, couldn't it?"

"It might be." Cody flashed a brilliant smile. "Or who knows, in fifty years we might look back on tonight and think it's about us. The only way we'll ever know if every one of those long, lost roads has truly brought us back to Honey Grove is if we bury the hatchet and get to know each other better."

"Think there might be a grander plan in all of this like they're singing about?" Stevie asked.

"We can hope so," he said and smiled.

She rolled the cold, sweaty beer bottle across her forehead. "Let's watch a movie or reruns on television."

"Reason?" Cody asked.

"Between the beer, the dancing with you, and you asking me out, I'm getting all emotional." She was bluntly honest—the only way she knew how to be.

"Is that good or bad?" Cody asked.

Stevie was wondering if she would wake up tomorrow morning in her own house and discover that everything that had happened was just a dream. There had been no crazy winter storm. Her van would be sitting in the driveway with no flat tires, and she would realize that she hadn't had a bad fall from a four-wheeler.

"It's all good," she finally answered. If this was a dream, she might as well enjoy it to the very end.

"I'm glad," Cody said as he turned off the music, picked up the remote, and hit the guide channel. "Looks like we've got reruns of *NCIS* and *Law and Order*, or we can bring up Netflix and watch something there."

"*The Ranch*," Stevie said without hesitation.

"Yes!" Cody nodded and punched in the right buttons on the remote. "What season are you on?"

"Two," she answered.

"I've been watching the third one, but I don't mind going back and doing season two again." Cody settled onto his end of the sofa.

How could he go from talking about a date on Sunday, to thinking about a television show? Stevie wondered. Her mind was still going around in circles, as she tried to figure out what she should wear to church, and how Addy and Mia would feel about her actually dating Cody. If the two of them decided that they didn't like each other, would that interfere with Mia being her assistant? Or worse yet, would the ranch stop calling on her to do vet work for them? If Sonny quit using her services, then how many other ranches would stop calling on her?

"Want another beer?" he asked.

"Yes, thank you." Her voice sounded strained in her own ears. "Maybe..." she started to say that dating might not be such a good idea.

"Maybe some pretzels?" Cody was already on his way back from the kitchen. "I was thinking the same thing."

Don't close the door when opportunity knocks, the voice in her head said. *Didn't you just tell him to face his fears? Well, take a dose of your own medicine.*

"Yes," she said again. "Pretzels would be great, and bring that package of chocolate kisses I saw in the pantry. I like salt and sweet together."

"You can have as many of my kisses as you can handle," Cody chuckled.

"Don't promise what you can't deliver." Stevie flirted right back at him.

"Want to give that a try?" Cody returned with half a bag of chocolate and an unopened one of pretzels.

She held up the kisses. "See, only half a bag. I could put away two bags between now and bedtime. Oh!" She clamped a hand over her mouth. "You were talking about real kisses. This is a failure to communicate. I thought you were offering me as many of these as I could handle."

"Sure, you were, but to clear things up…" Cody bent forward, tipped her chin up with his fist, and kissed her on the lips.

Stevie was glad that she was sitting down because her knees went all weak. When the kiss ended, her heart was pumping double time, and her pulse raced like she had just run a marathon.

"How many of those can you handle tonight?" Cody asked as he sat down on the other end of the sofa.

"As many as you can, Dr. Cowboy," she lied. One or two more of those and she would be unbuttoning his chambray shirt.

"We'll test that theory when you are completely well. Don't want to overload your brain with too many endorphins," he said with a grin.

"Or yours either," she told him.

Chapter Thirteen

$\mathcal{G}$lad to be free of the confines of the stall, Dixie and her adoptive sibling romped around in the corral while their mother, Maggie, kept a watch from a distance. Sonny sat in a lawn chair just inside the barn and kept an eye on all the alpacas plus the heifer and her newborn baby calf. Animals and humans alike seemed to be enjoying the nice warm sun and trying to ignore the breeze blowing down from the north.

"Can I get you anything?" Stevie asked as she dragged a couple more chairs over for her and Pearl. "There's water, bottles of sweet tea, and apple juice in the tack room refrigerator."

"I'm just fine," Sonny said, "but thank you. Getting to come out here and see the new babies is all I need today. Jesse and Cody are turning the cows back out into the pastures where they belong since the snow has melted down to where we can see grass. But for a few hours, I can enjoy seeing them milling about out there beyond the corral. They seem to be as happy as I am to see the weather getting back to normal. Only trouble with that is that spring will be here soon, and it's getting to where I can't do a damn thing except supervise."

Pearl tucked her scarf into her coat and zipped it up. "I'm just glad to see the sun and the temperature up in the forties today. Even the drifts in the shady areas should be melted pretty soon, and, Sonny Ryan, we're of an age where all we need to do is supervise, so stop your belly-aching and enjoy the day."

"You're probably right, but it ain't easy. We don't like the snow when it's here, but it sure helps the soil bring up good grass," Sonny pointed out into the corral. "Look at that little girl, darlin'. She's fitting right in with Maggie's new baby. Pearl, darlin', what are you going to name her?"

"I figured Mia would name her," Stevie said.

"Nope," Sonny sighed. "She thought she was going to sell the alpacas right along with her sheep, but I reminded her that I had paid for them, so they were mine. She's done very well since she came home, but she doesn't get to name the new babies. It's a reminder to her that choices have consequences."

"Tough love?" Stevie sat down on the other side of Pearl.

"I'm not sure who it's the toughest on," Pearl said, "Mia or us two old people who would like to step in and tell her that we'll make everything all right for her."

"I can't even imagine how hard that would be on parents," Stevie said.

"Letting them make their own choices, and then not rushing in and trying to make everything perfect when they make bad ones is probably the hardest part of being parents," Sonny said. "Speaking about Mia, I want to thank you for taking her under your wing when it comes to this vet tech stuff. I'm glad that she wants to pursue that in addition to the business end of ranching. She's going to make a good foreman someday."

"Hey, where is everyone?" Mia's voice floated across the barn.

"Back here," Pearl called. "We've turned the heifer and her calf and all the alpacas out into the corral. They're happy to be free of the stalls."

Mia sat down on a bale of hay beside Stevie. "The road crew just phoned the house and said we can get through to town now. We'll be weeks getting all the trees taken care of here on the ranch, and I bet they're awful in town too, but at least we can get out if folks need a doctor or a vet. Are you excited to be able to go home, Stevie?"

"Yes, I am," Stevie answered.

Who are you kidding? You or them? the aggravating voice in her head asked.

"But I'll sure miss having folks around me all the time," she admitted.

"You don't have to leave," Mia said. "Your van isn't fixed yet, so you could just stick around here for another week."

"I can use Mama's car until I can get someone out here to put new tires on my van," Stevie said.

"If you get bored, you can always come back and spend a few days with us," Mia offered. "I talked to Dad, and he says whatever days are good for you are fine with him. So once you get home, just let me know when I can be your assistant. I'll kind of be on call, like you are."

"Sounds good to me, as long as Jesse can spare you," Stevie said.

"I'm just so excited about working with you, and guess what?" Mia sucked in a lungful of air and let it out slowly. "Beau said he would love to go to church with me and come to Sunday dinner. Will you come too? It would help so much."

"I'd love to," Stevie said, and then remembered that she had a date with Cody.

He'll have to understand, Stevie thought. *Mia will want the whole family at the dinner so they can meet Beau, and Cody will want to pass judgment on the kid anyway.*

"Great!" Mia said.

Mia went out into the corral with the alpacas. She petted each one, giving the babies even more attention by crooning to them like they were human. "Poppa, what are you naming the new cria?" she asked.

"That's up to your nana," Sonny said.

"Since her sister's name is Dixie for that group and all these cats running around here are named for country music ladies, maybe we call her Patsy or Reba," Pearl answered.

"Reba sounds more Southern, don't you think, Stevie?" Mia asked.

"Kind of does," Stevie answered. So much for tough

love. She would bet dollars to cow patties that Mia had already said something to Pearl about naming the new cria Reba.

"Then Reba it is," Pearl said.

"I should get on back to the bunkhouse," Stevie said as she stood up, "and get all the things y'all loaned me washed and ironed."

Pearl laid a hand on her shoulder. "Honey, you don't worry with that. We'll just throw them in with our stuff tomorrow morning after Cody gives you a ride home."

"Thank you," Stevie said with a smile, "y'all have been so good to me. I've enjoyed getting to spend time with you."

A couple of huge icicles fell from the edge of the barn at the same time and broke into millions of pieces when they hit the barn floor right in front of the chairs, the noise sounding like someone throwing a brick through a glass window. Mia squealed and threw her hands over her head. Pearl jumped up and shielded Sonny's body with hers. Stevie dropped to her knees behind the lawn chair.

"What was that?" Sonny asked.

"Just icicles," Mia gasped. "Good thing you weren't sitting outside, Poppa. If one of those things hit you, Uncle Cody would be sewing you up."

The expression on Mia's face went from happy to scared to sad all in a split second, and then she said, "I'm going to the house now. Poppa and Nana, scoot your chair back a little way. There's lots more of those icicles just waiting to fall off the barn roof. I'll see y'all at supper."

Stevie straightened up. "That was a close call. It sounded like someone throwing bottles at us. Might be a good idea to do what Mia suggested and move both of your chairs back a couple of feet. You could still see the babies out there romping around." She looked up at several more icicles dripping water and threatening to let go of the edge of the roof.

Sonny got to his feet and moved his chair back a little way. "Wouldn't it be something if the Dixie Chicks and Reba ever got together on a tour?"

"If that happens, we'll buy the tickets, and all of us will go see them," Pearl told her, and whispered under her breath for Stevie's ears only as she moved her chair, "Mia is upset about something. Can you check on her?"

"I'll take care of it," Stevie said with a slight nod. "See you later, Sonny."

He waved over his shoulder.

Stevie found Mia outside the barn, bent over at the waist and sobbing so hard that she could hardly catch her breath. Stevie put her arm around the girl's shoulders and said, "Want to talk about it?"

Mia rose and wiped her tears on the sleeve of her mustard yellow work coat. "Yes, please, but in the bunk-house, not at home."

"Are you having second thoughts about inviting Beau to dinner?" Stevie asked as they made their way down the pathway, which was fast becoming a sloshy mess instead of being slick with ice.

"No, I really like him and want to see what the family thinks about him," Mia answered.

Stevie gave her some space, both mentally and physi-cally. She wanted to hug Mia and tell her everything was going to be all right, not to let things upset her that much, but she kept quiet.

When they were out of the cold and in the warm bunkhouse, Mia removed her coat and threw it on the rocking chair, then collapsed on the end of the sofa. Stevie sat down beside her and draped a supporting arm around her shoulders again.

"That icicle…" Mia stammered, "could have killed Poppa…" She hiccuped. "If he'd set his chair even closer to the corral like he usually does. It really scared me, and then I got to thinking about him not being…" More tears flooded her cheeks. "You know, not being here all the time."

"But he didn't sit closer because Pearl didn't want the cold breeze to hit him. She takes good care of him, so you don't have to worry," Stevie said.

"It breaks my heart that I disappointed him and Nana so much." Mia had gotten the crying jag somewhat under control, but she kept hiccuping. "I took what all they had done for me for granted, and I can't ever undo what I did. Every time I look at those alpacas, I think about how foolish I was."

"Sometimes, it takes a pretty hard shock to wake us up." Stevie went to the bedroom and brought back a box of tissues. "I wish I would have come home a year before I did, or that I would have started a vet service here when I first got out of school. I missed years and years with my mama."

"I can't bear to think of not having Poppa and Nana around." Mia pulled a tissue out of the box and blew her nose. "I would have never forgiven myself if something had happened to either of them while I was off blowing my money on Ricky."

"Neither of them would want you to worry like this," Stevie told her, "but I understand how you feel."

"Thank you," Mia said. "It's been a tough year. This time last year I just stopped going to classes so I could pay the bills on the apartment Ricky and I were living in. I wound up going through thousands of dollars that I had in my savings, then I sold my sheep, and we ran off together."

Stevie's phone rang, and she pulled it out of her hip pocket. "This is Stevie O'Dell," she said without looking at the caller ID.

"This is Raymond Green, and I've got a horse tangled up in a roll of barbed wire. I think she might need stitches," he said.

"I'll be right over," Stevie said and took down directions to his house, and then she remembered that she didn't have a vehicle. She held the phone out from her face and asked Mia, "You reckon we could use the work truck for an hour or so? Raymond Green has a horse with a problem."

"I'm sure we can," Mia answered as she dried her tears. "Does that mean I can go with you?"

"Of course," Stevie said. "You can even drive if you want to. We just need to get some supplies out of the van and put them in a duffel bag. We're going to have to untangle some barbed wire from a horse's leg and stitch up a gash."

Mia took her phone from her hip pocket and called her mother. "Mama, Stevie has to go check on Raymond Green's horse. Can we use the work truck, and is it okay if I go with her?" She listened for a few seconds and said, "Yes, ma'am."

Then she hopped up, picked up her coat, and said, "Mama says we can use the truck anytime we need it and if it hadn't been close by, we could have used her SUV. I'll jog up to the house, drive the truck to the barn, and pick you up." She was putting on her coat as she dashed outside.

Stevie dumped what was left in her go bag onto the bed, put a few things in it, and then threw an apple into the bag before she left the bunkhouse and jogged to the barn. By the time Mia drove up, Stevie had loaded what supplies she thought she would need out of the van and was waiting at the door.

"I know where Raymond lives," Mia said. "It's just a couple of miles toward town from here. We can be there in a few minutes. That poor horse has to be in a lot of pain. I've always wanted a horse, but Poppa says no. Daddy says that when he was a little boy Poppa had to put his horse to sleep, and that he'd had him for more than twenty years, even before they adopted Daddy and Uncle Cody and Uncle Lucas. Having to do that hurt him so badly that he wouldn't have another horse on the place." Mia rambled on and on the entire distance.

When Mia turned in to the lane leading up to the ranch house, Stevie interrupted her and said, "Keep following the path toward the barn over to the west. The horse is in the corral out back of that."

Mia nodded and kept talking. "It would break my heart to lose Maggie. She was my first hembra, and she's produced a cria every year for me. We're here." She braked and turned the engine off. "Can I help carry anything?"

"No, I've got it," Stevie answered.

Raymond met them at the gate and opened it for them. "She's gentle as a lamb. I've had her more than fifteen years, and I've been using a vet out of Paris, but he retired at Christmas. I'm sure glad that you're setting up a practice close by."

"What's her name?" Stevie asked.

"Buttercup," Raymond said. "I'm not against taking orders if you need help."

Stevie started by rubbing the horse's nose and speaking softly to her. "Hello, Buttercup. I'm here to help you. I promise to be as gentle as possible. Looks like you've got a nasty cut on your leg. We can fix that right up, and you'll be all better soon."

She dropped down on one knee and opened her bag. She removed a pair of wire cutters and began to snip the barbed wire away in pieces, a little at a time. "Good girl. You're doing just fine. We'll get this nasty old stuff off you in just a little bit and clean this up. Raymond, will you take all these pieces and put them in the trash, please?"

"Yes, ma'am," he said.

"And, Mia, get out that bottle of povidone-iodine and the chlorhexidine. That's what we'll use to clean the gash. From what I'm seeing, it's not deep enough to need stitches, but we'll treat it with some antibiotic and wrap the wound with a sterile bandage. I'd like to check on it every three days, if that's all right with you, Raymond," Stevie said.

"Anything you need," Raymond said, and nodded in agreement.

"How do you know whether to stitch or not?" Mia asked.

"It's a judgment call most of the time, but this is below the knee and it's not deep enough to see soft tissue. Stitching it would probably make it swell. We'll just wrap it up good, and you probably should keep her in a stall for a few days. Get her out and walk her for maybe twenty minutes each day," Stevie said as she cleaned the wound, treated it with antibiotic cream, and then wrapped it up. "How long has it been since she had a tetanus vaccination?"

"Two years last month," Raymond said. "I was waiting until the weather got better to call you to come out and vaccinate the cattle and get her up to date on her shots."

"I'll take care of her today, and we can make a date next week for me to come out here to check the cattle." Stevie took what she needed from the bag and gave the horse a shot. "That's a good girl," she said and then brought out the apple. "And here's your lollipop for not kicking me or throwing a fit."

Raymond removed his cowboy hat and scratched his bald head. "You're really good, Miz O'Dell."

"Just Stevie," she said, "and thank you. I love animals, and I think they should be treated with respect and love."

"Pretty good way to look at things," Raymond said. "What do I owe you?"

"I'll bring a bill when we check her in three days, or if you like, I can bill you at the end of each month for whatever services I render," Stevie told him.

"Fair enough. I'll be calling on you, so billing me will

make it easier for both of us." Raymond hooked a thumb in Buttercup's halter and gave a gentle tug. "Come on, baby girl. We'll get you in a nice clean stall, and I'll be out tomorrow morning to walk you around the corral."

"See you soon." Stevie gathered up her things and headed toward the pickup.

"That was amazing!" Mia said. "Were you serious about treating all animals with love?"

"Yep, I was," Stevie said.

Mia slid behind the steering wheel and asked, "Even the two-legged kind like Uncle Cody?"

"Only if he doesn't kick and eats the apple all in one bite like Buttercup." Stevie put her bag on the wide bench seat and got into the passenger side of the truck.

"I'm going to love working with you," Mia giggled.

"Right back atcha, kiddo," Stevie said.

* * *

Cody flopped down on the sofa that evening and said, "Dad got a hold of Bubba, the guy who owns the tire shop and wrecker service in Honey Grove. He can't get out here until Monday, but he'll bring four new tires out and put them on your van then."

Stevie brought two cups of coffee from the kitchen area and set them on the coffee table. "That was sweet of him to do that for me."

"He likes you," Cody said. "The whole family does."

"Well, I like them right back." Stevie sunk down in her spot on the sofa. "Where's Tex tonight?"

185

"He went home with Mama and Dad. He migrates between the three places, and we all spoil him," Cody answered. "Mia tells me that we're both going to be having Sunday dinner at the ranch house. What happened to our date? You afraid to be alone with me?"

Stevie kicked off her boots and drew her legs up onto the sofa. "I'm alone with you now."

"But now, we're roommates or friends, not a couple on a date," he argued.

"How about we go out the next Friday night?" she asked. "It's important to Mia that we all be there when Beau comes to dinner."

"It's true. I do want to meet the kid. But how about tomorrow night instead of waiting a week?" Cody asked.

"I'm going to be busy getting settled back into my own place tomorrow night," she told him, "but if you want to come over and have pizza and a movie night with me, then we could call that a date."

"Will I get a good night kiss?" he teased.

"I don't usually give those out on first dates," she answered.

"How many second dates have you been on?" he asked.

She cocked her head to one side. "Not sure that's any of your business, Doctor."

There was no getting ahead of this woman. "Ha! Fair enough," he answered. "But you can at least tell me if there was ever anyone serious, right?"

"There were a couple." She shrugged. "They were good guys—respectful and kind—but I backed away when they wanted a serious commitment."

"Same for me," Cody said. He had never discussed his past love life with anyone, but he found it a little liberating to talk about it, even in generalities.

"What was your fear of committing?" he asked. "Was it your father? Was he the perfect man in your mind?"

Stevie shook her head. "I don't have daddy issues, and I've known for years that my dad was far from perfect. He was a quiet man of few words, who loved reading and big band music. He left most of the business of raising me up to my mother, but I loved him and accepted things the way they were. I didn't hate him, and when he died suddenly at the end of my junior year in high school, I missed him something fierce," she answered.

"Then who was the perfect man in your life?" Cody asked.

"You, Cody Ryan"—Stevie locked gazes with him—"were the cowboy I'd built up in my mind to be perfect, even after you broke up with me. But believe me, I've found out that you do not belong on the pedestal I had you on, and for that, I'm very grateful for these past few days."

Cody finally blinked and looked away. "I've never been perfect, Stevie—far from it. I'm sorry that your idea of me has ruined what might have brought you happiness."

"I'm not." She shrugged. "Mama always said that God protects drunks and fools. Maybe I was a fool to have such an idea, but then again maybe having it kept me from making a huge mistake in my life."

Chapter Fourteen

*L*eaving Sunflower Ranch was a little anticlimactic the next morning. Stevie simply put the things that belonged to her in her go bag and tossed the clothing the folks at the ranch had loaned her into an empty laundry basket and left it at the foot of the bed. She had wanted to take it all home and launder it, but Mia wouldn't hear of it. She sent a text to Mia and told her where she could find the basket and got a simple one back that said, *OK c u later.*

She looked around the bedroom to be sure she didn't need to do anything else and sighed. She was excited to get back to her own house, but she'd made friends here— no, she'd been part of a family. That was even better than making friends, and she would miss it.

Cody knocked on the frame of the open door and leaned

on the jamb. "I thought we would grab some breakfast at the diner. We could call it our first date."

"Or we could just call it breakfast," she said.

"If I pay for it, and if I walk you to the door when we get to your house, then it's a date," he argued.

Date.

That was a word Stevie never expected to hear from Cody Ryan. She was happy that he asked her out, so why was she arguing with him?

Because I love the banter and the vibes it creates, she thought.

"You win," she said, "it's a date."

He picked up her coat and held it for her. She couldn't remember the last time she had a date. It had to have been at least a year before she came home to Texas. That would have been when she and Trenton, her second serious relationship, had broken up. He had been in advertising, was good-looking, and made a lot of money, but he was looking for a wife. When Stevie turned down the ring and the proposal, it was all over, and he had since married another woman only a few months later.

Wow! Can it really have been that long? she wondered as she picked up her go bag. She took one last look around the bunkhouse and made a mental picture of the whole place. She would miss being here with Cody and miss all the suppers and good times she had had with the whole Ryan family. She and Cody would date—that was a given—but things would never be quite like the time they had spent in the tack room and the bunkhouse.

189

"Ready?" he asked. "Need to get anything from the van or tell Dixie goodbye?"

"I'll drive back out here later this evening or tomorrow morning and get what I need," Stevie said around the lump in her throat. "I hate goodbyes, and I already kissed Dixie on the nose and told her to mind her mama."

With his hand on her lower back, Cody ushered her out to his work truck, and opened the passenger door for her. "I made sure Tex went with Mia and Jesse this morning, or else he would have pouted when he couldn't go with us."

"I wondered where he was." Stevie would even miss the dog lying on the sofa between her and Cody. "Are you and Jesse going after your truck today?"

"Soon as I get back," Cody said and nodded. "I'm sure the insurance adjustor will tell me that it's totaled. When they've made their decision, I'll go shopping for another one. If you want to go along, that could be our third date."

"What makes you think there'll *be* a third date?" Stevie asked.

"Because the third one is the charm," he answered as he drove around the side of the ranch house and down the lane to the road. "It's like this. You've been in two serious relationships, so this will be the third one. And now you don't have to measure me by me, because you know that I'm not perfect."

"Aha." She finally smiled. "A cowboy who admits he's less than perfect is rare."

"Then I'm a rare breed," he said with a grin. "But I do

have faults. I don't do well if I have a nightmare. I like to argue and flirt, and…"

"You love your family," she finished for him.

"That's a pro, not a con," he told her.

"Not necessarily. What if after the third date, your family doesn't like me, or doesn't think I'm good enough for you? What if you had to choose between them and a woman that you really like?" she asked.

"I'm not crossing that bridge until I come to it." He made a left-hand turn. "Look at all the trees that have been pushed to the side. This area will take years to recover from this storm."

Stevie just nodded, but she was thinking of all the years it had taken her to get from the crush she had had on Cody when she was a teenager to the way she was feeling that morning. Even though they had just left the ranch behind, she already missed it and the folks living there. In a little while Cody would walk her to the door of her house, and then he'd go on about his business, and she already missed him—even more than the ranch.

Going home to her own things and her own bed would be wonderful. But she began to mentally list all the reasons why she wished she could stay at the ranch a few more days.

The parking lot at the local diner was full, but then this was the time of day when the old ranchers gathered for coffee every morning. Stevie's father had had a standing date for breakfast on Saturday mornings with some of his friends when he was alive. Cody made a couple of laps around the parking lot before he found an empty space.

191

During that brief time, Stevie remembered being up early on a Saturday morning and asking her father if she could go with him when she was about six years old.

"No, you would be bored, sweetheart," he had said. "We talk about politics and taxes and those kinds of things."

"What's taxes?" she had asked.

Her father had patted her on the head, and said, "You'll find out when you are older. Now run along. Your mama has made pancakes for you."

"You're awfully quiet." Cody turned off the engine and turned to face her. "You having second thoughts about this date?"

"Nope, just thinking about my father. When he was alive, he used to have breakfast on Saturday mornings with his buddies at this place," she said.

"Dad used to come here a couple of mornings a week when he was able," Cody said. "I often wonder if he misses the times that he spent with the guys his age. He never complains, but I can see how much it peps him up when some of those older men come to visit him at the ranch."

"Ever think about driving him into town once a week so he could catch up with the whole bunch of them?" she asked.

"Yes, ma'am," Cody answered as he slid out of the truck. "I even offered, but he told me he didn't want to spend time away from Mama."

He jogged around the front of the vehicle and opened the door for Stevie. "He said she was the most important person in his life, and he didn't want to waste a single minute away from her side."

"That is so sweet." Stevie wanted that kind of lifetime commitment.

"Yep, it is." Cody slung an arm around her shoulders. "It's nice to walk beside a tall woman who can keep in step with me."

"Well, thank you, Dr. Cowboy, for that compliment," she said.

"Just stating the facts, darlin'," he said with a broad smile as he opened the door into the diner.

The buzz of several conversations ended the moment they walked inside the warm diner and found a booth. Old men and a few ladies over at a side table stared at them for a minute, then the whispers began, and the telephones came out. Stevie swore that she could feel the breeze off their arthritic thumbs as they sent texts to folks in Honey Grove. She would have loved to be a fly that could flit from one phone to the other, read the texts, and then make another round to check out the replies.

The waitress came right over to the table. "Good morning. Want to start off with...oh, I just now realized that you are Cody Ryan. Mia Ryan's uncle, right? I'm her friend Justine. I've missed getting to see her since the blizzard hit us."

"We met once when you came out to the ranch with your little boy. Matty, is it?" Cody answered and then introduced Stevie as Dr. O'Dell.

"Just Stevie," she said with a smile. "Glad to meet you. Mia has mentioned you."

"Tell her that I'll try to get out to the ranch this next

week. Now, can I get y'all some coffee or juice to start off the morning?" Justine asked. "Breakfast special this morning is two scrambled eggs, biscuit and sausage gravy, either bacon or ham, and a stack of pancakes. Or you can order from the menu." She pointed to the single sheet of laminated paper between the salt and pepper shakers and the old-fashioned napkin holder.

"Coffee," Stevie said. "Black."

"Same, and I'll have that special you've got listed right here with ham." Cody pointed to the item on the menu.

"Me too, only I want bacon," Stevie said.

"I'll get that coffee and have your order out in a jiffy." Justine put her order pad in her hip pocket and went back toward the kitchen.

"I like the hamburgers here almost as much as I like their breakfast," Stevie said. "But I've got to admit, the breakfast at the bunkhouse was even better."

"Well, thank you, ma'am. I try to keep a well-stocked kitchen and pantry. I missed bacon, eggs, and pancakes when I was in impoverished villages," Cody said.

Justine returned with their coffee. "Your orders will be out in a few minutes."

"Thank you." Stevie picked up her mug and held it in her hands to warm them for a minute before she took the first sip. "I believe we're supposed to talk on our first date. Tell me something about yourself."

"I'm a general practitioner or a family doctor, as I like to tell people. I don't like being tied down to a nine-to-five in an office, so I decided to put in a concierge practice where I treat the patients in their homes," he answered.

"I'm drawn to women with green eyes, and I really like the gold flecks in yours."

"Compliments of my father." She smiled across the table at him.

"Your turn," Cody said. "Etiquette for first date and all."

"I'm a veterinarian in a small town. I love what I do, and we have that business of being tied down to an office in common, so I take my van to my animal patients for the most part. For small animals that need spaying or neutering, I've turned my mother's garage into a little clinic," she answered.

"Well, now, that's something I didn't know. When Dolly weans her kittens, I should make an appointment with you to have her fixed," he said.

Justine brought out a tray loaded with full plates and all kinds of condiments. "Here you go, folks. Y'all enjoy, and just wave me over if you need anything else."

"Thanks," Cody said. "It all looks great."

She rushed off to wait on a man and a woman who had just come in with a couple of children. Stevie glanced out the window and noticed an SUV with an Arkansas tag. "Looks like those might be folks from out of state. If you were traveling with kids, would you stop at a local diner or find a McDonald's?"

"I'm not much of a fan of fast food." Cody salted his eggs and then used pepper for his gravy.

"Me either, except for hamburgers from Sonic." Stevie picked up a piece of bacon with her fingers and took a bite.

"Well, now, if we're talking hamburgers, I'm all in for a

good, old greasy Sonic burger," he said. "That can be our fourth date. We'll drive over to the Sonic in Bonham and order burgers, fries, and chocolate shakes."

"I might go out with you on the second and third date, just to get to the fourth one if you can guarantee me that," she told him.

"It's a promise," he said, and nodded.

Stevie had her coffee refilled twice and had finished her breakfast when she finally said, "We should probably go, Cody. You've got a truck to rescue, and I need to clean out the refrigerator and go to the grocery store."

"You're right, but this has been fun." Cody waved at Justine and she brought the check right over. He handed her a bill, told her to keep the change, and then slid out of the booth.

"Yes, it has and thank you," she said.

Cody was stopped by former patients twice before they finally made it outside, where dark clouds had begun to roll in from the southwest. They had questions about the rumors going around that he'd wrecked his truck out by Max's ranch and had been stranded for days. Cody took time to tell them the story of the buck that was the size of an Angus bull that had a rack a bushel basket wouldn't fit over.

When he and Stevie made it outside, Stevie nudged him and said, "You just made their day, and they're already on their cell phones telling everyone they know that they heard it from the horse's mouth about that wrecked truck."

"No, you did," Cody chuckled. "Now they can be the

first ones to tell their wives that the gossip is real, and that we were stuck in a tack room together for four days. Should we just go on to the courthouse in Bonham right now and make an honest woman of you?"

"Not until we have that fourth date, and I get my hamburger," she answered.

He settled her into the truck and drove the familiar road toward the school. Her house, which was located less than a block away, was a little two-bedroom frame house with a railing around the front porch and a small, attached garage off to one side. He parked in the gravel driveway and again got out of the truck and opened the door for her.

"You don't have to walk me to the door, Cody. Like I said before, you have things to do." She picked up her bag and slid out of the truck.

"My mama would peel the leaves off a peach tree switch and take it to me if I wasn't a gentleman." He tucked her free hand into his and walked up the three steps to the porch with her.

She fished her key out of her purse and started to open the door but noticed that he was frowning. "What's the matter?"

"There's water all over your porch," he said.

"Snow makes water when it melts," she said with a smile and then realized that the water was coming from under the door. "Oh, no!" she gasped and hurriedly opened the door. A flood of water rushed out of the house so forceful that it splashed both of them halfway to their knees.

"You've got busted pipes." Cody was already fishing his phone from his hip pocket. "I'll call city hall and get someone out here to turn the water off at the meter, then we'll see what we need to do after that. We might as well sit in the truck until they get here."

"Look in there," she gasped again. "It's six inches up the walls and..."

When he finished his call, he took her by the hand and led her out to the truck. "We can't do one thing until the water is turned off. Then we'll figure out the damage and what we have to do to fix it."

Tears welled up in her eyes. "But everything that was on the floor is ruined."

"We'll worry about that in a few minutes. They said they were already looking at a house not far from here that got flooded, so...look, here they are now," he said.

Stevie's mind ran in circles. All her mother's things would be waterlogged. The house itself would be a mess. There was no way she could live in there for weeks—if ever.

Two guys got out of a truck and hurried over to the meter in the front yard. One of them used a long tool to turn off the water and then yelled, "I'm so sorry you got flooded, Stevie. This isn't unusual with the older plumbing in these homes built back in the sixties."

"What do I do now?" she asked.

"Get what you can out of it. Soon as we get done a block over from you, we'll bring a pump and suck what water we can out of the house for you. Then you just have to wait until it dries and hire someone to come see if it's worth repairing," he answered. "Give us half an hour to finish what we've got to do, and we'll be back. We've got both the gas and electric companies over there with us. We'll bring them along to turn off those utilities. You shouldn't go inside until we do that for fear of getting shocked."

"Thank you," Cody yelled and then turned to face Stevie. "I'll take you back to the ranch. You can stay in the bunkhouse with me as long as you need to."

Stevie closed her eyes and gave herself thirty seconds to get over the panic, and then she said, "Back this truck up to the porch. As soon as they turn off the electricity, I'm wading in there. My clothing is hanging in the closet and should be fine, and there's pictures on the bookcase, and..." Tears began to stream down her cheeks.

Cody took her in his arms and held her tightly. "I'm so sorry, darlin'. I'll help you and together we'll load what we can in the bed of the truck. And I'm going to call Jesse. He can bring his truck, and Mia can drive Dad's. We'll take care of you, I promise."

"But your truck, and..." she stammered.

"It's sat in that ditch for almost a week. Another day isn't going to matter." Cody took a white hankie from his pocket and wiped away her tears. "I'm here for you."

"I can go to a hotel in Bonham," she sniffled.

"Oh, no, you will not." Cody shook his head. "After a shock like this, you need family around you."

Yes, you do. Her mother's voice was back in her head. *Don't worry about stuff. It can be replaced.*

Chapter Fifteen

I don't think I would be electrocuted," Stevie argued as she followed him out to the truck. "The water that washed out over us didn't shock us."

Cody glanced down at their wet jeans. "We should go back out to the ranch and get into dry clothes and bring rubber boots before we tackle this. Leave the door open so the guys can get in there and start pumping the water out."

"You are probably right," she agreed. "I'm afraid the house is going to be like your truck, Cody. Completely totaled."

"How's that?" He led her to his truck and helped her inside, where it was still warm. "It might take a while, but if the foundation is still good, it could be gutted and new drywall..."

"It's more than sixty years old." Stevie's voice sounded hollow in her own ears. "And as much as I hate to admit it, the floors have begun to slope a little. I can't bear to lose it, though. It belonged to my grandmother and then my parents, and it's the only house I ever lived in. I stayed in the dorms the whole time I was in college, and I lived in a small apartment when I worked at the clinic in Oklahoma City."

"We'll cross that bridge when we come to it." He started the engine, backed out of the driveway, and headed back to the ranch.

"Looks to me like we've got a lot of bridges to cross." She groaned when she thought about the garage. "Do you think the water would have gotten into the garage? It's attached, but it's on a slab instead of a pier-and-beam foundation. Mama's got boxes and boxes stored out there, and her car is parked out there. I haven't even started it up and driven it since she died."

"We'll just have to wait and see," Cody answered. "And, Stevie, life is full of bridges. Some we burn. Some we cross over with help from a loved one. Some we detour around. This could be a detour. You might just have to live at the ranch until it's all fixed up again. The upside is that you can make it all yours, and maybe that will be some sort of closure about your mother's death."

She sighed and wondered how many bridges she would detour around in the future. For now, she could live at the ranch, which was a blessing, but that was beginning to feel like charity.

Her phone rang, and she was glad to see Mia's name

pop up instead of someone calling about vet services that day. She would have gone out to wherever she was needed, but she wanted a few hours for all this to fully sink in.

"Hello," she answered.

"How does it feel to be home?" Mia asked.

"Not so good right now." Stevie's voice cracked, but she got control of it enough to tell Mia what had happened.

"I'm so sorry, but you can stay right here at the ranch, Stevie. If you're tired of bunking in with Uncle Cody, you can have my room, and I'll go stay with Nana and Poppa," Mia said.

"The bunkhouse is fine, and thank you," Stevie said. "We got wet when the water rushed out of the house, so we're on our way back to get into dry clothes."

"I haven't gotten the clothes that I loaned you, so there's stuff there, and I'll tell Dad that we're coming to help. He can bring his truck, and I'll drive Nana's SUV. We can store what's salvageable in the corner of the barn," Mia said.

"Thank you," Stevie said. "We're almost home, and as soon as we change, we're going back to town. Hopefully the electricity will be turned off, and we can get inside."

"You'll need rubber boots. I've got extras that I'll bring along," Mia said. "See you in a little while at your house. Dad does know where you live, right?"

"I'm sure he does, but it's about a block from the school. If you get to the house before I do, you'll probably see the vehicles from the city because they'll be pumping out as much water as they can," Stevie told her, "and thank you again."

"Hey, you don't have to keep thanking me," Mia said.

"That's what family is for, and just like Maggie adopted Dixie, we've adopted you."

"You are awesome, girl." Stevie tried to smile, but it didn't happen.

"I heard her," Cody said, "and she's right."

"Does that make you my brother?" Stevie asked.

"I hope to hell not." Cody turned in to the lane leading up to the house.

An hour later, three vehicles were lined up in the driveway at Stevie's house. The city guys were there pumping the water out into the ditch that ran along the front of the place. The electric and gas people had come out, shut off the utilities, and gone on to the next house with problems. When as much water as they could get out was gone, Stevie put on a pair of Mia's rubber boots and led the way inside. The sopping wet carpet squished with every step, and Stevie wanted to cry when she saw the condition of the sofa, the chairs, and the tables in the living room and kitchen.

"Let's go to your bedroom first," Mia suggested. "If your clothes are hung up, I bet they're just fine. I'll load them in the SUV. If they're wet, then we can put them in garbage bags and start laundry when we get home."

Glad that Mia had the foresight to think about where to start, Stevie just nodded and headed down the short hallway to her room. The bedspread had soaked up water from the floor and was wet all the way to the mattress. She opened the bottom dresser drawer to find wet pajama bottoms that already had black mold on them.

When she pulled the next one up open, everything was fine in it.

Mia threw open the closet doors and squealed. "The boxes on the floor are soaked, but your shoes and boots up on the shelf are good and so are your clothes. I'm going to take them to the SUV on the hangers."

Stevie went back to the kitchen and got a plastic garbage bag to use for all the things in her dresser drawers. Her suitcases were stored on the floor of her closet, so they would be ruined.

"The pipes under the sink burst," Cody yelled from the bathroom, "and the supply line to the toilet."

"The ones under the kitchen sink did the same," Jesse called out.

Stevie stopped in the hallway and stared at a picture of her and her mother hanging on the wall. "Oh, Mama, what do I do?"

Cody came up behind her and wrapped his arms around her waist. "I'll go to the grocery store and get some cardboard boxes to pack up all these pictures in. Even though everything on the floor is probably ruined, you'll have some keepsakes left."

Stevie turned around and laid her head on Cody's shoulders. "That's the most important things, right?"

"Yes, they are," Mia said as she passed them with a load of clothing in her arms. "All this other stuff can be replaced, but pictures and memories can't." She didn't stop but kept moving toward the open door. Every footstep made a sucking noise when she picked up her feet from the drenched carpet.

"My advice is that you shouldn't move anything but Stevie's personal things out today," Jesse suggested. "The insurance adjustor should see things as they are. You can come back after he's been here to take down pictures and think about the stuff in the kitchen cabinets, and such."

Stevie wanted to argue with him, but common sense said he was right. By Monday, maybe things would be dried out enough that she could make better decisions about the rest of her things. "Okay," she agreed, "I'm sorry you've brought so many vehicles. My clothing can probably all be loaded into the SUV. What about the rest of my vet stuff in the garage?"

"I checked out there," Jesse said. "It's backed up to the kitchen so the water from the pipes seeped through the wall, and whatever is on the floor is wet. The water didn't get up into the car or on the shelves where you keep supplies. Maybe you could just take what you have to have, like any medicines or that kind of thing."

"Want me to go out and start your mother's car for you?" Cody asked.

"Yes, please," Stevie said. "Keys are on the rack by the garage door. If it starts, I'll drive it out to the ranch."

She turned around and went to her room again, and started tossing all the dry things from her dresser and chest of drawers into one of the big garbage bags. "I'm a lucky woman to even have a place to go," she muttered, "so why..."

"Because this is your home," Mia said as she breezed into the room. "I'd be sad if this happened to the ranch house. It would even upset me if it happened to the bunkhouse or the empty place sitting over on the other property that Poppa owns."

"What other place?" Stevie asked.

"When my grandparents, Mama's parents, sold their ranch and moved out to the Panhandle, they sold their ranch to Poppa. It's got a house on it that hasn't been lived in in a long time," Mia explained.

Stevie made a mental note to herself to ask Sonny if he would rent that house if she had to tear down her family home. Then she said, "Your dad and Cody think it would be best if we just take my personal things until after the insurance adjuster looks at the place."

"I don't know anything about all that stuff," Mia said, "but if Daddy says that's the smart thing to do, I'd trust him."

Cody appeared at the door with a grin on his face. "The car started right up. That's the good news."

"And the bad?" she asked.

"Whatever was on the floor of the garage will probably have to be thrown away." The smile faded. "I hope it wasn't anything super important."

"Probably Christmas decorations." A wave of sadness swept over Stevie. She wished that she had put up a tree this past holiday. Maybe some of what was in the boxes would have been saved if they'd been on the tree instead of packed away.

"If we all take a load, we should be able to get the rest of this pretty quick," Mia said.

Cody and Jesse went to the closet, and each gathered up an armload of clothing. Mia reached up and took down as many shoe boxes as she could carry. Stevie threw the garbage bag full of things over her shoulder and took them out to her mother's car. Once she had put it in the back seat, she crawled in beside the bag and just sat there.

In a few minutes, Cody got in beside her, draped an arm around her, and pulled her closer to him. "I promise all our dates won't end like this one."

"If the second one does, there won't be a third," she said.

It's time to move on and make a fresh start. You've been looking for closure, and here it is, the voice in her head said. The boxes that she had kept all her journals and keepsakes in were soaked, and everything was completely ruined.

Back at the bunkhouse, she sat down on the edge of the bed and stared at the closed closet door. Cody had moved everything he owned out to the storage room in the main part of the house. Jesse had found a spare chest of drawers in storage and put it in there for Cody's personal things. Next week, they would rescue the rest of what was salvageable from the house and store it in the barn.

But right then, the entire impact of losing her home hit her.

"It would have been better if a tornado had simply taken it all in one fell swoop instead of having to face the destruction a flood can do to a house," she muttered.

Cody crossed the room and sat down beside her. "The insurance adjustor will be there tomorrow, and we can go back through the place again, once everything is dried out, and see if there's anything else worth saving. At least your mother's car started up, and you've got something to drive until Monday when the guy comes to fix your van."

"And we can save my vet supplies that are on shelves in the garage." She tried to hang on to a few positive ideas. "A lot of the things I use often are stashed in the van, so that's a good thing. I've got a roof over my head, friends who care about me, my clothing was all undamaged except for one drawer full of pajamas. My mother's voice popped into my head and told me that it was all just stuff. So why do I feel like I just fell into a black hole?"

"In the past few months, you've started a private vet practice. You've lost your last parent. You've been stranded in a winter storm with a baby alpaca and your arch-enemy. Now your house might not be worth saving," Cody answered. "That's enough to put a person without your strength over the edge."

"I don't feel so strong right now," Stevie said. "I'm grateful for everything, but inside, I'm a mess, Cody."

"Let's go up to the ranch house for supper. You need to be around people and family," Cody told her.

Stevie wanted to curl up on the bed, put a pillow over her head, and think about nothing, but after all the Ryan family had done for her, she couldn't do that. She nodded and stood up. "You are right. Maybe playing with little Sam and Taylor might make me realize that, like Mama said, it's just stuff."

Cody took her by the hand and led her to the living room, where he helped her into her coat. "I've lived among folks who had so little that I can agree with your mother."

Stevie just gave him a brief nod. They walked up the path to the house hand in hand, and just that small gesture made her feel better. Pearl must have been watching for them out the kitchen window because she met Stevie in the middle of the kitchen floor with outstretched arms.

"I'm so sorry about this," Pearl said as she hugged her, "but know that you are welcome here for as long as you want to stay. Sonny says we'll clear out the tack room and you can use it for your vet clinic."

"That's right," Sonny said from his place at the table. "We can put locks on both doors so the insurance people won't fuss at us over the drugs you need to keep handy, and you can keep your van parked in the barn so it will be ready to go when you need it."

"And for all that and for room and board, I want to pay you what's fair," Stevie said.

To her surprise Sonny nodded without an argument. "I've been thinking about that. How about you do whatever vet business we need done for free while you live on the ranch? But only your time is free. Whatever you have to use in the way of medicine or vaccinations will be billed to the ranch."

"That's a pretty good deal." Mia brought in one of the twins. "Can we add that I get to assist you with whatever that is?"

"Yes, you can, and thank you, Sonny," Stevie said. "That's a very generous deal."

"On whose end?" Cody chuckled. "Dad might figure out a way to keep you here through calving season and the spring vaccinations."

"If I can't, I bet Mia or Addy can help me out." Sonny laughed out loud.

"I won't let you down, Poppa," Mia giggled.

"And you can depend on me," Addy added as she put the second twin in a high chair.

Fate had to be playing out a hand, Stevie thought, and wondered what she would be dealt next. She glanced over at Cody to see him grinning so big she hoped that, whichever way the cards fell, things didn't get awkward between them.

Chapter Sixteen

The church parking lot was sparsely occupied that Sunday morning when the Ryan family arrived in three vehicles. Stevie had ridden with Cody, and even though he had said they would be going shopping for a new truck next week, she kind of hated to give up the old work truck with the wide bench seat.

"Penny for your thoughts." Cody parked between Addy's and his mother's SUVs.

"They're not worth that much." Stevie smoothed the front of her knee-length dark green skirt. "I was thinking about Tex not being able to ride in the front seat with us when you get a new truck. These days they all come with consoles and bucket seats."

"And here I was hoping you were thinking about sharing a hymn book with me," he teased.

"Do you know what that means to the old folks?" Stevie asked.

"Oh, yeah!" he said. "What do you say . . . *love*? Shall we make this a date even though we can't go out to dinner and for a long drive on dirt roads?"

"Why not?" She shrugged. "If this is a date, then we'll get to that fourth one faster, and we can get a Sonic burger."

As usual, Cody got out of the truck and rounded the front end to open the door for her. That morning, he wore starched and creased jeans and a plaid shirt with a Western-cut suede jacket over it. His black cowboy boots had been shined and his hat dusted off. He wouldn't be anyone's stereotypical idea of a doctor, but most people would think he was a rancher.

He ushered her across the lot with his hand on her lower back, and the whole family followed Pearl and Sonny down the center aisle. When they were about halfway to the third pew where the Ryan family always sat together, a young man stood and motioned toward Mia.

She peeled off to the right and sat down with Beau Martin—or that's who Stevie assumed he was since that's who would be coming to dinner with her after the services. He had auburn hair and a round face covered with freckles.

Pearl and Sonny sat down, and Addy and Jesse made their way to the middle of the row, leaving the last two places empty for Stevie and Cody. Stevie glanced across the aisle at the pew where she and her mother used to sit every Sunday morning. Nowadays, a middle-aged couple had taken up residence over there with their four daughters ranging in age from about ten to maybe sixteen.

The lady who played the piano hit a couple of chords, and everyone began to reach for the hymnals in the pockets on the backs of the pews in front of them. As luck would have it, there were only three hymnals: one for Pearl and Sonny to share, a second one for Addy and Jesse, and the one that Cody handed to her.

"Guess this means we're the topic of the gossip vine this week," he whispered.

"Or maybe folks are more interested in Mia and Beau than they are in us," she told him.

"Double their rumor pleasure," Cody said.

The man who led the singing at the church stepped up behind the lectern and said, "Good morning, everyone. It's good to see that some of you have braved the weather and come on out to services this morning. Will you all please turn to number two hundred forty-seven? We'll sing together 'When We All Get to Heaven.'"

Cody had a wonderful singing voice, but what Stevie loved most was the way her insides warmed with the touch of his fingertips against hers as they shared the hymnal.

When they finished the song, the song leader said, "And now Betsy and Justine are going to do a special song for Betsy's parents and Justine's grandparents this morning. Sharon and Thomas Walters were married fifty years this past week, and they weren't able to have much of a celebration what with the blizzard that we had, so they are singing this song for them today."

Justine and her mother, Betsy, made their way from the back of the church. They both picked up a handheld microphone from the top of the piano, and Betsy said, "This is the song that Daddy sings to Mama, so we thought it would be appropriate for their fiftieth anniversary."

"Happy Anniversary, Granny and Gramps." Justine waved toward the second pew. "I love you both and appreciate all the support you've given me through the years."

Betsy nodded at the pianist and she began to play "I Want to Stroll Over Heaven with You."

Stevie recognized the melody long before Betsy began singing the first words that asked the King for one more blessing—he wanted to stroll over heaven with the love of his life.

She only meant to peek at Cody's expression, but he was looking right at her, and they locked gazes. Was he wondering if heaven was big enough for the two of them, like she was? Or was he thinking of something altogether different? Everything around them suddenly seemed to disappear, and they were the only two people on earth. The moment couldn't have lasted more than a split second, and then Stevie blinked, faced forward, and focused on Betsy and Justine.

Stevie did the math in her head, starting with the year that Betsy had graduated from high school, and figuring out that she was in her early forties. The woman was only a few years older than Stevie and already a grandmother. That little bit of revelation set Stevie's biological clock to ticking so loudly that she could hardly hear the last of the song they were singing. Even if she had a child in the next couple of years, she most likely wouldn't be a grandmother until she was in her sixties.

I never got to be one, her mother said very loudly in her head.

Stevie came back to the present with a little jerk when the preacher cleared his throat. Cody touched her on the arm and asked, "Are you cold? Do you need my jacket?"

"No, I'm fine," she said. "I was just woolgathering and you startled me."

"Been there," Cody said, "done that many times in church."

The preacher said something about his sermon being about the fruits of the spirit from Galatians, but that was the last thing that Stevie heard. She went right back into her woolgathering and thought about all that had happened since her first tire went flat. In less than two weeks, she had gone from sitting on the back pew in church all alone because she couldn't bear to sit where she and her mother had sat, to sharing space with the Ryan family. If someone had told her the last Sunday she was here that she would be sitting with Cody the next time she attended services, she would have told them what they were full of—and it would not have been the fruits of the spirit.

"Hey, everyone." Mia came into the house holding Beau's hand. "I want you to meet Beau Martin." She made introductions, and he shook hands with each person, even little Sam and Taylor.

Stevie was just a tad bit jealous in that moment. She had never gotten to take a boyfriend home to meet her mother and father. She had attended her junior and senior proms as a single girl and had only stayed long enough to have her picture taken in front of the backdrop for the theme of the prom. Those were two of the pictures still hanging in the hallway of her house.

"Beau, you can go visit with the guys in the living room while I help Mama get dinner on the table. I hope you like ham," Mia said.

"I love home-cooked anything, but ham is about my favorite dinner," Beau said with a smile, "and don't worry about me, Mia. I like to visit about ranching." He sat down on the floor in front of the twins, who were still in their carriers. "Can I take one or both of them out and hold them? I'm really good with babies. I've got a niece who's about this age, and a nephew who's a little older. I'm their favorite uncle."

"Sure," Jesse said. "They'd love a little extra attention."

"Wow!" Stevie whispered as she locked arms with Mia and the two of them headed toward the kitchen. "Is he real? Jesse already likes him."

"How can you tell?" Mia asked.

"By his expression. His eyes are twinkling like yours do when you are playing with your little brothers," Stevie said.

"I hope you're right, because I really do like Beau." Mia stepped away from her when they reached the kitchen and started setting the table.

"What can I do to help?" Stevie asked.

"You can take the ham out of the oven and slide in the sweet potato casserole," Pearl said. "Then you can slice the ham. The electric knife is in the cabinet under the bar."

Addy hip-bumped Mia. "Why haven't you brought Beau home before now?"

"Because I'm not rushing into anything, ever again, amen," Mia answered. "Not even with him, even though he seems like a really good guy. He's the youngest of three kids, and his brother and sister are, like, ten years older than he is. I'm the oldest of three, and according to the internet, that's supposed to be a perfect match. But I'm not taking any chances, not even when statistics say everything is fine and dandy."

"Good girl," Pearl said. "But, darlin', you need to listen to your heart, not to the internet."

"You are so right, Nana," Mia agreed, "and my heart says to go slow, to build a friendship before a relationship."

"Yep, that love stuff only lasts a little while every day, but friendship takes you through the tough times." Pearl brought out a loaf of homemade bread and sliced it.

"Are you talking about love or lust?" Mia asked.

"Honey, you can call it whatever you want, but marriage is not another word for sex. Marriage is a sacred agreement between two people to live together and love each other through good times and bad and through poverty or riches. It's about sticking together side by side even when you want to shoot him and throw his sorry carcass out for the coyotes' supper," Pearl told her.

"Nana!" Mia gasped. "You never felt like that about Poppa. Y'all have had a perfect marriage."

Pearl stopped what she was doing and gave Mia a hug. "You just keep believing that. I wouldn't burst that bubble for all the dirt in Texas."

"She's right," Addy said, "and as much as I love your father, there are times when he's lucky that he's not breakfast for the coyotes."

Mia's blue eyes almost popped out of her head. "Mama! I thought you and Daddy never had a disagreement."

"We don't"—Addy took a bowl of cranberry salad from the refrigerator and put it on the table—"at least, not in front of the family. We settle our differences in the bedroom and then have amazing makeup..."

Mia stuck her fingers in her ears and started singing, "Fa-la-la-la."

Stevie laughed so hard that she had to peel a paper towel from the roll and dry her eyes with it. "How do you..." She finally got control, then got the hiccups. "Think you got here, Mia? Parents do have sex."

"I know all that, but I don't want to hear about it from my mama"—she shot a look over at Pearl—"or from my nana. I want to think that they found their kids under a cabbage plant in the garden or else the stork brought them on a stormy night. And besides, this is a first date with Beau. I'm not going to marry him or anyone else next week."

"Well, thank God for that!" Addy wiped her forehead in a dramatic gesture that was obviously fake. "I was worried about having to get a wedding planned in just seven days."

That comment made Stevie's thoughts go toward a wedding of her own. Would she want a long engagement, maybe live with a guy for six months or a year before they took that mile-long walk down the aisle? Would she even want the big dress and the wedding cake, or would she rather just take an hour out of the day and go to the courthouse?

"Oh, Mama," Mia sighed. "You don't have a thing to worry about. When I get married, I want the whole enchilada—the big dress, the flowers, and the cake. I want to have music and dance with my groom, and then with Daddy while you dance with the groom. I don't want to elope, and believe me, I will give you a lot longer than a week to plan the wedding."

"Well, that's a relief," Addy said, "but for today, let's get Sunday dinner on the table before those men start whining about starving to death."

Mia opened the oven and took out the sweet potato casserole. "Did I tell you that Beau likes to cook, and he fixes supper almost every night for his grandpa? Vernon never learned how to cook and was kind of lost after Beau's granny died."

"Sounds like Sonny." Pearl carried a platter of sliced bread to the dining room table. "It's a good thing he's got you girls and his sons to look after him if I die before he does. I insisted that my boys learn how to cook, clean house, and do laundry. Good thing I did since they're slow about getting married."

"Thank you for doing that," Addy said. "I'm going to teach Sam and Taylor to do all that too. I'm sure my sisters-in-law would love it if my brothers could cook. I don't think either of them knows how to even start a washing machine."

Stevie thought about the two serious relationships she had had in the past. One of those men had been a chef

219

at a fancy restaurant, and he hadn't wanted her to even enter the kitchen in his apartment. The other, a fellow veterinarian, couldn't boil water without burning it. In both cases, it hadn't been a question of whether he could cook or not that caused the breakup. But if she ever had sons, she agreed with Pearl and Addy. Guys needed to be able to do normal, everyday things for themselves.

Just like Cody does, she thought.

As if on cue, Cody appeared in the doorway and asked, "Can I do anything to help y'all?"

"You can tell all those guys to get their hands washed and come to dinner," Pearl said, "and help your father, only don't let him know you're helping."

"Will do," Cody said with a nod.

Beau was the first one to come into the kitchen. "Where am I supposed to sit? It's been a long time since I sat down to a meal with more than two people at the table."

"You can sit by me." Mia took his hand and led him to the back side of the dining room table. "We should have invited Vernon."

"He's having dinner down at the diner with his buddies like he does every Sunday after church," Beau said. "Sometimes, I go with him. I've learned a lot from those wise old guys."

"Like what?" Jessie brought in the babies and helped Addy get them strapped into their high chairs.

"Like what to do in a drought, the difference in big round bales and small ones when it comes to feeding in the winter, when to plow, and when to expect the cows to start dropping calves. Then there's the stories they tell about when they were young men just starting out and all the hardships and the good times they had," Beau answered.

Sonny took his place at the end of the table and hung his cane on the back of the chair. "You are a smart kid to know how to listen and learn."

"Thank you for that, sir, but sometimes, I'm not so smart when it comes to patience. I'm learning, but it's sure not easy. When does that happen?" Beau pulled out a chair for Mia and seated her before he sat down.

"You'll have to ask someone older than me," Sonny chuckled.

When everyone was settled into their places, Addy said, "Sonny, will you say grace for us?"

"I thought maybe Beau could do that for us," Sonny answered with just a hint of a smile on his face.

Stevie had no doubt this was a test, but Beau simply smiled and said, "It would be an honor." He bowed his head and said a short grace, thanking God for the beautiful day, the family, and the hands that prepared the meal. When he said, "Amen," Sonny was nodding, and Mia was smiling, even though her face was slightly red.

"Thank you, son," Sonny said. "Now, let's get this food passed around the table. I do love me some good ham. Tomorrow, I bet that Addy uses the ham bone to make us up a pot of red beans."

"You are so right," Addy said, "and some fried potatoes and whatever is left over from today's dinner to go with them."

"Do you put the ham bone in when you start the beans or wait until you add water the first time?" Beau asked.

"From the beginning," Addy answered.

"And you always save the bacon drippings from breakfast to use for the potatoes," Mia added.

"That's what Mama taught me, but I've never used ham for red beans. I bet Grandpa would love them fixed that way." Beau took the sweet potato casserole from Mia and scooped out a portion onto his plate. "Would it be all right if Mia shows me around the ranch after dinner? I'd love to see the alpacas and get a tour of the place."

"Of course," Sonny answered.

"Another test passed with flying colors," Cody whispered for Stevie's ears only.

"Why's that?" Stevie asked.

"Because he asked permission," Cody said out the corner of his mouth. "Mia's got a keeper there."

Stevie gave him a brief nod, and wondered if she had a keeper in Cody, or if this thing between them was just a flash in the pan.

Chapter Seventeen

Mia came into the bunkhouse, threw her coat over the rocking chair, and with a long sigh flopped down on the sofa. Stevie knew there were unspoken words behind that sigh, and they were not good. She'd done the same thing too many times to count since she was Mia's age.

"Coffee, tea, or beer?" Stevie followed Mia's example, and removed her coat but took it to her bedroom.

"Beer, unless you've got whiskey hiding here somewhere," Mia answered.

"Beer it is." Stevie headed to the kitchen. She'd seen Cody give Mia beer but never hard liquor, so evidently that was all right in the Ryan family. She took two long-neck bottles from the refrigerator, twisted the tops off both, and carried them to the living area.

Mia reached up, took one from her, and downed about a

fourth before she came up with a loud burp. "Beau would probably tell me that was cute, instead of saying that ladies don't do that."

"So, what's the problem?" Stevie sat down in the rocking chair on the other side of the beat-up coffee table.

"He's too perfect." Mia sighed again. "Mama likes him. Daddy and Poppa think he hung the moon, and I want to like him. I really do."

"But?" Stevie asked.

"He's even rich." Another long sigh, and she downed more of the beer. "He works at the feed store so he can get to know other ranchers, and he takes online classes to learn more about ranching, and his grandpa has already told him that when he dies, his big ranch will go to Beau," Mia groaned.

"What does that have to do with anything?" Stevie asked.

"He won't ever ask me for my money, and he's doing everything he can to learn to be a good rancher. He's a good man, but there's no sizzle like there was with Ricky. I wanted there to be, but it's just not there," Mia said. "Do you think it's because he's not as sexy as Ricky? Or maybe I'm just drawn to bad boys, and good guys don't do jack squat for me."

Stevie could commiserate with Mia. On so many of her dates, the sizzle, whether real or imagined, she thought she would feel with Cody wasn't there either. "I don't think it has to do with whether a guy is tall, dark, and handsome or even a little bit of a bad boy. It's..." She stopped when a hard knock on the door broke her concentration.

Mia set her beer on the table and hopped up from the sofa. "I'll get it. Justine was coming over this evening. Mama probably sent her down here."

"Tell her to come on in," Stevie said.

Mia raced across the floor and threw open the door. "Come on in," she said and then, "Beau?"

Stevie eased up out of the chair and tiptoed to her bedroom. She closed the door behind her. Mia needed privacy to sort things out with Beau. But when it was over, she would be there to help Mia explain to her folks how, even though he was perfect, Beau just wasn't for her.

She stretched out on the bed and stared at the ceiling. After a while, things were really quiet out in the main part of the bunkhouse, and the breakup, if it could be called that, was most likely over. She dressed in her pink sweats—a color that her mother said redheads should never wear—and put on a pair of fuzzy socks.

"Stevie, are you awake?" Mia's whisper came through the door.

"I'm on my way out if Beau is gone," Stevie answered.

"Yes, he is," Mia answered.

Stevie couldn't tell from the sound of her voice if she was relieved or sad about the decision she had made, but either way, she would probably want to talk about it. Stevie slung open the door and found Mia slouched on the sofa just like before.

"Did he take the news badly?" Stevie asked.

"Nope." Mia's blue eyes had gone from the worried look they had half an hour before to downright dreamy.

"You didn't tell him, did you?" Stevie asked. "Mia, you can't lead him on…"

"I'm not." Mia's face lit up in a smile. "I had left my gloves in his truck when we came home from church, and he brought them back to me. I invited him in and was honest with him, and he said he understood. I walked him to the door and tripped over Tex when he came running inside, and…"

"And what?" Stevie asked.

"He reached out and kept me from falling, then cupped my face in his hands, and…" Mia frowned just slightly. "Ricky was the same height as me, so he never had to raise my face for a kiss, but anyway, Beau kissed me, and there wasn't a sizzle. It went beyond that to pure heat. We wound up making out for a long time, and my knees went weak, and my heart was thumping."

"Did Ricky ever do that for you?" Stevie asked.

"Not like Beau did." Mia picked up her beer and downed the rest of it. "With Ricky it was kind of like I was flirting with something dangerous—something that Mama wouldn't approve of. With Beau, it was a totally different feeling, but from all the stuff I've read about relationships, I shouldn't be comparing one with the other."

"That's right, but when you've only had someone like Ricky in your life, that makes it kind of tough, doesn't it?" Stevie asked.

"Yes. I need chocolate." Mia got up and headed for the kitchen.

"There's chocolate cookies in the jar, and a package of miniature candy bars on the counter. I hope they are still good. I got them from the pantry in my flooded house. I'm glad the adjustor has come and gone so I can go in and save what I can, and then make a decision about how to redo the house," Stevie said.

Mia returned with the whole package of candy and a bowlful of cookies. "I'm going to have some milk. Want a glass?"

"Yes, please," Stevie said. "So, you think that you might go on a second date with Beau, then?"

"Oh, yeah! And maybe a third and fourth and twenty-fifth." Mia poured two glasses of milk and brought them to the living area. "But with this much passion, what happens when we have an argument?"

"Then you have amazing makeup sex like your mama told you about." Stevie took a glass from her, picked up a cookie, and dipped it in the milk.

Mia followed her example and dipped her cookie. "Did you and Uncle Cody have makeup sex in the barn? He said you were cranky, and y'all argued a lot."

"Nope," Stevie answered. "We're older and a lot more cautious than you two kids are."

"I'm nineteen and Beau is twenty-one," Mia argued. "We're not really kids."

"No, I guess you aren't," Stevie said.

"How do you know if a guy is *the one*?" Mia asked.

"You'll have to ask someone more experienced than I am," Stevie answered.

"I guess we can find out together," Mia said with a grin.

"Maybe so," Stevie said.

Mia finished off a handful of chocolate, half a dozen

cookies, and her milk, and then said, "I should be going. I know Mama and Nana are going to want to ask me all kinds of questions about Beau. I'm not going to tell them I had doubts there at first."

"Then I won't say a word about that either," Stevie said. "I'm just glad you got it all figured out and didn't lose an opportunity to get to know him even better."

"Me too," Mia said as she slipped her arms into her coat and shoved her stocking hat down over her dark hair. "Like I told Mama, I'm not in a hurry, but it will be nice to have a boyfriend—a real one who treats me and the family right. See you later."

Oh, to be young, Stevie thought, but before she could argue with herself over the cons of being nineteen again, Cody arrived bearing a brown paper bag that he set on the table. "Addy sent leftovers for supper."

Stevie got up and unloaded the bag. "There's enough food in here for two or three days."

"We would have loved to have that when we were stranded in the barn, wouldn't we?" Cody asked. "Hey, I hear that Mia spent a couple of hours with you this afternoon. Did she talk about Beau? The whole family thinks he's a good guy, and we're wondering if maybe the fact that we like him will..."

"No worries. She likes him a lot, and she even asked me how to tell if a guy was the one." She air-quoted the last two words.

"After only one day?" Both of Cody's eyebrows shot up. "That would almost be like love at first sight, which is downright crazy even for kids their age."

"I guess he kisses real good, and you don't need to knock that love-at-first-sight business." She put the container of ham in the refrigerator. "Didn't you ever wonder on a first date if the woman you were with could possibly be the one you would spend your life with?"

"No, did you?" Cody asked.

"I've never been on a date with a woman," Stevie answered.

"You know what I mean," Cody scolded. "Have you ever been on a first date and thought the guy you were out with was the one?"

Stevie hip-bumped him out of the way so she could put the pecan pie away. "Of course I have. It's normal, and after the second or third, I knew he wasn't the one and I cut him loose and stopped wasting my time."

"How do you know for sure if a guy is the one?" Cody asked.

"How do you men tell if a woman is?" she fired back at him.

"I have no idea. I never got that far into a relationship. Six months in one spot was usually the limit with the doctor program I was working with. That's not long enough to think about a permanent relationship." Cody helped put the containers of food away in the refrigerator. "Now you?"

"You already know that answer. I thought I'd missed my chance at *the one* because you were *that cowboy* and you had rejected me. I figured I'd be settling for someone who came in second in my heart," Stevie answered. "Now that we've had time to get to know each other, and for me to even bury the hatchet, I think that it takes getting to know each other a lot better than just one date and a make-out session to know if you want to spend your whole life with someone."

"You *really* are blunt," Cody said.

"You asked." She shrugged. "I answered."

"I wouldn't call what we had a make-out session." He got a bottle of water from the fridge. "Want one, or a beer, or a..."

"Maybe a bottle of orange juice," she answered. "And you are so right. What *we* had was not a bona fide make-out session."

From the change in his expression, it looked like Cody had seen the light. "Oh! So Mia and Beau did some kissing? When? In the barn when she was showing him the alpacas?"

"I don't tattle on my friends," Stevie said with a grin.

Cody handed off the orange juice to her and said, "If after our fourth date you know that I'm the one, will you be honest with me and tell me?"

"Of course I will, and I will also tell you if you are not the one, so that neither of us waste our time." She twisted the top off the juice, took a drink, and headed toward the sofa. "I guess, since you brought leftovers home, we aren't going to the ranch house for supper, right?"

He sat down at the same time she did, kicked off his boots, and propped his feet on the coffee table. "Right. Sunday nights we're on our own. So, movie, television, or..." He wiggled his eyebrows.

"Were you going to say strip poker?" she teased. "If that's

what you had in mind, then I don't play that until after the fifth date, and even then, you better be sure about dealing the cards. I do not have a tell, and I'm very good at poker. I won enough at the Thursday night games in college that my folks didn't have to give me spending money."

"Another surprise layer of the mysterious Stephanie O'Dell," Cody answered, "but I was going to say Monopoly."

"Sure you were," Stevie chuckled.

Before either of them could say anything else, her phone rang. She didn't recognize the number but answered it anyway. "Hello?"

"This is Bobby Blalock. Sonny Ryan called me this afternoon about a house that you own that needs repair, or at least a look over to see if it's worth remodeling. I've got an hour or two free in the morning if you could meet me there about nine," he said.

"I'll be there. Thanks for calling and getting to it so fast. Can you make up a couple of estimates for me to give to the insurance adjustor?" Stevie said.

"Yes, ma'am," Bobby said. "I'll bring the forms with me. See you there."

"Nine o'clock," Stevie said and ended the call, not sure if she was glad that Sonny had talked to him, or if she was a little aggravated that he had made the call rather than just giving her the name and number.

You wanted a family, her mother reminded her. *That's what families do. They get into your life and take care of you.*

"That was Bobby Blalock," she explained. "I'm supposed to meet him at the house tomorrow at nine."

"Do you remember Bobby?" Cody asked. "He graduated from high school a couple of years before I did. He never left Honey Grove but went right into construction with his dad. He took over the business when his father retired. Dad says he's really good at what he does, and he's honest."

"That's good, but I'm really afraid my house is like that truck of yours sitting out there by the barn—a total mess. Mama complained for the past few years that one side of the foundation was sinking and making the floor slope. I have to be ready to accept whatever happens, but it breaks my heart. And yet, Mama would tell me not to hang on to the past, just to get a new lease on life and move forward without looking over my shoulder." Stevie sighed.

"Sounds like something my mama would tell me." Cody drank down part of his bottle of water and then set it on the coffee table. "Do you ever hope you're as wise as they are when you get to be their age?"

"Only a dozen times a day, and especially when I hear her voice in my head," Stevie answered.

"Sometimes, I hear Dineo laughing or saying something cute, and I turn around to see if he's there before I remember what happened." Cody's voice seemed to crack a little and he stared off into space.

Stevie reached across the distance and laid her hand on his shoulder. "But we're glad for the memories those little voices bring back to us, aren't we?"

"Dineo was such a bright little boy," Cody said, and finally smiled. "I had even thought about creating a scholarship for him so he could go to a boarding school."

"Wasn't he in school over there?" Stevie asked.

"Yes, but those remote little schools wouldn't have challenged his mind. He was so bright, Stevie. He might have grown up to be a doctor if he'd had a chance," Cody said.

"You did what you could." She gave his shoulder a gentle squeeze.

He laid a hand on hers and said, "Thank you for that. Sometimes I play out scenarios in my head about what I could have done to prevent him and his father from being shot. If I'd grabbed him and run to the caves where we hid in dangerous times, or if Bodi had done the same thing, but it all happened so fast."

"That's because those people wanted the element of surprise," Stevie said, and remembered the shock she had felt when she turned around and Cody Ryan was standing right there in front of her in Max's barn.

"Let's watch something funny on television to take our minds off the sadness," he suggested.

"How about *Blue Collar Comedy Tour*? Last time I checked, it was on Netflix," she said, and nodded.

"What's that?" he asked.

"You've never seen it? It came out not long after we graduated from high school," she answered. "Comedians Ron White, Jeff Foxworthy..."

He picked up the remote. "Oh, I remember that, but I never got around to watching it. I was more into books than television back in those days when it first came out on DVD. Is it guaranteed to make me laugh?"

"If it doesn't, then you've got a heart of stone, and

there will be no second date with me." Stevie already knew that she was going to miss bantering with Cody and having his family around her every day when she got back to a place of her own and had to move away from Sunflower Ranch.

Chapter Eighteen

Stevie's house always smelled like scented candles. Her mother had especially loved gingerbread, hazelnut, or butter pecan that came in a jar. Ruth had burned one so often that the scent had permeated the walls, and that aroma was what Stevie was used to when she opened the front door. But that day, something nasty like musty old quilts or maybe a wet cat that had been caught out in the rain met her when she entered the place. The carpet was still soaking wet, and the tile in the kitchen had curled up on nearly every corner. She was glad that Cody and Addy had a full morning of appointments because she wanted some alone time with the house before Bobby arrived to give her an estimate on remodeling.

Anything that had been sitting on the floor was definitely ruined. Table legs were swollen, the sofa skirt had soaked up the water and carried it right up to the cushions. The same thing had happened with the dust ruffle on her bed and her mother's. Both mattresses and box springs had big brown spots on them from the dirty water. The adjustor that had come out on Saturday said there was no use in trying to salvage any of the furniture and had written up a report that said everything in the house was ruined.

"What do I do?" she whispered as she walked through the house and barely kept the tears at bay. "Do I tear this place down and rebuild right here on the same lot? Do I sell it and build somewhere else with more room for a proper vet clinic?"

"Hello! Anybody home?" a strong male voice yelled from the open front door.

Stevie whipped around. Bobby Blalock was a tall, lanky man with a crop of dark hair that was dusted with a sprinkling of gray around the temples, and big brown eyes that looked even larger behind thick glasses.

"I'm Bobby Blalock." He stuck out his hand. "We talked on the phone yesterday."

"Stevie O'Dell." She shook with him. "I'm glad you wore rubber boots. It's still a mess in here."

"Yep, I can see that. My son, Tilman, is under the house right now checking the foundation. Is it okay if I pull up some of this carpet, and maybe knock a hole or two in the drywall?" he asked.

"Do whatever you need to do," Stevie said with a grimace.

"I'll bring in my tools then," he said.

Stevie had expected that the carpet would have to

be taken out, but it didn't make it any easier to watch Bobby pile the soggy furniture to one side. He rolled the wet carpet to the middle of the room and slowly shook his head.

"Where are you, Tilman?" he yelled.

"Right here, Dad." A guy who looked like a younger version of Bobby, only his coveralls were muddy, entered through the front door. "Go ahead with whatever you need to do up here, but it sure doesn't look good under this place. Of course, it's muddy, but, Miz O'Dell, you've got a bad case of termites under there, as well as black mold."

Bobby drew back a claw hammer and knocked a hole in the wet part of the Sheetrock. Chunks of it crumbled like chalk, and more disintegrated as he pulled half a sheet free. He shook his head in disappointment and pointed to the studs. "I was trying to give you a little bit of hope, but I'm sorry, Stevie. See the Swiss cheese look in these studs? If this house was a person, I would tell you that it has bone cancer. This is dry rot." He pointed to part of the two studs, and then to the wet part below that. "And that is black mold."

Stevie looked at the mess and wondered if that had caused her mother's cancer to start or to be worse. She knew the house had to come down, but knowing did not lessen the disappointment one bit.

"I remember when you were a little girl riding your bicycle up and down this road with your red ponytail swinging back and forth," Bobby said. "I knew your daddy and your mama very well. Your dad and my mama worked together at the bank. I don't like to have to tell you this,

Stevie, but this house is not worth saving. You should have it torn down and have the ground treated to get rid of the termites. Then you can either rebuild right here or sell the lot, and that's my honest opinion on just what I've seen here."

"I was afraid that's what you would say." She sighed. "Thinking about doing that isn't easy, though."

"No, ma'am, I'm sure it's not. I'd hate to have to make that decision, but you could always build a new house on the same floor plan as this one since this is your child-hood home," he said. "I can check the other rooms if you want me to."

"No need. What do I owe you for this?" she asked.

"Not a thing, but I will write up something for you to give to the insurance company," Bobby said. "If and when you decide to tear it down, Tilman and I have the equipment to take care of that for you."

"Thank you," Stevie said with a heavy heart.

Both men left her standing in the middle of a spongy floor and went out to their truck. In a few minutes Bobby came back with a signed estimate form, and said, "I can't tell you how sorry I am. I can't imagine having to tear down my folks' place, but if it looked like this, I wouldn't hesitate to do just that."

"I appreciate your honesty," Stevie said.

"Can't be anything but that. My mama would take a switch to me if I was dishonest, even if I am over forty." Bobby smiled. "Just let me know if you need me to take it down."

"I sure will." Stevie waited until he was gone to let the

tears flow down her cheeks. "Damn it!" She wiped at them and stomped her foot so hard that it went through the floor and set her firmly down on her butt. She jerked her leg back up through the hole and groaned when she realized that her jeans were not only wet but torn, and that they were a pair that Mia had loaned to her. The cold air hit her butt when she stood up. She had not only poked her leg through the floor, and most likely tore Mia's jeans on a nail, but she had also sat down on the soaked carpet.

"Damn it!" she said again and then noticed that it wasn't water running down her leg but blood from a gash, and Mia's rubber boot was catching it. She went to the bathroom and wrapped one towel around the wound and took a second one with her out to her vehicle. When she got inside, she put the extra towel on the seat to sit on, got in, and called Cody before she even started the engine.

"Where are you and Addy?" she asked.

"At the ranch," he said. "We finished earlier than we thought. Want me to come to the house? What did Bobby say?"

"We'll talk about that later," Stevie said. "I fell through the floor, and I think I tore my leg on a nail. I didn't check to see if it was rusty or not, but I'm on my way home. Can you meet me at the bunkhouse? It might need stitches, and I know I'll need a tetanus shot."

"Are you sure you can drive? Do you need me and Addy to come get you?" Cody sounded genuinely worried.

"I can make it home. I've got it wrapped in a towel to keep from getting blood on Mama's car seat. See you in ten minutes or so," she told him.

By the time she reached the bunkhouse, blood was seeping through the towel, but by keeping her leg turned just right, she avoided getting any on the seat. She opened the door and got out carefully, then limped toward the porch. Cody and Addy must have heard the car's engine because they rushed out and helped her the rest of the way into the bunkhouse and onto a kitchen chair.

Cody already had his tools laid out on the table and dropped down on his knees in front of her to remove the towel. "Good grief, you really did a number on this. Addy, we'll need to cut her jeans off her, and this boot is ruined."

"These are Mia's rubber boots…" Stevie said.

"And they're the least of your worries. We buy these things by the dozens," Addy said as she began to cut the jeans away. We've got to clean it out first, and then it's going to need stitches. My guess is at least ten."

"Fifteen or more if we want to keep them close enough together that she doesn't have a bad scar," Cody said. "These first shots are going to sting a little."

"Ouch!" Stevie almost yelled. "That hurt."

"But it will numb your leg up so that you won't feel the stitches," Cody said.

"I know," Stevie said, "but I'm usually not the one on this end of the needle."

"I can't get at this thing from this position," he said with a frown. "I'm going to pick you up and lay you on the table."

Addy brought a pillow from the top bunk and had it ready to put under Stevie's head when Cody scooped her up in his arms and laid her out on the kitchen table. "There, that's much better. I swear, I can't let you out of my sight for five minutes that you don't hurt yourself, woman. The wound on your head hasn't healed, and now you've torn up your leg."

"Don't call me *woman*," she scolded.

"Okay, then *love* it is," Cody teased as he started suturing up the gash.

"Not that either," she told him.

Addy giggled. "You two remind me of how prickly Jesse and I were when he first came home. I'm going to get a tetanus shot ready. You want it in the arm or in the butt?"

"Arm," Stevie answered. The very thought of baring her butt in front of Cody caused heat to rise to her cheeks.

"When you get done, Mia and I have to go check on Raymond's horse," Stevie said, trying to take her mind off what was happening on the calf of her left leg.

"You really should stay off this at least for today," Addy said. "From that tear, I'd guess that you caught it on a nasty old nail when your foot went through the floor. I don't see any wood fragments, so that's a plus, but the nail could have been rusty. This shot and a round of antibiotics will take care of any infections."

"Does our local drugstore deliver medicine all the way out here?" Stevie asked.

"Don't need to," Cody said. "I've got samples that you can use, and you can't go to Raymond's on this leg. It's going to be numb from the knee down for a while."

"Mia can drive me," Stevie argued. "And all we have to

do is unwrap the bandage, check the wound, and re-dress the cut. I'll be back home in half an hour, tops."

"Mia is out in the pasture with Jesse," Cody said. "I'll drive you, and when we get back, you are going to sit on the sofa with that leg propped up, at least, for the rest of today."

"You sure are bossy." Stevie watched him meticulously put in the last stitch and secure it in place with adhesive tape.

Cody wrapped gauze around her leg. "It's contagious. I got it from you."

Addy chuckled. "Never a dull moment around y'all. Get ready for a pinch." She pulled up Stevie's T-shirt and gave her the shot.

"I hate needles," Stevie moaned.

"Most people don't love them." Cody finished wrapping gauze around her leg to keep the stitches clean—not totally unlike how she had treated Buttercup, only she didn't have to put stitches in the horse's leg. "I've got a set of crutches in the closet that you can use. They'll give you stability and keep you from putting too much weight on that leg until it heals. I'll dress the wound every day, and help you encase it in plastic when you take a shower."

"No baths for ten days?" she moaned again.

"That's right, but you can have showers, and I've even got a bath chair that you can use," Cody answered.

"I always thought those were for old people," Stevie said.

"I loan it to young folks like you who fall through floors," Cody said on his way to the closet to get the crutches.

Addy cleaned up the mess and tossed the disposable

suture materials into the trash. "I'll help you get that other boot and those jeans off soon as Cody brings the crutches."

"Thank you, Addy." She managed a smile. "Seems like I say that at least a dozen times a day."

"You are welcome a dozen times a day," Addy said, and nodded.

Cody brought the crutches out, leaned them against the table, picked her up for the second time, and set her feet on the floor. "Ever used these before?"

Stevie shook her head. "But I guess I'm about to learn." She crooked her leg back at the knee and started across the room.

"Doin' good," Cody encouraged.

"My work is done here, so I'm going back to the house to check on Pearl and the twins," Addy said. "Call me if you need anything at all, and I'll have Mia bring supper to y'all tonight so you don't have to get out again once you get back from Raymond's place."

"We've still got leftovers in the fridge," Cody said.

"But I heard something about beans and fried potatoes, didn't I?" Stevie asked. "Family meals are a bit of a treasure when you live alone. I seldom ever get beans, and I love fried potatoes."

"I'll send Mia down here with enough for both of you. I understand about family meals. When Mia and I lived alone, making dinner for two was a chore. There's no way to just make a little pot of beans." Addy followed her into the bedroom and closed the door.

Stevie unfastened her jeans but had to have help getting

them off. No more skinny jeans—at least not for ten days. "I'd better wear those cargo pants with the elastic waistband," she said.

"These?" Addy pulled them out of the closet and held them up.

"Yep," Stevie said, and nodded. "I haven't worn them in years, but I'm glad I saved them."

Addy helped her into them and said, "Just holler when you get ready for a shower. Either Mia or I will come help you. And before you say thank you, this is what sisters and nieces are for, even if they're pseudo-kinfolks."

"I'll repay you someday." Stevie pulled up the wide-legged pants.

"You already have," Addy said.

Stevie cocked her head to one side. "How do you figure that?"

"You're making Cody come alive again. Something happened just before he came home that bothers him, but he won't talk about it. You are helping him deal with whatever it is. Jesse said that he's even heard him whistling a time or two since he rescued y'all from Max's place." Addy waved over her shoulder and left the room without closing the door that time.

* * *

Cody was amazed at Stevie's determination and dedication, not to mention her sheer strength when they reached Raymond's place. She had mastered the crutches, and when she got to the barn where the horse was, she asked him to set a milking stool beside the horse for her to sit on. Other than that, she wouldn't let him do anything for her but hold her crutches. She sat on the stool, with her injured leg straight out, and talked to the horse the entire time she unwrapped the old bandage, treated the wound, and then rewrapped it.

"I heard she had a mishap this morning at her house when the floor gave way," Raymond said. "Most women would be laid up and whining after nearly tearin' her leg off."

"Yep, she is strong, but she's also bossy and stubborn as an old mule," Cody answered.

"I can hear you, and don't be calling me old, not when you're older than me, Cody Ryan," Stevie told him.

"I see what you mean," Raymond chuckled.

She finished up the job, stood up, and reached for her crutches. Then she took a carrot from one of the pockets of her cargo pants. "There you go, Buttercup. You were a good girl. In another week, you'll be running wild again. Only, from now on, I want you to watch where you're stepping."

"Don't worry about that," Raymond said. "I've had my grandkids go over every inch of this place, and they didn't find any more stray barbed wire. I think what happened is the blizzard blew it up here from somewhere else, and she got her leg tangled up in it."

"You're probably right," Stevie said. "I'll be back on Thursday to take care of her again." She turned back to the horse. "And next time I'll bring you a nice ripe apple."

"I reckon I could do what you're doing since you're wounded yourself," Raymond told her.

245

"I'll be fine by the end of the week and maybe even off these crutches," she said.

"All right then," Raymond agreed without an argument. "I'll feel much better about her if you check her out."

Cody wanted to pick Stevie up and carry her to the truck, but he respected her pride more than that. He did open the door for her and got her settled into the passenger seat. "Feeling coming back yet?" he asked.

"Oh, yeah," she told him. "I'm ready for a couple of pain pills, but just the over-the-counter ones, not the prescription kind."

"And maybe ready to sit on the sofa with your leg propped up on a pillow?" Cody asked as he closed the door and jogged around the vehicle to get into his side of the truck. He started up the engine and glanced over at Stevie. She was pale, and from her expression obviously in pain.

"I'll be glad to be still and let the pain medicine take effect," she answered.

"Maybe some chocolate would help," he suggested with a reassuring smile.

She leaned her head back on the seat and closed her eyes. "It sure couldn't hurt."

At the end of the lane, Cody turned out onto the main road. "I forgot to ask what Bobby said about your house."

"He said it has bone cancer." Stevie's voice cracked. "Black mold, termites, dry rot. It's not worth saving, so I guess the only thing to do is euthanize the place."

"I'm so sorry, Stevie," Cody said. "But please know, you've got a home at Sunflower Ranch for as long as you want."

"Before I can have it torn down and put the lot up for sale, I've got to pack up everything that's still usable and store it," she said with a sigh. "Everything in there has a memory of some kind. I'm not looking forward to doing that job, Cody."

"In my opinion, you shouldn't do that right now. For one thing, you don't need to be in a place like that until your leg heals, and for another, you've been through enough this past week without reliving every memory. Would you mind if I talk to Mama about getting someone to help you with that?" Cody asked.

"I couldn't ask Pearl to do that," Stevie said. "She's got to take care of Sonny."

"Mama knows people who would be glad to make a few dollars packing up everything for you," Cody said. "Remember, she and Dad have lived in this area their entire lives."

"That would be wonderful," Stevie agreed.

"Then I'll take care of that job," Cody said with a smile. "Now open your eyes."

"Why, so I can see more of my world falling apart?" she asked.

"No, because when your eyes are closed, all you feel is pain, both emotional and physical. When they're open, you can focus on things around you and ease that pain," he answered.

Her eyes popped wide open and she sat up straight. "Did you study psychology as well as medicine?"

"Had to take a few classes in it, and besides, coming from the background I did, psychology interests me," he

247

answered as he made a turn in to Sunflower Ranch. "We're almost home. I forgot to tell you that I'm going to drive Dad down to Dallas on Wednesday morning. Mama hates to drive in the city, so she volunteered me to do the job. We won't be back until Thursday afternoon. He has appointments both days for MRIs, X-rays, and other things. Will you be all right while I'm gone?"

Stevie shook her head slowly.

"You won't be okay? I can ask Jesse to take him, but the family thought that since I'm a doctor…"

Stevie held up a palm. "I will be fine. If we hadn't gotten stranded, and if my house hadn't flooded, I would be living alone and taking care of myself. Sonny needs you, and besides, you will understand what the specialists are saying about him. I just hope that the report is a good one."

"I really do admire your strength, Stevie, as well as your brains," Cody said.

"Thanks for that. I don't feel very strong right now," she admitted, "but Mama was right, it helps to have friends and family."

"And to have a Dr. Cowboy in your life?" He parked in front of the bunkhouse and turned off the engine.

She cut her eyes around at him, and almost smiled. "Yes, *love*…even a Dr. Cowboy in my life."

Chapter Nineteen

To drive from the bunkhouse to the barn on a bright, sunny day seemed more than a little bit silly, but the ground was still soft from all the melted snow, and crutches would sink with every step.

Cody had kissed her on the forehead at the crack of dawn that morning just before he walked out the door with his duffel bag and briefcase. "See you sometime tomorrow. Addy says to feel free to come up to the ranch house if you get bored."

"Be safe," she had said.

Stevie parked the car as close to the tack room door as she could get, and then got out and crutched her way inside. She had planned to go straight to her van and take stock of what was in there since she would be driving it for the first time the next day when she went to check on

Raymond's horse. But her phone rang as she started across the room, so she sat down on the wooden bar stool and leaned her crutches against the worktable.

"Hello, this is Dr. O'Dell," she answered.

"Oh, Stevie!" Gracie Langston moaned. "My Fifi just had two puppies, and I didn't even know she was expecting. What do I do? She's had them in my laundry basket on top of my towels, and they're all messy."

"You gently remove the top towel and wash it. Are the new babies nursing?" Stevie asked.

"Yes, they're fat little things, but how did this happen? I never let her out of the backyard, and I even had it fenced just for her," Gracie whined.

"Evidently, a male dog dug underneath your fence about two months ago and bred her," Stevie said. "If you don't want puppies a couple of times a year, you should have Fifi spayed."

"I bet it was that evil corgi that lives next door with Eva Taylor. She thinks she's better than the rest of us here in Honey Grove because her husband was a general in the Army, and they were in England for all those years. I hear she even has tea twice a day and keeps to English traditions." Gracie's tone went from a whine to dripping icicles in less than a minute and then back to just above a whimper. "My poor Fifi has to raise half-toy-poodle and half-corgi puppies. They'll be so ugly that I won't be able to give them away, and I'll have to keep them so Fifi won't be upset with me. Can you come over and be sure that she's all right?"

"Of course I will. What time is good for you?" Stevie asked.

"I've got a hair appointment in thirty minutes and a lunch with the Ladies Auxiliary at the church. Would two o'clock work, and do you think I should leave Fifi that long?" Gracie asked.

"Fifi will be fine, and I'll come by at two," Stevie said.

"That's wonderful," Gracie sighed. "I'm so sorry to hear about your mother's house. I heard that you're living out there at the Sunflower Ranch in the bunkhouse with Cody Ryan. I don't like to gossip, but..." She hesitated and then went on, "Do you think that's a good idea? Folks in small towns talk. Not that I would ever say a word, but there's already rumors going around about you and Cody."

Stevie rolled her eyes toward the ceiling and tried to keep her voice from betraying the way she really felt about people prying into her business. "I can take care of myself, Miz Gracie, but thank you so much for caring about me."

"It's the least I can do since your mother and I were such good friends," Gracie said. "But if things don't go well out there, I've got a spare bedroom I would be glad to rent to you."

"Thank you, again. I'll see you at two," Stevie said and ended the call. "Like I'd rent a room from her. I'd be crazy as a loon before dark on the first day." Stevie fumed as she picked up her crutches and headed out to the corral where the alpacas were kept these days. From the back door of the barn, she watched the two crias play for a few minutes, then closed the door and sat down on a bale of hay to pet Dolly and the kittens that had come out to greet her.

Her phone rang again, and the cats all scattered. Stevie pulled the phone from her hip pocket and a wide smile lit up her face when she saw Cody's name on the screen. "Are you there yet?" she asked.

"Oh, yeah," he answered. "They took Dad right in for an MRI, so I had a few minutes. Are you at the ranch house?"

"No, I'm in the barn. I've got a call out this afternoon," she answered, and then told him about Fifi's puppies.

"Those ought to be some weird-looking little dogs," Cody laughed.

"I'm wondering if Gracie will make Eva pay puppy support because her corgi is the father," Stevie said with half a giggle.

"Looks like it's going to be a long day for both of us. Will you text me when you get back to the ranch?" Cody asked. "I still worry about you driving on that leg. Maybe Mia should go with you."

"Yes, I will," she answered. "But I can do this on my own, and Mia is helping Jesse today. You just worry about Sonny."

"He'll be ready for the hotel room by the end of the day. I'm glad there's a restaurant attached to the hotel, so he won't have to get in and out of the truck so much," Cody said.

"That's great." Stevie frowned. "What's wrong?"

"Why would you think something is wrong?" Cody asked.

"I hear it in your voice," she answered.

"Nothing is wrong, but on the way down here, I got

to thinking about that old saying 'Out of sight, out of mind,'" he told her.

"Am I about to lose my Sonic hamburger on the fourth date?" she teased, but tears welled up behind her eyelashes.

"Not at all. I know it sounds crazy, but I miss you," Cody answered. "We don't see each other for hours most days, but knowing we are this far apart..." He paused so long that she checked her phone screen to be sure she hadn't lost service. "Well, that saying is bogus, Stevie. You are certainly not out of my mind."

"I'm glad," she said, and finally smiled.

"Here they are, bringing Dad out in a wheelchair," Cody said. "Now we go across town for the next appointment. Talk to you later."

"Be looking forward to it." Stevie ended the call.

She went to the van, tossed her crutches across the back seats, and slid the side door open. Things were in such a jumble that it took her all morning to get everything back into order. When she was done, she got out, eased the door shut, hobbled over to the big barn door, and pushed it open.

A limp was to be expected, but she wasn't doing too bad, so when she got back to the van, she put the crutches behind the seats and drove out of the barn. That done, she ignored the crutches and went back to close the door.

"The horse, Buttercup, didn't get crutches," she muttered, "and I'm as strong as she is."

Stevie drove into town, stopped at the diner and had a plate of nachos for lunch, and still had an hour to kill before her appointment with Fifi, so she went home—

to the house where she had grown up. She parked in the driveway, got out of the van, and left the crutches behind again. The house was coming down. There was no doubt about that, but she wanted to spend just a little more time inside to say goodbye.

When she had unlocked the door, she turned the knob and pushed, but it wouldn't budge. She had to get really tough with it but finally got it to open. Maybe that was an omen, she thought, something trying to tell her that she shouldn't tempt fate by going inside again.

"I won't stomp on the floor, and I will be careful," she muttered as she gingerly stepped over the threshold.

The house was as cold as death, and the musty smell was even worse than it had been when she and Bobby had checked out the floor and drywall. "You really have died, haven't you?" she said as she wandered back to her mother's bedroom.

She was glad that she had taken all her mother's clothing to a women's shelter right before Christmas. There was no way she could have ever let strangers come into the house and go through her mother's dresser drawers. But she was glad, too, that Pearl was going to get women she knew to come in and pack the kitchen stuff as well as what was salvageable out of the garage.

"I remember coming in from my senior prom and sitting in this rocking chair, Mama. You had gone to bed, and you were reading one of those thick romance books you loved. I told you that your Sunday school ladies would throw a hissy fit if they knew you were reading books like that"— Stevie smiled at the recollection—"and you told me that if it was all right with your father and all right with God, then you didn't care what they thought."

Stevie pulled back the lace curtains that now had mildew on the bottom. *I should adopt that idea for my own,* she thought. *I'll make things right with God and with Cody since we are trying to date, and everyone else can kiss my butt.*

That's not the way I said it. She could hear her mother giggling in her head.

"Nope, but it all means the same," Stevie whispered.

She made her way from that bedroom to her own room across the hallway and peeked in the door. Her first memory was of feeding her stuffed dogs in that room. Then there was all the excitement of getting ready for her first day of school, the mixed feelings when she went away to college, and then weeping uncontrollably when she found out her mother was dying. Her life was in that one room.

"Goodbye," she finally said and headed back toward the kitchen. What was in the upper cabinets was all salvageable, thank goodness. Her great-grandmother's gravy boat and cookbooks, and her mother's good china that Stevie's dad had bought for her on one of their anniversaries. She ran a finger across the stack of plates and the fancy cups and sighed. At least she would have that much to take with her when she figured out where she would build her next home.

"Hello! Are you in there?" Gracie's thin voice floated across the living room. "Oh. My. Goodness!" She had a hand to her chest when Stevie limped across the room, carefully avoiding the hole in the floor. "This is so sad. How can you bear it?"

"Mama would want me to take the good memories and not think about this," Stevie answered, and tried to change the subject. "Did you get done a little early?"

"Yes, and I worried about Fifi the whole time." Gracie wiped away the one lonely tear that was making its way down her face. "Ruth was such a good neighbor and a wonderful person. I'm glad she can't see what has happened to her beloved home. You are going to have it remodeled, aren't you?"

"No, ma'am," Stevie answered. "I'm calling Bobby Blalock to tear it down as soon as I get what can be saved out of it. If you're ready to go, I can check on Fifi now."

Gracie took one more look at the damage, sighed again, and took a step back, allowing Stevie room to force the swollen door shut and lock it. "Just think, if you'd been home instead of holed up in a barn with Cody Ryan, this wouldn't have happened."

"How do you figure that?" Stevie asked.

"Ruth taught you to let all the faucets in the house drip when it was freezing weather, didn't she?" Gracie asked.

"Never knew of her to do that," Stevie answered.

Gracie sighed again. "Well, I would have told you if you'd been home. But getting back to packing, I'll be glad to help you."

"Thank you, but we've got it covered," Stevie said. "I'll just follow you across the street and leave my van where it is."

"But what if you need to give the puppies shots?" Gracie asked.

"They won't need those for several weeks," Stevie said. "Are you sure you're going to keep both of them?"

"I've thought about it, and decided that I can handle three dogs, but I will need for you to take care of them if they're females. I sure can't handle more than three," Gracie answered.

"And if they're males?" Stevie stood on the porch as Gracie opened the door.

"I don't like boys," Gracie said. "That's why I never married. Men are demanding and want their way all the time, and they mess up a house and expect meals on the table every night. I remember how my daddy and brothers were, and I made up my mind that I was not going fall in love, and I didn't. My poor mama worked her fingers to the bone doing for my father and brothers. If those puppies are boys, Fifi can just be angry with me. I'll give them away."

Stevie didn't even realize she was holding her breath until she had let it out in a whoosh when she had crossed the room to the laundry basket in the middle of the floor and checked the puppies. "Two girls. What are you going to name them?"

"Well!" Gracie huffed. "They can't have a nice French name like Fifi. Maybe that one with the brown spot on her head can be Minnie, and the other one can be Mable. Oh, Fifi, how could you have done this to me? Now you'll have to share all the attention with these little girls of yours."

"They look healthy, and Fifi seems to be doing very well," Stevie said. "Just call me when they're about six months old and make an appointment to get them spayed.

But as soon as they are weaned, you'll need to get Fifi fixed or else you'll be having more puppies."

"I'll put it on my calendar right now. What kind of house are you going to build?" Gracie asked. "That lot isn't very big. I guess you could put up a two-story place."

"I'm not going to rebuild in that spot," Stevie said. "I haven't decided what I'm going to do just yet. I don't know where, or even *if*, I'll build right in town."

"Oh, really?" Gracie raised a gray eyebrow. "Surely you aren't thinking of building out there on Sunflower Ranch."

"I've got a while to think about it," Stevie said. "I'll just add today's visit onto the bill when I spay Fifi here in a few weeks. You have fun with the puppies. They can be quite entertaining." She escaped from the house with all its crocheted doilies and pink rose wallpaper, caught a breath of fresh air when she hit the porch, and would have jogged to her van if her leg hadn't been aching.

Gracie didn't even ask about my leg, she thought as she got in behind the wheel and started up the engine. She could just see the woman racing to get her phone out of her purse and start making calls. The cell phone towers were probably already heating up with the hot gossip.

She had barely made it back to the bunkhouse when her phone rang again. "This is Dr. O'Dell," she answered as she turned off the engine and answered the call, hoping the whole time that it was Cody and not Gracie.

"Well, hello, Dr. O'Dell," a familiar voice said.

"Rodney?" she asked.

"In the flesh, and a little less than four hours north of you," he chuckled.

"Is everything all right?" she asked her old boss. "How's the crew up there in Oklahoma City? Have y'all thawed out from the snowstorm?"

"Crew is fine and send their love," Rodney said.

When she heard that word, she immediately thought of Cody.

"We had to close things down for two days because we lost power, but we're up and running now," he answered. "And everything is great. I just got a huge promotion. I had two offers—my choice of going to Australia to run a clinic over there or moving to Las Vegas to open up a brand-new one."

"Congratulations," Stevie said. "Which one are you taking?"

"Las Vegas!" he said. "I don't want to live in Australia. Which brings me to why I called. I don't know how things are going in Texas, but the clinic here in Oklahoma City needs a supervisor if you want to come back to this area. Or since I didn't want the position in Australia, that one is open also. Would you be interested in either one?"

"Oh, my!" A vision of her house came to mind. Other than the promise of a few dates and a hamburger with Cody, there was nothing for her in Honey Grove anymore. "That's a lot to think about."

"I'm leaving in a week, and the folks in Australia said they'll need an answer in a week," Rodney said.

"They'd hire me without an interview or..." she started.

"When I turned them down," he butted in before she could finish, "they asked if I could recommend someone else, and I immediately thought of you. With your mother gone and no other family to keep you anchored, that would be a perfect job for you. I remember you saying that you wanted to travel, so I told them all about you, and they are very, very interested. They said they'd hold off posting the job until you talk to them."

"But..." Stevie stammered.

"But you can also step into my position here at the clinic. As you know it's more paperwork, more responsibility, and headaches, but a lot more money. Will you at least think about both jobs?"

"Yes, I will definitely think about them and give you an answer by Monday," she agreed.

"That's fair enough," Rodney said. "I'll be looking to hear from you then. Bye, Stevie."

"Goodbye," she said and laid her head back. Could she really leave Honey Grove? Could she walk away from Cody? Would she be giving up the opportunity of a lifetime? The chance to travel? Or to run her own clinic in Oklahoma? Only to have things fall apart in Honey Grove?

So many questions, and not one single answer.

Chapter Twenty

*S*tevie's mother had often told her that work would take her mind off whatever was stressing her. So, when she got home, she parked her van beside the barn and went to the tack room. All kinds of stuff had been left on the worktable—jars of screws, nails, tools, and even a can of paint. The small refrigerator had an apple in it that had probably come over on the *Mayflower*, and carrots that were growing beards.

"If cleaning this doesn't de-stress me, nothing will." Stevie removed her jacket and filled a bucket with water from the bathroom sink. She found a bottle of cleanser that was so old that the label had faded, but it still smelled lemony, so she poured some into the bucket, grabbed a sponge, and went to work on the refrigerator first.

When that job was done, she began to organize the

shelves. First by taking all the stuff from the cabinets and wiping them down, and by arranging all the items in a logical order as she put it back. "Mama, it's not working," she mumbled. "I'm still tied up in knots worrying about the house, the job offers, and this *thing*, whatever it is, with Cody."

Her phone pinged, and she dragged it out of her pocket to find a message from Cody: *We are at the hotel. Will call this evening. Dad is exhausted.*

Her thumbs quickly typed, *Okay.*

She had just hit send when her phone rang. She hadn't realized that it was suppertime until she saw that the call was from Mia and checked the time.

"Hello, Mia," she said.

"Daddy has a volunteer fire meeting in town this evening, and they always have it catered in by the diner. It's just us girls, and the twins of course. You are coming to eat with us, right?" Mia asked.

"Be there in just a few minutes." Stevie rushed through putting the last of the things on the shelf, decided she'd better use the crutches to go to the house, and made sure her van was locked before she started that way. Mia was waiting with the back door slung open when she arrived.

"You should have called. I would have come and got you in the work truck," Mia scolded her. "And why is your van at the barn? Are the alpacas all right?"

"Don't be nosy," Pearl called out.

Stevie leaned the crutches against the washing machine and limped on into the kitchen. "Alpacas are fine. I had a few hours after I checked on Gracie Langston's poodle and her two new puppies, so I cleaned the tack room. Mama told me that I could relieve the stress of my problems with hard work, so I gave it a try."

"Did it work?" Mia asked.

"Nope," Stevie answered. "Maybe I didn't work hard enough."

"If you cleaned that nasty tack room, you worked plenty hard," Addy said as she set a pot of potato soup on the bar. "We're doing buffet style tonight."

"Smells and looks wonderful," Stevie said. "Is it okay if I wash up in the sink?"

"Fine by us," Pearl told her. "Anyone who will tackle that part of the barn can wash their hands anywhere they please. Want to talk about your problems? Got to do with the house?"

"That's part of it, and thank you for getting a crew together to pack everything for me. I went by there today and said goodbye to the house. Does that sound crazy?" Stevie asked as she washed and dried her hands. "It's like I'm grieving for something that has no life and never did."

"Oh, honey." Pearl filled a bowl with soup and carried it to the table. "That house has been very much alive. If the walls could talk, they would tell about the day Ruth brought you home from the hospital and how she was so proud of you for following your dreams. That's just two incidents that come to my mind."

"What about this house?" Mia asked. "What would it tell us?"

"Too many things to count," Pearl said, and smiled. "I'll

say grace for us right here at the bar." She bowed her head and said a quick prayer, asking God to bring Sonny and Cody home safely and giving thanks for all the natural things that they could enjoy. "Amen. And now back to memories in a house. Sonny was raised right here in this place, and all three of our boys were as well. Then we had the privilege of you and Addy coming to live with us during some tough and lonely times."

Mia took her food to the table. "I never thought about it like that. I guess you really did need to say goodbye to your house, Stevie. But you mentioned puppies? Gracie didn't say anything about puppies at church last Sunday, and she's always telling us something about Fifi."

"Well," Stevie said with a giggle, "she's embarrassed that her precious poodle has been out slumming with the neighbor's corgi. They will be some strange-looking dogs if they get poodle hair and short legs."

Pearl laughed. "Gracie is probably mortified."

"Hey, I heard from Cody," Stevie said. "He says that they're in the hotel and Sonny is exhausted."

"Sonny called me just before you arrived," Pearl said. "He sounded so tired and said that Cody had ordered pizza delivered to the room, and that as soon as he ate, he was taking a shower and going to bed. This trip always wipes him out."

"Do they have any tests results yet?" Stevie asked.

"No, that's what they'll talk about tomorrow morning," Pearl answered. "His last appointment is for a consultation at eleven o'clock, and then they'll start home. Sonny and I will probably stay home until after the weekend. The snow is melted now, and it's time we got back to our own schedules, anyway."

"And that is?" Stevie asked.

"We have Sunday dinner together, and pop in and out when we want to," Addy said.

"But we don't have supper here every evening," Mia added, "and I'm going to miss that."

"We all need time apart as well as time together," Pearl said.

Did Fate have a hand in that call from Rodney? Stevie wondered. *Did it come when Cody and I are apart for a couple of days so I can think about it without distractions?*

* * *

Cody made sure that Sonny's cane was right beside the bed, and that his dad was snoring before he called Stevie that evening. When she didn't answer on the fourth ring, he started to hang up and send a text, but then he heard her voice.

"Hello," she said. "Sorry about that. I was just getting out of the shower."

"Then you're wearing nothing but a towel?" Cody teased. "I'm closing my eyes and getting that picture in my mind."

"I'm wearing your terry cloth robe, and it smells like your shaving lotion," she answered.

"Even that looks sexy. Is the belt tied or untied?" he asked.

"It's your imagination, so just picture me however you want," she joked.

"I miss your teasing," he chuckled.

"I miss you," she said.

"Well, there is that too," Cody admitted.

"Will you be home in time for supper? I've got something I need to talk to you about, but not on the phone," she said.

"We should be home in the middle of the afternoon," Cody answered. "I'm dreading the consultation tomorrow. I'm afraid the best news we can hope for is that the disease hasn't worsened. I didn't realize how much Mama does to help Dad until today."

"At least you get to have more time with him. Treasure every moment," Stevie said. "I went back to the house today, Cody. I made peace with tearing down the place as soon as things are packed and moved out."

"That's a good thing. Do you feel better now?" he asked.

"Much better," she answered.

"Mama told Daddy that you had spent some time cleaning the tack room," Cody said. "You didn't have to do that."

"It was either that or clean the bunkhouse, and the tack room needed it worse," she told him. "I was working through some issues."

"Get it all settled?" Cody asked.

"Not one bit," she answered, "but I've got until Monday, and we'll talk about it when you get home."

"Oh...kay." He hoped that this talk wasn't to tell him that she'd found a house in town to rent. He didn't want her to move out of the bunkhouse. "Will you save me a hug to go with the talk?"

"Of course," she said. "I meant it when I said I missed you. Mia has arrived. I should go now."

"Good night... *love*," he said.

"Good night, Dr. Cowboy," she fired back.

He could have talked with her until midnight about anything or nothing, teasing or serious, and he felt just a little cheated when they had to end the call after only a few minutes. He watched a couple of reruns on television and then went to bed. The next morning, he woke up five minutes before six to find his father already up and dressed.

"You going to sleep all day, son, or are we going down to the restaurant for some breakfast and then get on out of this place? I'm ready to go home," Sonny said.

Cody sat up and rolled the kinks out of his neck. "Me too, but you've still got a couple more appointments today. The last one should be over by noon."

"I'm glad these things are only once a year," Sonny groaned. "I don't like hotels and being away from my own bed and pillow."

Cody thought of all the places where he had slept on a canvas cot without a pillow, maybe catching a couple of hours of sleep at a time. He would have been so glad for a spotlessly clean, warm or air-conditioned hotel some of those nights.

"Give me time to take a shower to wake me up, and then we'll go get some breakfast," Cody said with a yawn. "How hungry are you?"

"I could probably eat half a ham and two dozen eggs," Sonny said with a wide grin. "I've been up for an hour and already had that last slice of pizza and talked to your mother. She's making me an apple pie, and we're going back to our regular way of doing things. I love all you kids, but I like my regular routine."

Cody made his way to the bathroom. "Me too, Dad."

"Think anything will ever come of whatever this is between you and Stevie?" Sonny asked.

Cody turned on the shower and adjusted the water, then stepped back to the door. "Who knows? She's a complicated woman."

Sonny's chuckle came from down deep in his chest. "Aren't they all? I've got a feeling this is more about you than it is about Stevie."

Cody nodded. "Dad, am I too old to think about starting a family? I'm almost forty."

"I thought that might be what was worrying you," Sonny said. "I wondered the same thing when we adopted you and Lucas, and it was for nothing. I wasn't a young whippersnapper when we got you boys. Sometimes a little age comes with a lot of wisdom when it comes to raisin' kids."

"Well, us three boys sure had a good role model, so I hope you are right," Cody said and closed the door.

When he had showered, shaved, and gotten dressed in fresh jeans and a plaid shirt, he came out of the bathroom to find Sonny leaning on his cane.

"I thought maybe you'd drowned in there, son," he said. "Now I see you were just primping for Stevie."

"Maybe I was hoping for a beautiful nurse at the doctor's office where we're going," Cody teased.

"Son, it don't take a genius to see that since you and Stevie were stranded you've got blinders on when it comes to any other woman," Sonny told him. "I've gathered up all my stuff. Get yours together, and we won't have to come back up here when we finish breakfast."

"Yes, sir," Cody saluted.

Sonny shook a finger at him. "Don't be a smart-ass, or I'll whoop on you with this cane."

"You haven't lost your sense of humor," Cody said as he put all his things in his duffel bag, and then picked up his father's small suitcase.

"Who says I'm teasing?" Sonny's old eyes sparkled.

* * *

Stevie awoke on Thursday morning after dreaming about kangaroos and emus all night. Her roommate in college had told her that dreams were an omen of things to come. As she put on a pot of coffee and unwrapped a miniature Mr. Goodbar that morning, she wondered if the omen was telling her that she should go, or if it was warning her to stay in Texas. She had binge-watched *McLeod's Daughters* after her mother's death, and remembered an episode about emus—or was it another bird something like them?—that invaded the countryside every so often. Were her dreams telling her to stay away from Australia?

When the coffee stopped dripping, she poured herself a mug and filled a bowl with fruity-flavored junk cereal. "It says fruit right there on the box, so it has to be good for me." She remembered telling her mother that more than

269

once, and every time, Ruth would just shake her head and laugh. While Steve ate, she opened her laptop and researched the small town where she would head up the vet clinic if she chose to go to the land down under. From what she could see, it didn't look much different from the place on the television show. Leaving the actors out, she closed her eyes and thought about the countryside, the problems, and all the other factors that came from living so far away from a city.

"Am I ready for that kind of heat and living?" she asked herself. "But it would be the adventure of a lifetime, and if I didn't like it, I could resign…"

She picked up her phone and called Rodney.

He answered with "Hey, did you already make up your mind? Which one are you taking? We've got a pot going in the office here, and I've got money on Australia."

"I haven't made up my mind, but tell me more about the position in Australia," she said.

"Aha, so you *are* leaning that way. They'll pay for your flight, and there's a small apartment about forty yards behind the clinic that will be yours free of charge. You will have to sign a two-year contract. I had my lawyer look it over, and it can't be broken. If you don't stay two years, then you have to give all your salary back to them. That's what made me decide on the job in Las Vegas. That and the fact that my wife took one look at that apartment and said there was no way she was raising our two daughters over there for two years. Other than that, it's a good deal, especially for someone who is single and has no family," Rodney said.

"Okay," Stevie said. "I'm still weighing the pros and cons. I'll let you know by Monday."

"Fair enough," Rodney said, "but I will tell you this. If Darlene had been willing to go, I would have taken the job. I've always been interested in that part of the world."

"And besides all that, you really would like to win that bet they've got going at the office about which place I'm going to choose, wouldn't you?" Stevie asked.

"How did you know?" Rodney laughed out loud.

"I know all of you," Stevie answered.

Rodney chuckled again and said, "I'll look to hear from you sometime over the weekend or Monday at the latest."

"Talk to you then." Stevie ended the call, finished her breakfast, packed herself a sandwich for lunch, and drove her mother's car out to the barn so she wouldn't have to use crutches. She still needed to think, and the tack room was far from finished.

Her hair stuck to her sweaty neck as she swept the floor. She stopped long enough to tuck the errant strands back up into her ponytail and had started to mop when the door opened. She didn't need anyone to tell her that Cody had made it home earlier than planned, or that she looked and probably smelled horrible. The afternoon sun caused his body to be nothing more than a silhouette, and even though she wanted to hug him, she hung back and kept the mop in her hands.

He crossed the room in a couple of long, easy strides. When he picked her up, the mop hit the floor with a thunk, and he spun her around half a dozen times. "I missed you, Stevie O'Dell, so much," he said when he finally set her down on the floor.

"I'm a mess...you're early..." she stammered. "I was going to go home and get cleaned up."

"*Home!* That's the important word," he said. "I've never been so glad to be back here on the ranch again, and we were only gone two days." He wrapped his arms around her and then kissed her.

When the steamy, hot kiss ended, her knees felt like they had no bones in them. "Welcome home, Dr. Cowboy." She had to catch her breath between words.

"Best place in the world... *love*," he whispered.

Chapter Twenty-One

The tack room hadn't been so clean and organized since Cody and Jesse were fourteen and fifteen and had to straighten it up for punishment. That memory put a smile on Cody's face as he passed through the room on the way to the barn. He and Jesse had snuck out of the house after bedtime one night and met a couple of boys who were old enough to drive out on the road.

Jesse came through the back door and shook his head. "Are you remembering what I am?"

"Yep," Cody said with a grin, "but we agreed the party was worth it."

"It was at the time but spending every evening cleaning this place taught me a lesson," Jesse said.

"When Mama says no, she means no, and Dad will back her up on it," Cody said.

"That's right."

"Just think about those twin boys you've got and how much trouble we used to get into when we were kids and teenagers," Cody teased.

"Yes, but that old barn out near Windom where we used to party has been torn down, and kids today would rather sit in front of a television and play video games than go out to an abandoned barn and drink beer." Jesse shook his head in disgust.

"History just might repeat itself." Cody raised both eyebrows. "Sam and Taylor might be more interested in girls and beer than video games."

"That's a bridge way on down the road," Jesse said. "Right now, they're more interested in a bottle of formula, and the only women in their lives are their mama, sister, and grandmother."

Before Cody could say anything, his phone rang, and when he saw that it was Nate, he said, "I should take this. I'll meet you out at the pasture in a few minutes."

Jesse waved over his shoulder as he left the room. "See you there. Tell Stevie hello."

Cody answered the phone on the fourth ring. "Hey, Nate. Where are you these days?"

"Houston," Nate answered with his thick British accent. "I thought I was done six month ago, but I'm restless and about to go back. Want to go with me?"

"Nope. Where are you off to this time?" Cody asked.

"South Africa," Nate answered. "The company I'm working for now has built a fairly good-sized new hospital with a surgery and about thirteen rooms near Nieu-Bethesda. I've been asked to be the chief. I've got a surgeon lined up, but I need another doctor, and I thought of you. It's a one-year contract instead of six months, and the area is beautiful. I've been over there overseeing the building, and now I'm back recruiting a staff. The village has a population of less than two thousand, but we'd serve a large area. Interested?"

"It's still a no," Cody said.

"Will you at least think about it a few days before you give me your answer?" Nate asked.

"My dad's condition is gradually getting worse, and I'm needed here in Texas," Cody said.

"What if I sent you pictures of the town and the hospital?" Nate asked. "It's not as sophisticated as a big medical facility here in the states, but it's a far cry from a mud hut or a tent."

"I'd love to see the pictures, but—" Cody started.

Nate butted in before he could finish. "Sending them to your phone right now. I'm really excited about this project, mate, and I hope it's just the beginning of several more centers we can put up in the next ten years. You'd be getting in on the ground floor with me, and you know that we like working together."

"We did have some good times," Cody agreed.

"Think of those and all the people you could help if you put your name on the dotted line," Nate said.

"I'll think about it, but don't get your hopes up," Cody said.

"That's fair enough. I'll look to hear from you in a few days, then. Cheers, old mate," Nate said, and ended the call.

Cody took time to scroll through the pictures. Compared to the hospital he had just been in with his dad, the facility looked really small, but when he remembered working out of a one-room place with a generator for power, it was downright beautiful. The photo of the village, which sat at the base of a lush green mountain range, was different from anywhere he had been sent before. If his dad hadn't been on the decline, or if Stevie hadn't come into his life, he would have jumped at the chance to work with his old friend.

He tucked the phone back into his hip pocket and got on one of the four-wheelers, intending to join Jesse in the west pasture. If it wasn't too wet, they would be plowing that morning. He hadn't even had time to start the vehicle when his phone rang again. This time it was Gracie Langston.

"Dr. Ryan," he answered. "What's your problem, Gracie?"

"I've got strep throat and maybe pneumonia. A fever for sure. Fifi's puppies have made me sick." Her tone sounded downright nasal. "The doctor's office doesn't have any appointments available, and I need help. I could die before Monday."

"I doubt you're going to die, Gracie. But I'll be there as soon as I can." Cody slung his leg off the four-wheeler and jogged to the ranch house.

Addy and Mia were both in the kitchen when he got inside. "Hey, Addy, sounds like Gracie Langston has a fever and is asking if we can come check her out so she doesn't die before the doctor's office opens on Monday. You free?"

"Dying, huh?" Addy chuckled, knowing her neighbor's hypochondriac tendencies. "Yeah, I can go with you. Watch the boys for me?" Addy asked Mia.

"Sure thing," Mia replied.

"And will you call Jesse and let him know I'll be back as soon as I can?" Cody asked.

"Of course. And if Dad needs me to go help plow, I'll call Nana to come babysit until you get back. And if Gracie has to go to the hospital, you can bring Fifi and her puppies home with you. I'll babysit them until she gets well."

"Oh, no!" Addy shook her head. "If those dogs come to the ranch, you'll never let them go back. If Gracie has to be away for a few days, she can hire someone to go to her house and take care of her animals."

Addy tossed Cody the keys to her SUV and grabbed a sweater on her way out the door. "I saw Stevie's van leaving a few minutes ago. Where's she off to?"

"Glen Watson needs a cow checked for something or other, so she's on her way to Dodd City," Cody said as he got into the SUV and started the engine. "Do you remember me talking about Nate?"

"Your doctor buddy?" Addy asked.

"He called this morning, and..." He told her what Nate had offered him as they drove into town.

"Are you thinking about taking him up on it?" Addy asked.

"I told him no," Cody said. "Dad might need more and more medical help. Jesse needs me on the ranch. It takes both of us to do what Dad used to do on his own. Before long, we'll be hiring summer help and then…" He paused. "There's this thing with Stevie."

"But your heart kind of aches for the job, doesn't it?" Addy asked. "I remember when I first came to the ranch. I missed nursing so much. I knew I was doing good here as a personal nurse to Sonny, and the ranch was a good fit for Mia. But…" She shrugged. "All I can say is it wasn't easy. These days, at least, I get to be your nurse. But don't ever let me keep you from doing what your heart is telling you to do."

Cody hadn't even thought of how taking the job would affect Addy. "Hey, I'm not going anywhere," he assured her. "There will always be job opportunities, but right now I want to spend all the time that I can with Dad." He parked in front of Gracie's house and took his doctor bag from the back seat.

Gracie met them at the door and motioned for them to come on into the house. Pink floral paper covered the walls. Frilly lace curtains hung over the windows. Doilies were under every lamp, on top of every table, and even graced the backs and arms of her rose-colored sofa.

"Where do you want me so you can check my throat and lungs?" she asked. "I'm so afraid that you're going to call an ambulance and send me to the hospital. My poor Fifi might grieve herself to death…" She stopped to pull a tissue free from a box and sneeze into it. "If I'm not here to take care of her."

"Let's set you on a kitchen chair," Addy suggested, and brought one out to the middle of the living room floor.

Cody took her blood pressure and temperature. "Low-grade fever, but your blood pressure is good. Let's take a look at that throat and listen to your lungs.

"Quite a bit of drainage going on there," he said, then put the stethoscope on her back. "Take a deep breath and let it out slowly. Again. One more time. Lungs are good. I think you've got a good old common cold. You just have to let it run its course. I want you to take a vitamin C every day, and a Tylenol every four hours to help with the achy feeling. If you aren't feeling a bit better in forty-eight hours, call me, and Addy and I will check on you again."

"I'm so relieved that I don't have to leave Fifi," Gracie sighed. "Her sweet little baby girls are too young to be left without a mother."

"Okay, then, call if you need us again." Addy patted Gracie on the back. "I'm sure you'll feel better in a couple of days. We send out bills at the end of the month, but if you want to pay us today, then..." She told her the amount.

Gracie looked at her like she was crazy for just a moment, then shuffled over to a desk covered with fig-urines and wrote out a check. "I wasn't thinking about you charging since you don't have a real clinic."

"But he is a real doctor, and you didn't have to get out and drive to Bonham to the emergency room where they would have charged you twice this amount. You did say the clinic here in town couldn't see you until Monday, right?" Addy asked.

"I expect you are right," Gracie said. "I remember when doctors used to come to the house all the time."

"Take care of yourself. Lots of liquids and rest," Addie said.

Gracie waved them away with a dirty look.

When they reached the SUV, Addy fastened her seat belt and asked, "Now *that* emergency is over, what is this thing you were talking about with Stevie? Are y'all more than friends?"

"I'm not real sure what we are right now," Cody said. "We flirt. We're comfortable around each other, but there's a sizzle there too. What does all that mean?"

"That the two of you are very attracted to each other," Addy said with a smile.

* * *

Glen Watson was one of those old farmers who wore bibbed overalls, chambray shirts buttoned all the way up to the top, and a straw cowboy hat no matter what the season was, and who always had a smile. And he never left her side when Stevie was taking care of his livestock.

"Want to come in for a cup of coffee or a piece of pie?" he asked when Stevie had finished checking his milk cow and vaccinating her.

"Thank you, but I'd better be getting on back to the ranch," she answered. "You tell Linda I said hello."

"Will do, and you do the same for me to Sonny." He lowered his chin and looked up at her over the top of his glasses. "And, honey, don't you pay no mind to all these old women and their gossiping. What goes on between you and Cody Ryan is your business."

"Thanks for that too," Stevie said, and smiled.

Glen walked her out to the van. "I was right sorry to hear that you have to tear down your mama's house. I understand you kind of fell through the floor and cut your leg up real bad. That why you're limpin'?"

"Yes, sir." Stevie got in behind the wheel.

"Well, you just drag that sumbitch if you have to, girl. We need us a vet like you around these parts, someone who will come when we call and not tell us we have to bring our animals to town for them to check. You will just bill me at the end of the month like always, right?" Glen asked.

"I sure will," she answered.

He shut the door for her, then stood back and waved until she couldn't see him in the rearview anymore. "I can't leave folks like Glen," she said as she turned left onto the county road leading back to the ranch. "I'm just now building up a decent practice here in Honey Grove."

You are talking to yourself again, the voice in her head reminded her.

"I know, but I've got to figure this Australia and Oklahoma City thing out and make up my mind about one or the other, or neither before I talk to Cody about it," she muttered.

Chapter Twenty-Two

Maybe Jesse was right, Cody thought as he drove his new pickup truck into town to buy a load of feed that morning. He had been too busy to actually go into town and look at trucks. He had liked the one he had totaled enough that he asked the dealer to order one just like it. Since the Ryans had always bought their vehicles from the same dealership with the same business, the manager even offered to deliver the one they had on the lot to the ranch. Cody had planned to have Stevie with him when he took the first ride in it, but she and Mia had gone off on a vet call, and besides she'd been acting strange for two days now. She had said she needed to talk to him about something when he got home from Dallas, but when he remembered to ask her about it, she was evasive, and distant.

For the past few days, she'd been distant and almost

cold toward him. She'd answered his questions with a simple yes or no, and when he teased her about it, she just shrugged it off.

"What did I do wrong?" he muttered as he backed the truck up to the loading dock of the feed store, got out, and went inside.

"Hey!" Beau Martin came from behind the counter. "What can I do for you today?"

"I need as many bags of feed as you can possibly load on that truck out there," Cody said. "And put them on the ranch bill. How are you today, Beau?"

"I'm good." He beamed. "Mia and I are going out tonight. Dinner and a movie over in Paris. Got any suggestions for a good restaurant?"

Cody almost said Sonic for burgers, but he didn't. "You want fun or fancy?"

"I want to impress her," Beau answered, "so I guess fancy."

"If you really want to impress her, ask her where she would like to go and what movie she would like to see." Cody had been surprised when Stevie wanted to watch *The Ranch* and when she kept talking about a Sonic date. "Sometimes it's not where you go or where you eat but just getting to spend time together."

"Well, that would sure enough take the worry out of the evening. Thanks, Cody. I appreciate it. She's so beautiful, and way out of my league. I don't want to blow things with her by…" He paused. "By taking her someplace cheap and making her feel like she's not worthy of a five-star restaurant."

"You are so welcome," Cody said.

"I'll get right on that feed, and I'll get an invoice made up soon as I get it all loaded." Beau started for the storeroom.

Cody followed right behind him. "I'll help with that." He hoisted a hundred-pound bag of feed on his shoulder and tossed it over in the bed of the truck.

"Is this a brand-new truck?" Beau asked as he tossed a bag over the side. "Last time you came for feed you were driving an older truck."

"Yep, just got it delivered a little while ago," Cody answered. "I've been using the ranch work truck until we could rescue my old truck and the insurance claim could be filed."

"And you brought it to the feed store?" Beau was visibly shocked. "If and when I can afford to buy a fancy truck like this, I hope I'll be taking Mia out for a ride in it, not messing it up with ten bags of cattle feed."

Cody bit back a grin. "With that in mind, do you think you should be taking advice from me about where to take Mia for supper tonight?"

Beau shook his head. "Nope, but that was good advice."

"Well, what would you do when you would like to take your girlfriend out for a ride," Cody asked, "but she has been cranky for two days?"

Beau shrugged. "Man, that's above my pay grade, but if you figure it out, don't forget how you deal with it, because someday, I might need that advice too." He tossed the last bag over onto the pile in the truck's bed and headed back into the store. "Let's get you an invoice made up, and don't tell Mia that I asked about where to take her."

"My lips are sealed, but only if you never mention that I said Stevie was cranky," Cody agreed.

Beau tapped a few keys on the computer, and two copies of the invoice rolled out of the printer. "You're all ready to go. I hope Stevie gets over her cranky spell soon."

"Me too." Cody signed one copy, handed it back, and took the other with him. "See you next time around."

"Thanks again for the advice." Beau said.

"Sure thing." Cody waved and disappeared back through the supply room. He stepped down the concrete steps to the ground, got into his truck, and turned the radio on to his favorite country music station.

* * *

Stevie had spent the whole morning and part of the afternoon vaccinating cattle on a ranch way out beyond Dodd City. When she finished, she was tired, dirty, and hungry. She drove home with the radio blaring and planned to drag out her laptop that evening and enter all the invoices she had stuffed in an envelope on the front seat of her van—right after she had a long, soaking bath. That way, she could get her billing done early the next week—maybe for the last time in Honey Grove if she decided to take the Australia job.

The rich aroma of roast beef met her when she entered the bunkhouse. She wasn't even aware that Cody had put it in the oven since she had left earlier than he did that morning. She took long oven mitts out of a drawer and put one on each hand, then brought the blue granite roasting pan out of the oven and removed the lid. The potatoes, carrots, and onions were all done perfectly, and the roast fell apart when she tested it with a fork.

She left it on top of the stove, turned off the oven, and headed straight to the bathroom, where she adjusted the water in the tub and dropped her clothing on the floor. Days had passed since she fell through the floor and had to have stitches in her leg, and in those days, she had only had a shower each day with a plastic bag taped to her leg.

She wanted a bath. No, that wasn't right. She needed to feel warm water around her so she could think. She had removed a lot of stitches from animals, and taking them out of her own leg couldn't be a bit different. She went to the utility closet where Cody stored all his supplies, and found a disposable suture removal kit. In no time at all, she had removed the stitches, and the little black spider-looking things were lying on the vanity. The tub was nearly full, so she turned off the faucet and sunk down into the warm water.

"I will never take a bath for granted again," she said with a long sigh.

She vowed that before she got out, she would have her mind made up about Australia. She would tell Cody about the offer and her decision over supper. Maybe then she would have some peace.

"We can see if a long-distance relationship can work," she said. "We would have two weeks before I have to leave, and I'm talking to myself again."

That comes from being an only child, the voice in her head whispered.

Was that what had defined everything about her? she wondered. Including her problem with making a decision. Growing up, she hadn't made friends very easily, especially after being made fun of by her classmates. In college, she had been of those nerdy students who studied all the time and didn't have time for close friendships.

The water turned lukewarm and then downright chilly, but she refused to get out of the tub until she had made up her mind. Finally, when she was covered in goose bumps, she admitted complete failure and flipped the lever at the end of the tub with her toes to let the water out.

When she was dressed in warm sweats and had brushed her wet hair out, she left the bedroom. She was surprised to see that Cody had set the table. She hadn't heard him come in. He had poured two glasses of sweet tea, and when she made it across the living area to the kitchen, she noticed he had already made each of them a salad. Now, he was busy slicing a loaf of homemade bread, most likely sent down from Pearl and Sonny's house.

"Are you in a better mood?" Cody asked.

"What makes you think I've been in a bad mood?" She brought butter and salad dressings from the refrigerator.

"You've been all buttoned up and refusing to talk to me," he answered. "What's on your mind, Stevie? Are you tired of living here with me? Tired of being around people all the time? Do you want to move out, and you don't want to tell me?" He brought the platter with the roast, potatoes, and carrots all arranged beautifully on it to the table and went back for the basket of bread.

"The thought of moving is my problem, but not just

moving out of the bunkhouse," she admitted. "I've tried to make up my mind about something for two days, and I'm no closer to making a decision than I was when you were gone off to Dallas with your dad." She took a deep breath and let it out in a whoosh.

"Whoa! Let's just have a silent grace so we can both say our own individual prayer before we talk," Cody suggested.

Stevie bowed her head and closed her eyes. *Lord,* she prayed silently, *please let me make up my mind before I raise my head. It's not fair to Cody, or anyone else for that matter, for me to sit on the fence about it any longer, and besides, this indecision is driving me crazy, and about to ruin whatever hope we have for a relationship.*

When she finally raised her head, Cody was staring at her. "You want to eat or talk or both?"

"Both," she said. "I'm hungry and this looks delicious."

"I'll go first," Cody said. "I accused you of being cranky, but after I said my prayer, I realized that I haven't been easy to live with lately either. Remember me talking about my friend Nate?"

"Yes...*love.*" She squirted dressing on her salad, then loaded her plate with pot roast and vegetables. "I couldn't forget good old Nate and his British accent."

"Well, he called and asked me to come to South Africa with him to help out at a new clinic." Cody loaded up his own plate. "I told him no right off the bat. I don't want to look back someday and regret not spending as much time with my dad as I can."

"I understand." Stevie took a drink of her tea. "I wish I'd had more time to spend with Mama before she died.

You've got an opportunity that I didn't have. You know that Sonny isn't well, and that things will gradually get worse. Mama told me about her cancer, I moved home, and she was gone not long after that. But I also understand wanting to go follow that dream and be a part of something that would help others."

She opened her mouth to tell him about the job offer from Australia and the one in Oklahoma City, but took a bite of carrot before she said a word. She had to make up her mind, act on her decision, and then never look back with regrets, like he talked about, before she opened up to anyone.

"But that doesn't stop me from wanting to say yes," Cody admitted. "After traveling like I did for all these past years, I get the itch to go back where I can be a real help."

Stevie swallowed so fast that she almost choked. "And you think you're not a help here? You are building up a pretty decent practice among folks over a three-county spread as a doctor who will make house calls. And besides, Jesse needs you on the ranch, not to mention how tough it would be to tell everyone goodbye if you took that job."

Are you talking to Cody or to yourself? she asked herself.

Cody slathered butter on a thick slice of bread. "Ranch help can be hired, and if I wasn't here, folks would go back to sitting in an office waiting room in town like they did before I got here. I'll probably get over the desire to travel when I've had time to put down some real roots. I just don't think I can do it in this bunkhouse, so I'm going to talk to Dad about moving into the vacant house over on the property he bought from Addy's folks."

"Then your mind is absolutely made up?" Stevie asked.

"Yes, it is. Family is everything." Cody said.

Stevie was hoping that he might say she was why he was staying in Honey Grove. But when she thought about it for half a second, she was glad that he hadn't. If she was the only thing keeping him here, he could easily resent her later for being the reason he had not followed his dream.

"Now, your turn," Cody said.

"I don't want to talk about it until I've gotten off the fence and made a decision," she said.

"How long is that going to take?" Cody looked worried.

"It's like this," Stevie said. "Since my house has to be torn down and I don't have any family left, I don't have any of those roots that you talked about. I do have a good foundation for my vet business, and we have a date, and other things keep getting in the way."

Cody started to say something, but then did what she'd done earlier—he took a long drink of tea before he spoke. "Sounds like you're trying to make up your mind whether to stay in Honey Grove or not."

"Exactly," she acknowledged with a nod and then told him about her offer to either relocate to Oklahoma City to her old clinic or go to Australia for two years. "I know I've been cranky. If these offers had come before the house flooded, I would have said no, but now I'm wondering if that was an omen."

Cody didn't say a word until she finished. "I don't want you to go," he whispered, "but I can't stand in your way if that's your dream. You're right, you don't have a reason to stay, without family to hold you back, but maybe you and I could plant some seeds and see if together we could find some roots."

In that moment, Stevie listened to her heart and made her decision. "I'm going to call Rodney tomorrow and tell him that I appreciate his offer, but I'm staying in Honey Grove. I've been promised a fourth date, and that burger and fries means a lot to me."

Cody pushed back his chair, rounded the table, and tipped up her chin with his fist. The kiss was both sweet and hot at the same time, and it sealed forever the decision she had made. No matter what happened, she was determined that she would never look back with wonder if she'd made the right choice.

Chapter Twenty-Three

Stevie's lips still felt warm from Cody's kiss when Mia knocked on the door and yelled that she was bringing peach cobbler for their dessert. She set the plastic container on the table and pulled out a chair for herself. "We had lots of leftovers, and I know you like any kind of cobbler, Uncle Cody. Looks like I timed it just right." She reached out and picked up a carrot with her fingers and popped it into her mouth. "I didn't have supper, and I'm starving. Beau is picking me up in…" She checked the time on her phone. "Thirty minutes. He's so sweet. He asked me where I wanted to go, and what movie I wanted to see. When I was with Ricky, we always did what he wanted to do. I know! I know! I shouldn't compare them. They're as different as a fresh cow patty and a diamond ring, but it's tough not to, when Ricky is the only other guy I've been with or dated."

"I'm going to put off having my dessert for a little while and go check on Dad," Cody said. "After that long trip, I should be taking his vital signs every day. You ladies can have some time to discuss the dating game while I'm gone." He pushed back his chair and stood up.

"You think all we talk about is you guys when you're not around?" Stevie asked.

"I hope so." Cody flashed a smile on his way out the door. "Be back in a few minutes."

"I'm glad that Poppa isn't any worse, but I was hoping that specialist would tell him he was getting better," Mia sighed.

"Not any worse is a good sign," Stevie said. "It's kind of like being in remission if he had cancer. We'd be tickled with that news, right?"

"I suppose so," Mia sighed again, "but I still believe and hope for a miracle."

"You got one when you met Beau," Stevie told her.

Are you talking to her or to yourself again? Her mother's tone seemed to be happy.

"Amen to that," Mia said.

"Where are you going tonight?" she asked.

"We are going to Sonic in Sherman," Mia answered. "I'm having a double bacon cheeseburger, double fries, and a chocolate shake, and then we're going to see that new spy movie that just came out last week."

"Sounds like a perfect date. What made you choose a spy movie?" Stevie asked.

Mia finished chewing another carrot before she answered. "It's about kick-ass women spies, and I like action films." She checked her phone again. "Beau isn't the type to be late, and I'm ready to go, but I should brush my teeth. I don't want him to taste carrots when he kisses me."

"Have fun." Stevie started to serve herself some cobbler, but then decided to wait and have dessert with Cody.

* * *

Cody drove the mile from the bunkhouse to the other side of the ranch where his folks now lived in the old foreman's house, a small two-bedroom frame house. He found his father and mother sitting on the front porch swing bundled up in coats. Sonny even had a blanket around his legs.

"What are y'all doing outside in the cold?" Cody called as he got out of his truck, went up onto the porch, and hiked a hip on the railing.

"We're celebrating," Sonny said. "Today is the anniversary of our first date all those years ago. I wasn't allowed to take your mother out in my old pickup truck, but her daddy said I could sit on the porch swing with her and we could talk. Every year, we do this to remember that we fell in love that night."

"We sit on the porch swing for one hour," Pearl said, "because that's how long my father said we could spend together, and then Sonny had to come inside the house and visit with my folks the rest of the evening."

"Our hour is up." Sonny pushed the blanket to the side and used his cane to steady himself as he got up from the swing. "Let's go have coffee and some of that apple pie your mama made today."

Cody folded the blanket over his arm and followed his folks into the house. "Mia brought peach cobbler to the bunkhouse, so I'll pass on the pie, but I would like a cup of coffee."

"What's on your mind this evening, son?" Pearl asked.

"Can't a guy come see his parents without..." He paused as he laid the blanket on a ladder-back chair in the foyer. "Something being on his mind?"

"Yes, but I know you." Pearl made sure that Sonny was seated at the table, and then she got down dessert plates and ice cream from the refrigerator. "Sure you don't want just a sliver?"

"Maybe a tiny piece," Cody said as he poured three mugs of coffee. "I want to save room for some of Addy's cobbler too."

"Boy, as skinny as you are," Sonny chuckled, "you could eat this whole pie and a cobbler too, and still need to gain weight. You've got muscles, but you could use thirty more pounds."

"Dad, I'm six feet, four inches tall, and I'm pretty much at the right weight for my height now that I've put on ten pounds from eating such good food since I've been home." Cody carried all three mugs to the table and then sat down. "If I keep having double portions of dessert, I figure, by summer, I'll have to buy new jeans."

Pearl cut the pie and put a scoop of ice cream on the slice she set before Sonny. "How much is just a tiny piece?" she asked Cody.

"Half as much as you gave Dad," he answered. "You

were right, Mama, I do have something on my mind, but I probably need to start from dirt…"

Sonny chuckled again. "I remember the days when you were a little boy, and I'd ask you a question. You always had to give me an hour's worth of backstory before you ever got around to answering it."

"And you got to where you would say, 'Just the facts, son, not the story from back when God made dirt.'" Cody was so grateful his dad's illness hadn't stolen his memories and his mind.

Pearl slid his pie across the table and then cut herself a slice. "That's right, but we've got time, so give us the full story."

"You remember me telling y'all about my doctor buddy, Nate?" Cody asked.

"The British guy, right? I always kind of thought of him like Ducky on *NCIS*," Sonny answered.

"He called me last week, but before I tell you the story and show you the pictures, I want you to know that I turned him down." He told them what the conversation had been about between bites, and after he had shown them the pictures on his phone, he ended with "I want to be here in Honey Grove, living on Sunflower Ranch and doing exactly what I'm doing."

"Something tells me that's not all." Pearl finished off her pie.

"This is kind of like Fate, but Stevie got a similar offer." He sipped his coffee and set the mug back down. When he had finished that tale, he said, "But we talked tonight, and decided that we would like to see if we might be able to put down roots together. She deserves something more than a bunkhouse, and she has all that stuff from her mother's house that I'm sure she would like to have around her."

"Then why don't the two of you move into the house over there on the other part of the ranch? The one over on what used to be the Hall Ranch," Pearl suggested. "Lucas called us earlier today and postponed coming back for another year. He said that he wants to get more into horse therapy to help kids with disabilities, and he has an opportunity to do that. If he comes back at some point, the bunkhouse will be plenty big enough for him to stay in."

"Lucas has always been the quietest one of us and needed more space for himself than me and Jesse ever did," Cody said. "But I actually drove over here to ask if I could move into the old Hall house you mentioned, Mama, and to ask if it would cause a problem if Stevie and I live together. We need to find ourselves before we rush into anything more than that."

Sonny laughed so hard that he had to wipe his eyes on a napkin. When he finally stopped, he asked, "What exactly have you been doing all this time, son?"

Cody hadn't seen his father laugh that hard in weeks. "Well, Dad, I guess I lost my mojo, because we've just been roommates. I want to ask her to take it to the next level, and move in with me, but I didn't want to do that unless I could have the house. She's special, and she deserves more than I can probably ever give her, but that would be a good start."

"Yes, it would," Pearl agreed. "And of course, we don't have any issues with you asking Stevie to share the place with you. She's practically like family already."

"Thanks to both of you, and for the pie, Mama," Cody said.

Pearl handed him a key ring with two keys on it. "We won't say a word about it until she says yes, and, son, I'm so excited for both of you."

"Me too," Sonny said. "It's way past time that you started putting down those roots you mentioned. And Stevie is a good woman to help you with that."

Cody gave them both a hug and whistled all the way to his truck. He went by the barn and stopped by the corral where Maggie and the crias were. He used a length of baling twine he found in the barn to tie one of the keys around Dixie's neck. She fussed about it at first, but when Maggie came over and loved on her, she accepted it a little better.

"You be a good girl and don't lose that. I'll be back tomorrow to get it back from you," he said as he petted Dixie on the head.

When he arrived back at the bunkhouse, Stevie had cleaned up the table and divided the cobbler into two dishes.

"I waited to have dessert with you," she told him. "Want a glass of milk to go with it?"

"That sounds great," he answered.

"How's your dad? Vitals all right?" she asked.

"Well, damn it!" he said. "We got to talking, and I forgot to check him. I'll do it tomorrow after church. They were sitting on the porch..." He told her about it being the anniversary of their first date.

"That is so sweet. That's the kind of relationship I want." Stevie brought out two tall glasses of milk to go with their dessert.

"Me too," Cody agreed.

* * *

The next morning, Stevie managed to listen to the minister's sermon on being at peace with yourself, with God, and with your family—at least part of the time. Not even God could have found fault with her for stealing glances at Cody and being almost giddy with happiness that she had finally made her decision. She had even called Rodney that morning and told him she'd be staying in Honey Grove. Now it was done and finished, and she was ready to sink a root or two into the ground.

At the end of the service, Mia and Beau were the first to step out into the aisle. They looked so darned cute together that Stevie had to work hard to keep from sighing.

"Mama, I'm going to Beau's house for dinner today," Mia told Addy. "He came to our place last week, and he and his grandpa have invited me to their ranch today. I'll be home in time to help with evening chores."

"Have a good time," Addy said.

"Thank you, Miz Ryan," Beau said and smiled. "I can't wait to show Mia around our place, and if I'm late getting her home, I'll help her do the chores."

"How about I help you with *your* chores at your ranch,

and then you come home with me for supper and maybe watch a movie this evening after you help me with chores?" Mia asked.

"I'd love that," Beau said and smiled again at her.

They went on ahead of the family, shook hands with the preacher, and were already gone by the time Cody and Stevie made it out to the parking lot. Not a single cloud floated in the sky that morning, and warm sunshine had melted most of snow that was piled up at the four corners of the lot and had looked like small dirty mountains the week before.

"See y'all at the house?" Jesse called as he put Sam into the car seat, and then reached to take Taylor from Addy's arms.

"We're going out to dinner today." Cody raised his voice above the noise of more than a dozen vehicles leaving. "See y'all later."

"Oh, so we're going out?" Stevie asked when Cody opened the door for her and she had gotten into the truck and fastened her seat belt. "The new smell is still here."

"Have you ever bought a brand-new car?" Cody asked as he slid behind the wheel.

"One time, and I brought it with me when I came back to Texas, but I learned real quick that I needed a van to do my work," she answered. "So, I traded it in. The van wasn't exactly new, but it was in good condition. A vet had owned it before, so it was already tricked out with bins I needed. The tires needed replacing, and you know the rest of that story. Where are we having dinner?" she asked again.

"Sonic," he told her, and drove out of the parking lot.

"I thought we'd go over to Bonham and have burgers and fries."

"That sounds great, but this is not our fourth date," she told him.

"All depends on how you look at it. It could be our fourth if you count it my way. First was breakfast at the diner. Second was when I kissed you the first time, and third was last night when we decided to stay in Honey Grove," he told her. "That would make this our fourth, and it's also your first ride in my new truck, so we're celebrating."

"You had me at a hamburger and fries. Who cares about counting?" she laughed. "Are you still happy with your decision to stay in Honey Grove?"

"Are you?" he fired back.

"Yes. I've already called Rodney, so it is now set in stone," she told him. "I'm going to get in touch with Bobby Blalock tomorrow morning and tell him he can tear the house down as soon as all the stuff is out, and I'm at peace with that too. I also decided I want to do the packing myself so I can make decisions about what to save and what to throw in the trash."

"Sure you are ready for that?" he asked.

"Yep," she answered.

"Then I'll help you," Cody said. "Together, we should be able to take care of it in a day, and I can hook one of our cattle trailers onto the truck and bring it all to the ranch."

"Thanks," Stevie said.

Driving from Honey Grove to Bonham when there was

no snow on the roads took only fifteen minutes, and the Sonic was right off the highway. Cody pulled into a place and rolled down the window, hit the red button, and a voice came through the speaker. "Welcome to Sonic. I'll take your order when you are ready?"

Cody glanced over at Stevie. "Were you serious about a burger?"

She leaned across the console and raised her voice. "I'll have a double bacon cheeseburger with no onions, double fries, and a large chocolate shake."

"Is that all?" the voice asked.

"No, just double that order," Cody said.

"Your total is on the screen. Cash or credit card?"

"Credit card," Cody said as he slid his card into the slot.

"Thank you, sir. Your order will be right out."

"Are we going for a long drive when we finish eating?" Stevie asked.

"We can, if you want to, but I have something I'd like to show you back at the ranch," Cody said.

"And then a nap?" She covered a yawn with her hand. "I didn't sleep so well last night. Probably from worrying about telling Rodney no on the Australia offer."

"Regrets?" Cody asked.

"Not a single one, but it was pretty nice of him to recommend me for the job, and I hated to disappoint him," Stevie answered.

"I can't believe the sassy Stevie O'Dell has a soft heart," Cody teased.

"Believe it...*love*." She winked. "I can't believe you are going to let us eat in your new truck. I wouldn't let anyone even have a soft drink with a lid on it inside my new right-off-the-lot car when I first got it."

"The fact that I'm letting you eat in my new truck just goes to show you how special you are to me...*love*." He unfastened his seat belt, leaned across the console, and kissed her on the cheek.

Warmth and contentment filled Stevie from the inside out at the touch of his lips on her face. Those two things seemed like two diametrically opposed feelings to her. Sexy heat and peace at the same time. But maybe, just maybe, that was exactly what she had been looking for all this time—stability with a steaming hot cowboy.

* * *

After they had eaten and had a nice slow ride back to the ranch, Cody parked his truck out by the barn and helped Stevie out of the passenger side. "We've been neglecting Dixie for the past few days. I thought we'd take a few minutes to check on her."

"You don't think she has forgotten me, do you?" Stevie asked.

"She'll never forget you, darlin'," Cody answered as he slipped his hand into Stevie's and led her through the barn and out into the corral.

"What makes you so sure?" Stevie asked.

"Because I'm living proof that it's impossible to forget you," Cody whispered, and then kissed her on the cheek.

"That is so sweet." Stevie's eyes lit up when she smiled. "And there's my sweet Dixie."

The cria came running from the back of the lot over to her, and Stevie stooped to hug the baby around the neck. "What is this? Who put a string around your neck?"

"I did," Cody admitted. "There's something on it just for you."

"What is this key to?" Stevie asked as she removed the string.

"It's a surprise I'd like to show you," Cody answered.

"Did you find a house for me to rent?" she asked.

"No, but come with me and I'll show you what that key opens." He held out his hand.

She put her hand in his without a question, which made him feel like the luckiest cowboy in the whole state of Texas.

"I love surprises," she said.

Cody parked in front of the house on the ranch that Sonny had bought from the Hall family when they had moved out to the Texas Panhandle. He had been over to the place when he and Jesse were plowing or moving cattle from one pasture to another, but he'd never really paid much attention to the house itself.

"Is this the old Hall Ranch?" Stevie asked. "I love the wraparound porch. Can we get out and sit on the swing? It's a beautiful day."

Cody thought of what his folks had told him about their first date, and smiled at the idea of sitting on a porch swing with Stevie when he asked her to move in with him.

"It was the old Hall Ranch, but it is part of Sunflower Ranch now, and yes, we can sit on the swing." Cody got out of the truck with plans of helping her, but she slid out on her own and beat him to the porch.

"You are ruining my reputation as a gentleman." Cody took her hand in his, and they crossed the wide porch and sat down on the swing together. "Looks like this old swing could use a coat of paint. What color do you see it as?"

"Yellow," she answered without hesitation. "Sunflower yellow, and the house could use a paint job too, and I would make it white instead of gray."

"Why yellow?" Cody asked.

"Because that's my favorite color and because it's part of Sunflower Ranch," Stevie answered. "Are y'all getting it ready to sell or something?"

Cody was more nervous than he'd ever been on a first date. "Or something...*love*," he finally answered.

"Okay, Cody, something is going on. I can tell by the gleam in your eyes, and you're teasing me with that word again. And I've got this key." She held it up, still on the baling twine. "Does this open the door to this house?" she asked.

"I've fallen in love with you over this last month, and I know this is maybe too fast, but would you move in with me?" Cody asked. "And, yes, darlin', that is the key to this house. I have one just like it, and I want us to live together."

Stevie's brows drew down and she frowned. "Cody, we have been living together for weeks."

"But that was as roommates with a few kissing privileges. I'm asking you to move in with me here, with a real future in mind—in this house. There's four bedrooms inside. You can have one all to yourself until you are ready..."

Stevie stood up and sat back down, only this time she was in his lap. She pulled his face to hers in a long, passionate kiss. When it ended, she said, "Yes, yes, yes. I'm really in love with you, Cody. That infatuation I had as a teenager has grown into something serious and deep, but if I'm going to live with you, I want all the benefits. I want to share my life with you. My whole life... *love*."

He wrapped his arms around her and drew her close enough that he could feel her heart beating against his chest. "Do we have to wait until we move in to start that sharing a bed and being totally intimate?"

"Lord, I hope not!" She whispered, "But could we take a look inside before we make it official?"

"Of course we can." Cody said. "I don't want you to be disappointed in the place. Mama says it might need some cosmetic help."

"I'm pretty good with a paint roller, and besides, as long as we're together, that's all that matters." Stevie stood up and started for the door.

"Don't I get to carry you across the threshold?" he asked.

"That's for the next step. Right now, we're just moving in together." She opened the door and went inside.

* * *

If a person could float on air, Stevie was doing it on the way back to the bunkhouse. She was moving in, as in really *living with*, Cody Ryan. They were going to have a house and room to put all the things that she could salvage from her house in town before it was torn down.

I'm going to sleep with him tonight, she thought, and then panic struck. *What if I disappoint him? What if he changes his mind? I may not have braces, but I'll never be a trophy girlfriend.*

"You're awfully quiet," Cody said as he drove from what would soon be their home back to the bunkhouse. By walking, it would only be a mile, but driving meant going back to the farm road, traveling half a mile to the main road, and then another one to the lane leading up to the ranch house on Sunflower Ranch. "Thinking about what color paint you want to use for the inside of the house?"

"No, I was worrying about whether or not you will be happy with me in the bedroom," she answered.

"I can always depend on you to be brutally honest, can't I?" Cody said.

"I can't change who I am," she told him.

"And I'm so glad you can't. That's just one of the things that I love so much about you, and, honey, you could never disappoint me—not ever." He turned in to the lane and drove right past the house.

"I hope not too, because I really love you," she said.

He parked in front of the bunkhouse, and this time, she waited for him to come around the truck and open the door for her. Instead of waiting for her to unfasten her seat belt, he reached across her lap and did it for her and then scooped her up in his arms. He asked her to open the door for them, and once they were inside, he locked it behind them and didn't stop until he had gently laid her on the bed.

"Today is a big step for both of us, and I may carry you over the threshold when we move into our house too. The third time will be after we've said our wedding vows." He leaned down and his eyes went all dreamy.

She barely had time to moisten her lips before the kiss, and this time it wasn't only scorching hot, it was full of promise for the future. When it ended, she wiggled free and stood up. "Did you just propose to me?"

"No, I didn't...*love*." He drew her close to him and hugged her tightly. "What I said was just a promise of a proposal. When I really pop the question, you won't have to ask."

Stevie pulled away from him, kicked off her shoes, and pulled her sweater up over her head. Cody's eyes changed from dreamy to downright hungry when he saw the black lace bra. She pulled his Western shirt free from his pants, unsnapped it from the bottom to the top in one fell swoop, peeled it down his arms, and tossed it on the floor with her sweater. He gasped when she ran her fingers through the blond hair on his chest and then undid his belt and slowly unzipped his jeans.

"My turn." He unzipped her long denim skirt and strung kisses down her belly to her bare feet as he slid the skirt down to the floor.

"I feel like we're the only two people in the world right now," she whispered.

"We are, darling," he said, "and we're going to feel like this real often in the next fifty or sixty years."

Epilogue

Five months later

The wedding was a simple affair held in Stevie and Cody's living room with just the immediate family and Beau. The preacher stood in front of the fireplace, and Cody and Jesse were to his left. Cody's palms were sweaty, and he could hardly lasso one of the thoughts that kept circling through his mind. He had worked so hard on his vows, and now he was afraid he would forget them.

Mia started the music on the CD player, and then Stevie appeared in the doorway on Sonny's arm. Sunshine poured through the window, putting all kinds of highlights in Stevie's red hair. She wore a simple off-white dress and had a ring of tiny yellow roses in her hair, and Cody thought she had never looked more beautiful. His mouth went dry, and he wanted to cross the room and kiss her right then and there. He knew she was walking so slowly because Sonny had to lean on his cane, but to Cody she was floating to him like an angel straight from heaven.

When they were standing in front of Cody, she let go of Sonny's arm, and he focused on his son. "Son, I want you to love this woman like I have loved your mother. Become one in heart, mind, and spirit with her. I'm putting my blessing on this union and I'm hoping that you live to enjoy many years together. And"—his father's old eyes twinkled—"produce lots of grandchildren for me and your mother to enjoy."

A few chuckles filled the room, but Cody just nodded. "Yes, sir, I'll do my very best."

Sonny turned to Stevie. "We are glad to welcome you to the Ryan family, and what I said to Cody goes for you too."

"You've got my word that I will make it happen," Stevie said.

"Your word is good enough for me," Sonny said, and then shuffled over and sat down beside Pearl on the sofa.

Stevie handed her bouquet of yellow roses to Mia and took Cody's hands in hers. "I wrote pages and pages of vows. Then I realized that in all my worry about vows, I was saying something from my mind, not from my heart. So, I tore them all up and decided to let my heart speak today. It says that it's been in love with you since I was a teenager. In those days it was just puppy love, and that doesn't last forever. It also says that what we have isn't just for this life, but it's deep enough and strong enough to last through all eternity. That's because it takes your heart to complete mine. Without it mine would stop pumping, and I wouldn't survive. So, today, Cody Ryan, I will happily change my name from O'Dell to Ryan, but it's more than just a name change for me, it's accepting you as my husband, and promising to cherish, respect, and share our lives...*love*," she said with a grin.

Cody chuckled and stared into her eyes. "I didn't know that I was only half-alive until we got stranded together in that winter storm. You complete me, and I vow to honor, to cherish you, respect you, and to love you even beyond my last breath."

"Well, it looks like this couple have said their vows, so now, there's little left to do but go on with the ceremony"— the preacher held up two gold wedding bands—"so let's just get on with the exchanging of rings."

When that was done, the preacher said, "I now pronounce you husband and wife. Cody, you may kiss the bride."

Cody pulled her to his chest and said, "I love you, Stevie Ryan."

"I love you right back, Dr. Cowboy," she whispered.

Then he sealed their vows with a long kiss. When it ended, Mia handed the bouquet back to Stevie, and the preacher said, "Folks are waiting in the fellowship hall on all y'all. There's food, cake, and presents for you to enjoy before you leave on your honeymoon. If whoever is taking family pictures will take mine with the bride and groom first, I'll go on ahead and help my wife and the other ladies with the final touches."

Beau stepped up with a camera. "I'm the photographer today. I've only ever taken wildlife pictures, but I'll do my best."

"But before that begins, I have a little present for Stevie." Pearl stood up and hugged the bride and groom. "This tradition started when I married Sonny. My mother-in-law gave me a bag of seeds from her sunflowers, and I planted them by the cattle guard at the end of the lane leading up to Sunflower Ranch. When Jessie and Addy got married, I gave her a bag of the seeds from my sunflowers, and she's planted them at the back of the ranch house. This is for you, Stevie." She put a bag of seeds in her hands. "I thought you might plant them at the end of your house. They'd look really pretty blooming by that yellow swing."

"Oh, Pearl"—Stevie wiped away a tear—"this is the best present ever."

"When you have children, just pass on the tradition." Pearl handed her a white hankie. "Dab those tears away and get ready to smile for the pictures."

Cody took the time to brush another sweet kiss across Stevie's lips. "This is the best day of my life, darlin'."

"Mine too," she said.

"I can't even begin to tell you how happy I am." Cody's lips met hers in one of those kisses that still made her knees go weak.

When it ended, she whispered, "Let's get this reception over with so we can come home and you can take me to bed, cowboy."

"No *Dr. Cowboy* or *love?*" he asked.

"Nope, just cowboy, and you're all mine for a whole week of our stay-at-home honeymoon," she said.

"No, darlin', I'm all yours forever," he whispered.

Don't miss
Lucas Ryan's story,
coming in late 2022.

About the Author

Carolyn Brown is a *New York Times* and *USA Today* best-selling romance author and RITA finalist who has sold more than eight million books. She presently writes both women's fiction and cowboy romance. She has written historical and contemporary romance, both stand-alone titles and series. She lives in southern Oklahoma with her husband, a former English teacher who is not allowed to read her books until they are published. They have three children and enough grandchildren to keep them young.

For a complete listing of her books (series in order) and to sign up for her newsletter, check out her website at carolynbrownbooks.com or catch her on Facebook/Carolyn BrownBooks.

Enjoy the best of the West
with these handsome, rugged cowboys!

TEXAS HOMECOMING
by Carolyn Brown

Dr. Cody Ryan is back in Honey Grove, Texas, much to the delight of everyone at Sunflower Ranch—everyone except the veterinarian, Dr. Stephanie O'Dell. So he can't believe his fate when a sudden blizzard forces them to take shelter together in an old barn. Cody's barely seen his childhood crush since he left, so why is she being so cold? As they confront the feelings between them, it's clear the fire keeping them warm isn't the only source of sparks. But once the storm passes, will Stevie and Cody finally give love a chance?

Connect with us at
Facebook.com/ReadForeverPub

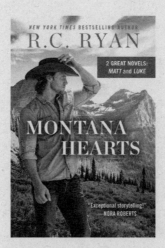

MONTANA HEARTS (2-IN-1 EDITION)
by R.C. Ryan

Fall in love with two heart-pounding Western romances in the Malloys of Montana series. In *Matt*, a raging storm traps together a rugged cowboy and a big-city lawyer who can't stop butting heads. But when one steamy kiss leads to another, will differences keep them from the love of a lifetime? In *Luke*, a stubborn rancher thrown from his horse is forced to accept the help of a beautiful stranger. But as they begin to feel sparks, will secrets from the past threaten their newfound feelings?

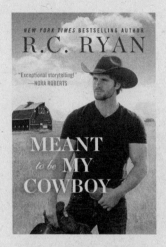

MEANT TO BE MY COWBOY
by R.C. Ryan

Fresh off a bad breakup, Annie Dempsey has rules for her new life in Devil's Door, Wyoming: no romance, no drama, and steer clear of the Merrick clan—her family's sworn enemies. But when a charming stranger steps in to protect Annie from a sudden threat, rules fly out the door. Because her mystery hero is...Jonah Merrick. As she hides from a dangerous pursuer at Jonah's ranch, they can't deny the chemistry pulling them closer together. But can they put their family rivalry aside to make room for love instead?

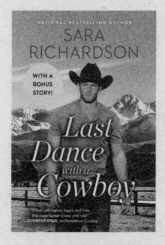

LAST DANCE WITH A COWBOY
by Sara Richardson

Leila Valentino will do anything to keep her grandparents' Colorado winery afloat. Even partner with August Harding, the first—and last—man to break her heart. The cowboy's investment offer could save the business, but her grandparents have no idea how close they are to going under. So Leila insists that August pretend he's back in town for her. When their faux relationship starts feeling for real, a second chance seems possible—but can August convince Leila that this time he's not walking away? With a bonus story by Carolyn Brown!